Carl Weber's Kingpins:

ATL

Carl Weber's Kingpins:
ATL

Brick & Storm

www.urbanbooks.net

Urban Books, LLC
97 N18th Street
Wyandanch, NY 11798

Carl Weber's Kingpins: ATL

ISBN 13: 978-1-62286-730-1
ISBN 10: 1-62286-730-0

First Trade Paperback Printing November 2016
Printed in the United States of America

10 9 8 7 6 5 4 3 2 1

This is a work of fiction. Any references or similarities to actual events, real people, living or dead, or to real locales are intended to give the novel a sense of reality. Any similarity in other names, characters, places, and incidents is entirely coincidental.

Distributed by Kensington Publishing Corp.
Submit orders to:
Customer Service
400 Hahn Road
Westminster, MD 21157-4627
Phone: 1-800-733-3000
Fax: 1-800-659-2436

Carl Weber's Kingpins:
ATL

by

Brick & Storm

Chapter 1

Saint

Jonesboro, GA
Neighborhood of Goodman

Ever wonder why niggas in the hood always fighting to live then, basically, living to fight? I mean, the homie Pac wasn't fucking around when he asked that same question himself. Too many of us are just scraping by trying to make it, trying to give pieces of ourselves for the area we live in every gotdamn day only to end up with a bullet inches from our heart. Or with a bullet blasting out our brains or spine, dying on the hot or cold concrete with trash blowing over our bodies as if our lives, the purpose of our being born in this fucked-up nation, ain't meant shit. Ultimately, it really didn't.

Yeah, but anyway. Pac ain't have the answers, and here's a nigga like myself sitting on the top of my crib overlooking my community, my neighborhood, while staring at the sparkling lights of the Roanoke enclave of Jonesboro wondering the very same thing. Jonesboro was one city. The shit was split up into two halves: the haves and the have-nots. Roanoke was the come up, where all the rich White, Black, Asian, Hispanic, and whatever else lived.

While their poor counterparts lived in my area of Jonesboro: Goodman. Shit was just that simple. One side of Jonesboro was rich and prosperous: the haves.

That was the Roanoke neighborhood. The other side of Jonesboro was the hood of all hoods. That was Goodman: the have-nots.

We all were one with the same county, same city, but separated by a set of railroad tracks built back in the days of segregation. True story, it ain't like nothing really changed, except we now we're separated by class and money. Oh, well.

"Saint!"

Goodman was a chill place mixed with a lot of fucked-up situations. Like, on some real shit, as I enjoyed the taste of my Black & Mild mixed with some Kush—a sweet type—several rounds had gone off within the same hour window. Somebody was dead; that was verified by the late-ass flashing lights of five-o. Where I was at, I saw the niggas who did it. Saw one run past the towing yard where I lived, and saw two others hop back in a junky silver Impala. I clocked the license plate, too, out of habit.

In my business management books for my online classes, I was doodling. Nothing but scribbles lined the border and I placed the number of the license plate in it. Nothing in me was a snitch, so that's not why I did it. The reason it was there was because of my job. I worked two of them: one, a regular job as a tow truck driver/ mechanic for my mother's towing company, and another as a part-time runner for our area big man, Blanket.

Blanket was a kingpin, a drug lord, the leader of one of the most known drug havens in metro Atlanta. Since I was a kid, that nigga's name rang heavy in the streets. The shooting took place in Blanket's zone. I had to note the shit, so that I could erase some motherfuckers for acting up when they weren't supposed to. So, when I wasn't taking online classes for the sake of my mom's business, and working for her, I ran the streets for extra dough for my apartment, for my mom, and to keep our area straight.

"Saint!" I heard again.

Leaning back on my hands, I spit several sunflower seeds on top of the head of the nigga who yelled my name.

"Uggg, you stay a bitch-ass nigga," was shouted at me and it made me flash my teeth in a deep laugh.

"And you stay holding deez nuts. Whatcha want, Sinner?" I lackadaisically said back.

The sound of this fool climbing up to where I was had me glancing his way. He was dressed in the similar type of clothes I wore when I wasn't working: black boots, loose-fitting black jeans, a medium-size shirt, and a black-and-white casual jacket around his waist. I gave a scowl when I stared at my twin brother. He had my jacket on. Pushing up, I rushed him and landed him on his back. I was in my gray work overalls, which made it easy for me move around for what I was about to do. Thumbing my nose, I aggressively reached out for my twin; then we started scrapping like we always did. At twenty-one, my twin was called Sinner and I was called Saint. We were assholes with some good qualities, cut from the same cloth, though we didn't facially look the same.

We both were six feet tall with natural red hair. Mom always said we had our father's cinnamon brown skin. I had a patch of hair on my chin, where my twin had full beard. My tats were on my neck, shoulder, and back, where my twin's were on his hands, forearms, and neck. We both had the same brown eyes and body type, a muscular average-athletic build, kinda like Usher when he was younger. We both played basketball in high school, so I guess that was why we were made how we were. Sin and I also had the same movements. If it was dark enough, you'd think we were identical when we weren't. We also had our own language, twin talk.

"Niggahhh . . . Saint . . . Santana, fuck, get off me!" Sinner shouted.

Yanking my jacket off of him, I pushed off him, backed up, and ran a hand through my wooly red fade. "You always taking my shit. Just walking up in my place and claiming shit, nigga. What you want?"

Running a hand over his large, cottony red afro, Sinner laughed as if he didn't give a shit. He never gave a shit about taking my material things. So when he slid a hand over the hair lining just his jaw line, then slid his hands in his jeans, I just shook my head and listened to him talk.

"Unk said Blanket is looking for you," he said matter-of-factly.

The notorious Blanket was employer to both of us. No one knew who Blanket was, or saw the nigga, but we knew he had eyes on everyone in Goodman. All things guns, drugs, sex, and more went through Blanket. Smaller dealers were on the block, but even they knew not to fuck with Blanket, except for Guerilla. Guerilla was the other kingpin of metro Atlanta, the only nigga stupid enough to go head up with Blanket. For as long as we could remember, Guerilla had been around too. In the hood you were either on Blanket's team or you were a fucking monkey.

Anyone who rolled with Guerilla had to be offed, no questions about it. The hatred between Blanket and Guerilla was so deep that there had been times where both my brother and I had been asked to roll up on his corner in the Goodman hood, and trail his crew. A week later, whoever we followed would disappear and the distribution flow would revert to Blanket.

It was some foul, crazy shit, but it was what it was. We survive however we can. Funny enough, Blanket stressed responsibility with our kills and to never let a bullet fly stray. If so, it was our heads.

"I'm where I always am. Tell that nigga that I'll get at him in a few here," I said over my shoulder as I took several steps back to where I was sitting, and dropped back in my seat.

Sinner's footsteps followed. He sat by my side, took my bag of sunflower seeds, and tossed some in his mouth, spitting out the shells as we spoke. "Mom hit me up. She said stop turning off ya cell and routing pickup calls to the house."

Frowning, I stretched a boot out and stared at the back of my twin's tattooed hands as he dug in my bag of sunflower seeds. Maya Black, formally Payne, Ms. Maya, or Auntie Maya in our neighborhood, called the shots in our family. At forty-two, our mama was the baddest bitch around according to the old heads in the area. No lie, my mom was a beautiful woman, but that's not why she garnered that title. After my pops died when we were around eight years old, my mom and uncle became the heads of Black Towing and Rentals.

Before that, she ran a little sweetshop in the back of the establishment. Something she did for the kids in the neighborhood and to keep me and my brother out of her hair. We Blacks were well known and something like royalty in the area because of the founder of Black Towing, my grandfather, Sonny. Founded back in the start of the seventies when my grandpops left the Army after serving in Vietnam, Sonny found himself in Jonesboro, Georgia, due to the Greyhound bus he was riding on breaking down in the town.

He and a friend were heading to Miami for some sun, but that all changed when he stayed at a hotel in the Goodman neighborhood. How I remember my grandpops telling it, he was grabbing a pop when a fly sista with a big red afro and a bow in her hair walked by in the baddest pair of jeans that showed off an ass for days. Grandpops explained that he had never seen a sista in person with red hair like hers who wasn't mixed up. He'd only seen it in *National Geographic* magazine with the brothas and sistas in Africa who use a special mud to tint their hair red. That's how red it was, he told us as kids. Long story short, he spit some game, they ended up hooking up, and he permanently made his home in Goodman with her. My grandma Inez and my grandpa Sonny married. My uncle Jarvis was born; then my dad Will followed a year later.

During that time, Grandpa Sonny used his G.I. money to open the towing shop, and money they comped back was used to help build up our part of Goodman. Man, it was rumors that my grandpops was a smooth man. If you ever saw that movie with Denzel Washington as a notorious drug dealer? Yeah, supposedly my pops had some swag like that, connections like that, but no one could ever prove that shit. I knew that no one in the family believed that shit, either. He was a normal dude from New Orleans who had a love for cars and who loved helping the community any way he could, so there was no truth in the whispers about that at all.

Anyway, my grandparents ran the business for years until my grandpa died the week my mom and dad had finally gotten married. It was the same day my pops died, too. Both of them ended up shot in some freak accident as they were driving to turn in the marriage license. Funny enough, about two months after that, my grandma Inez died from a broken heart and that was that. My mom and Uncle Jarvis ended up taking over the shop and here we were today.

Before all of that, the shop was where my mom and dad met, outside of high school. My mom begged my grandpa to work for them because she wanted to do something different from the girls in the neighborhood.

She later told my brother and me that it was to get close to our dad. My mom always told us how she fell for a boy everyone called Rooster because of his red hair and his brother Red. How he used to walk her home with her best friend from school, even though she never asked him to, just to protect her, he'd say. Life was simple back then.

In our part of Jonesboro, everyone knew to come to the Blacks for anything. The same could be said today, except now the environment was different. My mom stopped the sweetshop and we now did block events in the spring and summer. Though Jonesboro, as a whole, was run by drug lords who stifled the county, there were a few people who tried to push to bring back the safety in our neighborhood of Goodman. Even with the property taxes going up, people's houses being taken from them, people dying from bullets every day, and even though my brother and I helped in a lot of that shit, Goodman might have been hood, but it still had a lot of soul.

But, yeah. Where there's good, there's bad. Guess my twin and I were somewhat of a disappointment to my grandfather's legacy, due to the bad we helped bring about. Oh, well. He and my pops never should have died.

"I'm going to make my pickups. She needs to stop stressing," I said, annoyed. Glancing at my twin, I gave him a look. "I'm working, right? Why can't you do it, Will?"

Will Black Jr., aka Sinner, gave a quick laugh then smirked at me. "Because I run the front desk, Santana, and since Mom is happy with me today about me having a gallery show with my class, I get to do what I want!"

Of course. Will was the spoiled one because he came out of the pussy first whereas, because I looked like our dead pops more, Mom always stressed responsibility with me. Will was at Atlanta Metropolitan College, the bulk of my fam's money going to helping him study graphic design, whereas I was online with some of it helping with me learning business management. For years, it was like we had flipped roles. He acted younger and I acted older. I wasn't complaining, but the shit always annoyed me; though, we loved each other without question or issues.

Sinner tossed the bag at me and I snatched it out of midair. Then he spoke, "We're kings in a valley of weeds."

I sighed and replied, "If we don't handle the overflow then our yard starts to look weak."

"Right," Sinner said while staring at the same city view as I was. Sinner always quoted our mom with that line, but he was right.

I always came up to the roof just to get a feel of something normal. I didn't have to think of my mom, who I loved; didn't have to think about work, or the streets, or our natural talent for killing. I could think about classes and acting normal while staring at Roanoke, dreaming of building up my family's wealth. Roanoke owed Goodman. Fuck them and how they did us.

"A'ight, let's get busy then." Standing, I popped some seeds in my mouth then threw the bag back at my brother while cleaning up my books. "Mom's just going to be pissed that we in the streets as usual. She'll get over it."

Sin gave a goofy laugh then agreed.

Our mother hated everything that was the streets. Yet, she knew everything that always went on. She hated Blanket. Hated Guerilla. Hated Royal Realty who were sweeping through the hood taking houses from us poor motherfuckers, just to flip them and gentrify our hood. Word in the street, the Royals were scaring people, especially old people, into selling their property. They also were known for using eminent domain. My mom hated that family with her lifeblood.

So, whenever she heard about us being in the streets, or saw us doing what we do, my brother and me always got a foot in our ass because, as she saw it, we had no reason for helping a dealer. Yet, bills were always late, the shop was being threatened to be taken away, and niggas stayed breaking in our spot.

So, yeah. We ain't have a reason. Fuck that. My brother and I were a product of our environment. Bang, bang.

Anyway, we both ended up in my apartment over the tow shop. I moved in to stop the thief. Sinner lived with our mother in his own place built as a separate apartment in the basement of her large yellow Craftsman-style house. Always close, the house was only a block away. I glanced at the graffiti art resting on the surface of a canvas my brother made out of junk hanging on the main wall of my bedroom. Quickly dressing, I pulled on my boots that opened at the top, pulled my straps on, added a layer of protection, buttoned up my short-sleeve top over it, and put my watch on.

I brushed my chin beard, then slid the brush in my back pocket. As I headed out, I stopped to stare in exasperation at my twin. Nigga was digging in my fridge, going at the food my mom had stocked it up with. On the counter was a sandwich, which I jacked, took a bite of, and walked off with.

"Let's go, asshole. We got money to make," I said, slamming the screen door of my place.

After that, we both ended up in my black GMC Yukon XL, driving out of the gates that surrounded the family towing yard. Music cranked up, hyper rap blasted and we headed to our zone. A zone was a local hub where a part of Blanket's crew reigned. It was nestled on the other side of Goodman, near the northeast tracks. Our shop was at the city exit. We rode through the block, watching our front and back.

Smoothly turning down MLK Drive, we rode past a large green bungalow house with a gang of rides outside of it. I slowed down to make sure everything was good and Sin spoke up: "Dee Dee is having a party. We got invited but you know how you are around Dee Dee."

"Yeah, I want to choke her ass. Shawty doesn't know not to keep touching my dick," I said in annoyance.

"Ha! Your, dick, my dick. Her throat, her kitty. She stay trying to snatch," Sin added, laughing. "Hold up, slow down. Roanoke tags."

Slowing down, I waited for a silver Audi to park. As it did, my brother watched the car empty out with a gang of females. Ass, breasts, and curves were on display even though they were dressed in tight jeans and cropped tanks. I found myself biting my lip with a smirk, until my gaze latched on to the driver: a shorty with a wild mane of kinky, curly sandy brown hair. Miss Pretty Dark Butterscotch was laughing and, as she smiled, a large gap flashed. Baby girl was a unique breed, something that drew my attention with her mother Africa earrings and gold necklace on her chest that said HIPSTER RICH.

"Damn, they bad. Drop me off when we get done with work, man. I don't give a fuck about how Dee Dee may act."

I rolled my eyes and kept the ride pushing. "Sin, they ain't checking for us. Straight up extra. Ro-girls, you know how they are."

My brother hung out the car, looking back at the females as I drove away. "I'm saying, Saint. Bet we can turn some of them out."

"Yeah, we can, but watch us catch a case. Them black Roanoke girls are just as bad as them hoes cash-chasing an NFL player and later trapping him with a kid or hollering bullshit. You know that. Remember what happened to Eddie?"

"Man, Eddie was stupid anyway fucking with that white Cuban Ro-girl. Daddy was a cop, too? Man, fuck outta here." The sound of my brother lighting up was the end of that convo.

We made it to our destination, our zone house: a red brick abandoned old-school post office near our downtown. As we climbed out, I still had Eddie on the dome. Eddie was a star football player who got mixed up with the wrong type of female. His girl got pregnant, she tried to get an abortion, and said he raped her. When that turned out to be a lie, the girl ended up having the baby and tried to put it up for adoption. In the end, Eddie got the kid, but he also lost his chance at playing in the NFL. He now worked at Royal Realty with their Goodman construction company.

We heard music blasting as we stepped into our place. We gave head nods to our boys, Sin dropped on the couch, and I headed to the bar to talk to our fellow bodyguard Jelly Roll.

"Yo, Jelly, did the package come through?" I stood, arms crossed, staring at a nigga who was so skinny you'd think he was drawn into reality. When this nigga's eyes got wide, I frowned and stepped back. "Where is Marvin?"

"Ah, see, he got tied up at the border, Saint," Jelly said, putting down his plate of lemon pepper chicken wings to lick his fingers.

"How?" was all I asked. Everyone knew Blanket didn't fuck around with missing product. If Marvin hadn't shown up with it, it meant only one thing. He stole it and was getting high of that shit, yet again.

Staring everywhere but in my eyes, Jelly got ready to open his mouth with a, "Sorry," and my fist went flying into his face.

"You let that nigga go off with our shit? And he's near the border? So basically our shit is possibly in

Guerilla's hands and Marvin is getting high off the rest? Motherfucker!" Somewhere in my stomping, my gun slid in my hand and somewhere in me kicking the fuck outta Jelly's face, that gun went off and a bullet flew in his hand.

After that, Sin and I were back in the streets of Goodman hunting down Marvin.

Chapter 2

London

"Oh, my God, Brash, I cannot believe I let you talk me into coming over here," I said again.

I shook my head and looked around. I had to admit, I was scared to be over on this side of the tracks. I had no idea why I agreed to go to a party I had no business going to. I didn't really have many friends and that wasn't because I was ugly or had a nasty attitude. It's just that I never knew if people really liked me or my status. Daddy was the big man on campus, per se, and no, he wasn't a drug lord or thug or anything of the sort. I mean, unless you called him a corporate thug, because that he was. Daddy traveled all over the world for his job. Owning one of the top house-flipping businesses in the South, Daddy had worked his way from the bottom to the top. Royal Realty was a name everyone knew, no matter what side of the tracks you were from.

I didn't live in the hood. Actually I lived across the tracks in Roanoke, a neighborhood of Jonesboro, Georgia. I lived on the side where the rich folk resided. If Daddy could help it, I'd never cross the tracks into Goodman. But that was the hood he had come from and he still had family there. There were literally train tracks separating the two neighborhoods. There were times when I was younger I could see kids, all dirty, nappy-headed, and dingy looking, watching me from across the tracks when Daddy would take me out shopping.

As a kid, it never occurred to me to not look down my nose at them. In my head, I was better than them. It wasn't until Mama tore into my ass with a leather belt once that I changed my whole attitude.

"Look at those dirty, stinky, nappy-headed niggers," I'd said, only repeating what I'd heard Daddy call some of his brothers.

I was only eight at the time. Mama had been so embarrassed, her eyes widened and I could literally see the blood pulsating underneath her light skin. We were standing outside of Reed's Pharmacy talking to Mayor Dixon and his wife, who were both white, when I'd said it. Daddy always called Mama a redbone; well, that day she got as red as I'd ever seen her. She excused herself and yanked my arm so hard the ice cream cone I had in my hand fell to the ground. I didn't understand why she was so mad at me because Daddy had always said the N-word when he was mad. Yes, he was a black man, but if another black man pissed him off, Daddy would let the N-word ring from here to hell.

Mama drove home so fast that I didn't even think we stopped at any stoplights. That was the first time I'd ever gotten my behind beat. She beat me like I'd stolen something, all the while preaching about me being just as black as those people across the tracks. Once she was done, she packed a bag and had me wait in my room until Daddy got home from work. I remember them arguing about how he had spoiled me and made me think my shit didn't stink or that I was better than folk from across the tracks.

Mama barely raised her voice at Daddy, but that night she lit into him like a firecracker. Next thing I knew I was being taken over the tracks to my Daddy's sister's house, Auntie Nikki. That weekend changed my little rich life.

I'd never heard so much cussing, smelled so much used chicken grease and weed, or seen so many roaches or so many unruly kids a day before in my life. Auntie Nikki treated me like a slave that weekend. While her seven kids sat around doing nothing, my eight-year-old hands and feet were tired from cleaning, cooking, and serving them all day. When my parents finally came to get me, I was done for.

Still, Daddy made it his business to always tell me to stay away from there and, suffice it to say, after that weekend, he really hadn't had to say much else. Oddly enough, over time, Mama's views of Goodman changed too. She went from telling me not to look down my nose at people, to looking down her nose at them. I didn't know what had changed her mind. However, I tended to be easily influenced any time I hung with my best friend.

I knew to stay away from the other side of the tracks, but Brash had always been able to talk me into doing the most stupid shit. At nineteen I was on my way to becoming a second-year college student. Engineering was my major and my parents were pretty stoked about that. I kept a 4.0 grade point average and because of that I was one of my only friends who had my own place at nineteen. That was a big deal for me because, even though all my friends lived in the same upper-class neighborhood I grew up in, none of their folks would pay for them to have a place.

But Daddy had always been the one to give me everything as long as I did what he asked. I had to keep an A average in school. I had to always make curfew and always be respectful to him and Mom. I had no problems doing any of those. They came easy to me. So my father never had a problem with spoiling me. Brash always joked that the man I married would have to have money like Daddy or he would be in for a rude awakening. I often laughed it off since I had no plans to get married anytime soon.

But, yeah, Brash asked me to go to this party with her. I didn't want to go. For one, I wouldn't know anyone there. Two, it was on the other side of the tracks and Daddy was still adamant that I never set foot there. And three, Brash always got into some shit any time we went out together.

Even though Brash lived the upper class life same as me, the girl could blend into any ghetto you put her in. She was loud, obnoxious, always smacked gum, and dressed like she was either in a nineties or a Beyoncé video. People would never think she came from money and class or that she was the daughter of a senator and a judge. People already wondered why her name was Brashanay anyhow.

"Girl, they named me before they knew they were going to get up out the hood. They were sixteen when they had me," she always told us. "Daddy was talking about me legally changing my name, but fuck that. I ain't ashamed of my name or who I am."

Anyway, back to the topic at hand. It was a Friday night and all week Brash had been talking about the party. I'd spent my first two weeks of summer doing nothing. I needed that break from classes so I'd been sleeping and binge-watching shows on Netflix.

"Girl, you need to get the fuck up out this house. All you been doing is studying and shit. It's summer. You on break. Hit this party with me, sis," she said, smiling like she had won a million dollars.

Unlike me, Brash didn't want to go to college, but if she wanted to keep getting her monthly $1,500 allowance from her parents, she had no choice. She picked the easiest thing she could find, which was cosmetology, much to the chagrin of her folks. But Brash was good at doing hair and nails so it worked for her.

"Yeah, but it's over in Goodman, Brash, and I don't really want to go over there," I whined.

"Because of your racist-ass, prejudiced black-ass pappy. You need to tell that nigga not to forget where his black ass came from," she fussed.

I frowned as she spoke about Daddy. People didn't understand him. He wasn't racist. How could he be? He was a black man himself, but he was prejudiced. Daddy didn't even visit his sister a lot. When she needed money for rent last time, Daddy made her walk all the way over to our house to get it. Walking from Goodman to our house in Roanoke was no small feat. For some reason, the man just hated Goodman and the people who lived there, even though he was always giving back to that neighborhood.

"Brash, don't speak about my daddy like that. You know he's a good man. He just don't like hood folk."

She rolled her green eyes. "Girl, whatever. Your daddy is the worst kind of black man. He the kind who get a little fucking change and forget where he came from. Turning his nose up at folks and shit. Them people in the ghetto or 'hood' ain't no worse than them white folk he be up under all day. Quiet as kept, that white nigga he do business with looks like a damn pedophile. I'd rather hang with hood niggas and ghetto bitches before hanging with child predators. Now tell yo' daddy to sip on that tea," she spat.

I sighed hard then got up from the couch. It wouldn't be the first time Brash went on a rant about my daddy. For some reason, she didn't like him. I didn't really know why other than the fact that she didn't like that my folks and her folks thought they were better than other black people because they were in a higher tax bracket. But Brash would take anybody to task. She'd always been outspoken and unafraid.

Still, I didn't care what anyone said, Devon Royal, my father, was a good man. He may not have liked the ghetto mentality many of the people across the tracks maintained, but he still helped a hell of a lot. He sent trucks of toys during the holiday season and trucks of food for all major holidays. He gave money to schools and charities. All he wanted was the betterment of our people. And the people of Goodman knew that. Daddy was like royalty to them. He was a king in many of their eyes.

"Stop it, Brash," I said, walking into my kitchen. "Daddy just wants people to see the world from different lenses, and what does that have to do with me not going to this party anyway?" I asked, annoyed.

"Because you only not going because he has made you be afraid to be around other black folk. Anyway, you're going with me so you ain't got shit to worry about. And Laylah told me she was going."

Laylah was my cousin, Auntie Nikki's youngest kid. She was only seventeen, but she had a three-year-old kid and was always in the know about everything. Laylah and I were good friends as well as cousins, but she and Brash were best friends, too. I didn't even know Brash knew my cousin until she was talking about a girl she knew who was pregnant about three years ago. She was helping the girl out with money and clothes for the baby. Come to find out, it was Laylah. And I only found out because I walked in Brash's room one day to find her head between my pregnant cousin's legs. They claimed they weren't a couple. They both kept boyfriends, but I'd seen them fight one another when jealousy reared her ugly head. Nobody knew about them but me, and they preferred to keep it that way.

"You and Laylah always going to some damn party," I said. "Whose party is it anyway?"

"This girl named Dee Dee. Everybody going to be there," she said excitedly. "Her brother going off to Duke to play college ball so they throwing him a going-away bash and it's Dee Dee's b-day."

"Girl, how do you know so much about what be going on over there?" I asked then shook my head.

Brash rolled her eyes. "Because I'm a people person and shit. So you going or what?"

After a few more rounds back and forth about why I didn't want to go, I finally gave in to her constant begging.

"Okay, fine, Brash. I'll do it."

Brash was already rolling her hips as Chris Brown blasted through the loud speakers talking about hoes not being loyal. She was five feet six with dark skin. The thing that attracted most dudes to Brash besides the fact that she was beautiful was that she had green eyes. I'd never seen a dark-skinned chick with green eyes before Brash, but since her pops was half white, I saw how it was possible. We all were dressed similarly in hip-hugging jeans and tank tops. Name-brand wedge sneakers were on our feet. My hair was in its natural state. Brash had a sleek ponytail. Laylah had her micros pulled up into a cute bun.

My cousin Laylah was light skinned with a big, round ass. People often told her she looked like a young Faith Evans. She was everything every video girl you had seen was about. She knew that shit, too, and used it to her advantage a hell of a lot. Two more girls Brash and I knew from high school were with us: Marsha and Brandy. They, too, were just as banging as the rest of us. Marsha was a plus-sized chick, but she put any of us smaller girls to shame. The girl carried herself like she was the best thing happening; same with her sister Brandy. Both were brown skinned with flawless skin and even better makeup skills.

"This shit is popping," Brash yelled. "Look at all these fine niggas. They don't grow 'em like this in Roanoke. They just don't."

I noticed Laylah roll her eyes, but she didn't say anything. I swore it felt like we were walking a red carpet as we made our way to the front door. Most of the guys tried to grab a hand, ass, hips, anything they could to get our attention. Actually Marsha and Brandy were snatched up first by these two buff dudes.

"Yo, yo, let me and my bruh holla at you two right quick," one had said as he grabbed Marsha's wrist.

She smiled wide. She and Brandy left us to our own devices before we even got in the house. Quiet as kept, I was scared as shit. I felt as if someone was going to yell "Worldstar" at any minute. I'd heard gunshots as we were riding through to get here. The smell of weed, fried chicken, and grilled meat scented the air. Different colognes and perfumes attacked my nose. Girls in booty shorts, short skirts, and high heels turned their noses up at me as I passed through. I had to wonder if I stank or something. Dudes had on Tims, bandanas, and low-hanging jeans. Gold grills and chains almost blinded me.

I saw two dudes arguing underneath a tree. One shoved another and all I could think was, *Jesus, please don't let me die here tonight*. I knew that sounded horrible, but Goodman was like a war zone. Every day I listened to the news somebody had come up missing, someone had been found dead, or some kind of drug bust was happening, not to mention the everyday crime that occurred like breaking and entering and assaults.

But surprisingly, as the night progressed, I found that I was having fun. The inside of the house wasn't as bad as it looked outside. Furniture had been moved out of the way so the spacious front room was a dance floor. The kitchen and backyard were crowded with people dancing, eating, and talking. A spades and dominoes game was going on. There was a loud and competitive pool game going on in the basement.

"Nah, nigga, run my shit," I heard a dude yell. "Fifty dollars a game, nigga. I'm up two hunnard. Run my shit or catch a fade."

I shook my head as I looked around. I had a drink in my hand but hadn't touched it, so I dumped it in the trash. The purple fuzzy liquid wasn't something I was used to drinking. I was hot and sweaty. Me, Brash, and Laylah had been dancing our asses off. We'd whipped and nae-naed, bunny hopped, juked, and twerked until my hips, thighs, and arms burned. No, I wasn't from the hood, but I was always up on the dances. Dancing was my hobby. Any dance that came out, I was on it.

But, as any time when Brash and I were out, I should have known some shit was about to pop off.

Chapter 3

Saint

So, I had a deep pet peeve. Though I was a runner for Blanket, I hated having my time wasted by searching for a nigga. Yo, the shit really grated my nerves. Everyone knew that about me. I was stickler about my time. You do some stupid shit that you knew was fucked up, why must I be the one to correct that shit? Yet, there I was, fixing some bullshit that Jelly knew was a fuck-up.

When I got elected to be a runner and chosen to watch over my own zone house with Sin, I specifically recruited my nigga Jelly Roll. He and I went back since diapers and I had deep trust with him. Bringing him in on something simple, like being my additional eyes and security, helped Sin and me keep our part of the hood in check. Now, I knew the nigga had several flaws, like he couldn't retain water. You tell him some shit and he forget it an hour later. He always had to be around some new pussy and food and he stayed getting high when he wasn't doing specific protection work.

Seeing him there with that plate of food, and his eyes bloodshot, let me know already that he was thinking stupid and had left Marvin to his own devices. Because I knew that I'd have to search for this roach-ass nigga, my anger got the best of me, so I shot Jelly. Tomorrow I planned to check on dude, but fuck. He just fucked up some mad money for Blanket and just helped out Guerilla at the same time.

The sound of rubbing drew my attention. Sin sat scanning the areas where Marvin could be, while rubbing his hands together.

"I know you pissed and all but, shit. We need to make this quick. I want to hit up Dee Dee's. You know she always has the best pussy at the party, right?" Sinner said, licking his lips.

"Nigga, you stay on the pussy," I said just because I was still annoyed.

Sin looked at me with an expression that said I had three heads and it made me laugh and him smile wide.

"Nigga, pussy is life. Like, that shit is the ebb and flow of everything and nothing. Pussy creates. Pussy saves lives—" he started until I interrupted.

"Yeah, and if you get the wrong pussy, that shit can be foul, as in crazy as fuck. Pussy also almost got you locked out with a kid, remember that?"

Sin thumbed his nose, and focused on the houses we passed. Though it was night, people still were in the streets doing them. I drove past some young dudes sitting on their porch lighting up, as several others stood in front of the porch talking shit. All of them had on oversized white T-shirts, sagging basketball shorts, and Js. Because I was looking for Marvin, I rolled down my window to see. Every dude outside that house gave me a, "What up," then let me know that they hadn't seen Marvin in the area.

Frustrated, I sped off and rolled my window up.

"Check it, how are you going to hit me with some past shit? The Lord was on my side that day," Sin finally replied.

I laughed because I remembered how relieved my brother was that he hadn't gotten Dee Dee pregnant. "But you still fuck around with Dee Dee though? Where they do that at?" I said, bugging up.

When Sin dropped his head back and sighed, I knew what he was going to say before he even said it. "Naw, see. You know firsthand why, though. That ass always talking to me. I can't help it," he explained, making a curving motion with his hand.

He was right about that. Dee Dee was known for having a fly ass. Just juicy and shit. Old to young always wanted to know if her cat was fat because of that ass and, from experience, I knew it was. But honestly, Dee Dee and I used to be cool before she started using her body to trap me and my brother. We used to chill in front of the towing shop outside of the gate and talk about music. The girl had a voice on her and I always thought that she'd go somewhere with it, but she didn't, which was disappointing and annoyed me. Sin used to love her to sing to him while he spray-painted; now he was trying to do his all not to get trapped by her.

"And best believe I haven't really been fucking with her like that in some months after all of that. When she got her period, I stepped back. Now we're chillin'."

"Yeah, while she's chillin' with me too," I said with a grin.

Reaching over, pushing my head to the side, Sin laughed in pride. "Right. You shit talking but you were digging her out too."

"Man, look, we both hit her up when we bored, but I always make sure not to let Dee have any samples from me. She is extra as fuck sometimes." I shook my head remembering all the crap Dee put us through with going after us, and I laughed.

"True. Which is why we need to hit up that party. New pussy means no more Dee or her thirsty-ass friends."

"Wait, though, some of them are sexy as fuck and very resourceful. Let's slow down on that talk, man," I said, knowing we both were shit talking about leaving Dee and her friends alone.

For me, I never once thought about going outside of Goodman to hook up with any other broads. To me, Goodman girls were the best girls. They came in all flavors of chocolate and caramel, each mama unique and special. Now, some were crazy and extra but my brother and me didn't care. We liked spice sometimes because it helped when we got bored. So, the idea of linking up with new females, such as Roanoke neighborhood girls at Dee Dee's, did intrigue me. That was the only neighborhood in Jonesboro I didn't involve myself with. However, outside of the new pussy, I had my mind on other things like finding Marvin.

Saving the best for last by pulling into the Crack, an area everyone in Goodman knew users lived and hid, after not finding Marvin where he usually went, we ended up on a one-way street. Slowing down, I parked in front of a tall brownstone. Singe marks were on the brown brick. Moss curled over spots of the roof. Trash was in the little bit of yard there was and people sat on the concrete steps. In front of the old, ratty joint hella people were in the yard, drinking, dancing, and taking whatever drugs they could. Blue lights flashed inside of the spot, while music blasted.

"This dusty nigga is having a party?" Sin said with a tilt with his head.

"Looks like it," I said in annoyance. "Or he's selling our shit when he's not supposed to."

I turned off the car's engine, thumbed my nose in thought, and got out. In the Crack there was no loyalties. People who have dealings with all the gangs in Jonesboro could be found here, which made it hard for some runners to find people. Sinner and I, we didn't have that type of problem. No matter what, we always found people who would point out who we were looking for because of who we were.

Which we hoped would be the case now.

There was the scent of funky-ass, bad-grade weed and chemicals saturating the air when I stepped into the place. Everywhere I walked, I felt something crunch under my boot, or it stuck to the wooden floor. House music made my ribs rattle and people brushed against me as they drunkenly danced around the place.

"Damn, I hate coming over here. All I smell is piss, ass, and pussy," Sin spat out with a frown on his face.

I bowed my head coughing and almost covered my nose. He was right. It did smell like that.

"'Scuse me? You see a nigga by the name of Marvin, or Mad M?" I asked a skeleton-thin blond white chick who kept eye-hustling me.

She gave me a weird smile as she flipped her hair to the side while asking, "Who?"

"Marvin," I said with an irritated sigh. "Mad M. He's about six feet. Color of that oak door, beard, gray eyes?"

"You got some M? I'll buy some from you," the chick said, not even paying attention to what I asked.

"Nah, bitch." Pushing her away, I walked off.

Sin was across the way near some stairs. He signaled to me that he was going up and I gave a nod.

I continued searching around the place, my skin crawling. While I was walking a roach parachuted from the ceiling to land on my shoulder. For a second there, I almost shot up the whole house. I fucking hated the sensation of bugs crawling on me, and having that nigga land on my shoulder and try to holla at me did not help my already pissed-off mentality.

Having checked the back of the house and the kitchen, when I stepped out someone came up on the right of me. "Ooo, let me play in ya hair, daddy," I heard in my ear.

Hot breath that smelled like tart ass whisked under my nose.

My reaction was quick and something I couldn't hide. I twisted my face up and held my breath, trying not to gag while I looked down at a shawty with dyed red hair dressed in a micro dress. Gotdamn this broad had the scent of decay on her, like she tumbled in nothing but trash. My heart went out to her, because she looked to be my age. Though her arms were bruised with marks, I could see that she wasn't a real-deal junky. Not like the addict I just walked away from. No, this chick still had a healthy shapeliness to her. It was just her eyes that were full of sadness behind them that let me know she was on something.

I held my hands up while taking several steps backward. "Nah, mama, I'm good. But you can help me with something else."

"Yeah?" she said, suddenly shifting into an embarrassed gaze.

Damn. I knew that many people who ended up in this place didn't really want to be there, that they all had stories to tell. This girl in front of me was no different, so I checked myself and gave her respect. "Yeah, mama." I reached out and gently took her hand. "I'm looking for this grimy nigga. About six feet tall. Skinny, gray eyes. Goes by the name Mad M?"

The girl looked away from me, holding her hand while chewing on her lower lip. She then slyly looked up at me. "Mad M? Marvin? Yeah. He went upstairs. Just got done handing out some crazy product."

"Yeah? I hope you didn't take none of that shit, did ya?" I said, hitting her with a flirting tone.

"Nah. Poppa didn't collect any yet to give me for"—the girl looked around, then up and down at me, stopping on my dick—"stuff."

Annoyance hit me. So she was a prostitute. Usually that shit didn't bother me, but it was the vibe this girl was giving off that had me on edge, like she was being forced. So, I stepped up to her, and whispered in her ear while holding her waist, "Why don't you do me a solid since you just helped me out here?"

"Yeah? I can. What is it?" she happily asked while scratching her arm.

"Show me who poppa is," I calmly asked. Leaning back, she looked worried, and I held my hands up. "Promise, I mean no harm."

Giving me a smile, she pointed. "Right there, bald guy."

"Ah yeah?" Looking at the bald biracial-looking nigga with tats on his neck, I gave him a "what up" with my chin, and he turned my way.

"Thanks, mama," was all I said as I pulled out my Glock and let a round go off.

Several screams let out around me, but mostly people were too high to give a damn. Some folks screamed then went back to doing them, while others started searching the dead man's body.

"Oh, my God! Why you do that?" the girl screamed at me.

"Chill the fuck out and listen to me. What is your name?" I said, gripping her arm.

The girl continued to struggle and tug until she realized that I wasn't letting up. "Niecy," she said, sniffling.

"Look. The rules of the Crack is this: no pussy selling here, a'ight? I want you to hit up Dove Street and link up with a Miss Linda, okay?" Shaking her so that she would look me in the eyes, I stared at her hard. "Do that. If I don't see you there when I check in later in the week, I'll find you and kill you. Do you understand me, Niecy?"

Niecy sniffled then tugged. “Wh . . . why you do that? You said you weren’t going to harm him.”

“Right, and I didn’t. Harm and kill two different things, mama. Besides, you helped me and you remind me of an old pic of my grandma. So I’m helping you. Fair exchange. Now head out. Don’t come back to the Crack, a’ight?”

A loud commotion and banging started. Niecy gave me her okay and I let her go with little bit of cash in her hand. I watched her run out and glance at me, this time with something like a thank-you in her eyes. She disappeared into the darkness outside. While I rolled my shoulders and checked my Glock, I rushed to where Sin was now banging down the stairs after a nigga holding a large bag. Immediately I knew who it was: Marvin.

Nigga was in nothing but his boxers as he ran through people, pushing them out the way. Because my brother didn’t play, I followed him as he sprinted out the house. I jumped down the concrete stairs, hopped in my ride, and sped off following them both, trailing after my crazy-ass brother.

I shifted gears with a shake of my head, and sped up. When he led me to a dead-end alleyway between two brick buildings, I hopped out my ride to run up on my twin, who was choking Marvin against a brick wall.

“Nigga, you get no more chances,” I heard him shout.

Marvin shook with buck eyes, rambling about Guerilla giving him no choice. Breathing hard, Marvin huskily rushed out, “They told me to sell what I got at the Crack. Said . . . said they’ll kill me if I didn’t. I had no choice!”

That’s when my brother stood and let his Glock pop off. “No, Blanket gave you no choice.”

I walked up on Marvin, then kneeled down to look into his fading eyes. His mouth flapped slowly like a guppy. Blood curled and spilled from the edges of his pale lips.

The quietness of death always intrigued me. I wondered if Marvin could think clearly now. Sighing, I ran a hand down my face and hoped he heard me. "You could have told family, nigga. But instead you steal from family and giveth that bread to the enemy? Yeah, you had other options and that wasn't one of them."

A buzzing on my hip drew my attention to my cell. I saw that I had a page to tow a car. Pressing my Glock to Marvin's temple, I pulled the trigger and watched that light finally flicker out of his eyes.

I slowly stood up without any conviction over what happened. I turned to walk away, and spoke over my shoulder: "Call Choppa to handle the body. Search Marvin's place, and recoup whatever product we can find. We'll handle the Guerilla's contact later. Uncle Red is paging me to tow an Audi over on MLK, so I'ma head over there to pick up that truck and change. Let Blanket know where the issue started. We'll handle the loose ends."

"A'ight, twin," my brother said in a disjointed voice I was very familiar with.

My twin pulled out a blade. Observing him, I quickly added, "Don't carve up that nigga's face this time, man."

"Damn, but—"

"We don't have time for it, man. If I can't remove ears, fingers, or a tongue, then you can't carve him up. So, get back to Blanket's business," I said with a chuckle because my brother was staring at me with a crestfallen face.

"A'ight, then, I'm on it, twin," Sin said in sadness.

While he shook his head I heard him say, "Wasteful, Marvin. Fucking wasteful, nigga."

I rolled my shoulders and popped my neck and my twin did the same. We were Saint and Sinner. When Blanket was crossed, we handled the loose ends or it was our asses. Otherwise, we were the Blacks, just two niggas trying to survive Goodman while wondering when everything would change.

Chapter 4

London

I had made my way to the bathroom when I heard Brash's name coming from some chick's mouth in the bathroom. "I'm so sick of those bitches from Roanoke coming over here taking our niggas, man. Sick of that shit," some chick said.

"Tell me about it. Soon as them hoes come around, these niggas start acting brand fucking new. You see how Dusty and Lank all over them big bitches," another girl asked like she couldn't believe men would be interested in Marsha and Brandy because they were plus size.

Another girl chimed in. "I'm telling y'all, they only get wit' them bitches for the guap, trust me on that shit. It's always about the money."

"And then Laylah done brung that bitch Brash and that gap-tooth bitch up in here. Them hoes out there shaking they ass like they the shit. Busted-ass bitches. I should snatch that damn chain off that gap tooth–ass broad, though," the first girl said.

"Ho got a hair fulla nappy-ass hair and them niggas acting like she a bad bitch or some shit. Gap-teef bitch got Slade and Darren all over her. I don't understand that shit," the second girl said.

I figured Slade and Darren must have been the two dudes I had been dancing with. I wasn't attracted to them, but they could damn sure dance.

"And they only on that black bitch Brash 'cause she got green eyes. Other than that, them niggas wouldn't be fucking with that black bitch like that," the third girl said. "Fuck them hoes and, bitch, where Saint and Sinner asses at? They was s'posed to be here."

I heard an exaggerated sigh. "Them niggas be acting too brand new sometimes," the second girl said.

"Dee Dee, I still can't believe you fucked both them niggas," the third girl squealed.

"I sure the fuck did and what?"

I figured out that the second girl was Dee Dee. As soon as she had seen Brash she was all smiles and here the broad was talking trash behind her back. Oh, I couldn't wait to tell Brash.

"The 'what' is why you act like can't nobody else fuck 'em now," the first girl said. I detected a bit of attitude in her voice.

Dee Dee snapped, "That's because you can't, bitch. Those two dicks belong to me and if I see either one of you bitches trying to hit, you will proceed to catch these hands, ho."

The first girl tsked. "Whatever, bitch. I'ma tell you right now, if Saint even looks like he wants to fuck, he can get it. We just gon' have to fight about it later. Shit. Red-haired motherfucker fine as fuck and you talm'bout a bitch can't hit. You crazy out'cho head."

"You a nasty-ass bitch if you fuck behind me, ho," Dee Dee said.

"You two, please don't start this shit tonight, okay? Damn," the third girl cut in.

Just as she said that, she snatched the bathroom door open and came face to face with me. My eyes narrowed and I could tell by the look on her face she knew I'd heard something.

"Can I help you?" she snapped.

She was pretty enough. Dark brown with a long, straight weave. Her makeup was on point and she was prettier than I'd assumed she would be. She had on short shorts, some combat boots, and a cut-up shirt that showed her perky breasts.

"I need to use the bathroom," I said.

Another girl snatched the door open. She was paper sack brown. One side of her head was shaved off, and the other side had a long, curly weave. The style fit her heart-shaped face perfectly. I could tell she had gray contacts in her eyes, though.

"Go to the one in the basement," the girl snapped.

"I can't," I said.

She frowned and snatched the door open wider. She folded her arms and leaned her weight on one thick leg. "Why the fuck not?" she asked with much attitude.

"Someone is having sex in there."

The third girl—she was tall, at least six feet—appeared from behind the door and they all stared at me like I'd done something to them.

"Well, you can't use this one so I don't know what'chu gon' do," the one with the shaved head said. I knew she was Dee Dee based on her voice.

I found myself getting annoyed. "Well, is there anywhere I can use the bathroom?" I asked.

"Porta-potty out back," Dee Dee said with a smirk.

I studied her for a moment, trying to see if I had done something to the girl. "I'm sorry, have I offended you in some way?" I had to ask.

Dee Dee chuckled then looked at her girlfriends. The three women gave me an up-and-down stare then shook their heads. "Girl, bye," Dee Dee said then slammed the door in my face.

I shook my head and found myself walking back down the hall to find Brash. My bladder was screaming. I'd tried to go to the basement to use the bathroom first but walked in on a dude with another dude bent over the toilet. They looked as if they had just been caught red-handed robbing a bank. I quickly shut the door and rushed away. I could have sworn it was the same two dudes I'd seen arguing earlier. I'd heard stories about gay thugs, but had never seen no shit like that up close and I never wanted to again.

I finally found Brash hugged up in a corner with some cute dude who had locks. He reminded me of, oddly enough, my brother, DJ. Now I always thought Brash had a crush on DJ but I never said anything; however, any and every dude she had hooked up with looked like my brother or had the same characteristics he did.

I tapped her shoulder. "Brash, come go outside with me so I can pee," I whispered close to her ear so she could hear me.

The guy had her locked to him at the hips. His hands were on her waist and he kept licking his lips and looking down at her like he wanted to eat her alive.

"Find Laylah," she responded.

"I don't know where she is!"

"Where Marsha or Brandy?"

"I don't know, Brash! Come on, man. I need to tell you something anyway."

She huffed and puffed. "Damn, man. I'll be back, Paul," she told the dude.

"I'll be here, shorty," was all he said in return.

She giggled then took my hand. We made our way to the backyard. In the corner, where not too many people were, was the dark blue porta-potty.

Brash pulled out her phone and turned on a flashlight app. We both scanned the inside of the potty. It didn't look like it had been used at all. And I was thankful for the seat covers. I put a few down then squatted so I could handle my business.

"So how you know Dee Dee?" I asked Brash.

"She cool people. When I come over here to do hair and shit, me and her kick it from time to time."

"You like her? Consider her your friend?"

"Why you asking me that? You jealous?" she joked with a laugh.

"No, but I did hear her and her friends talking about us in the bathroom."

Brash snatched the door to the potty open. "What she say?"

I was used to Brash being abrasive so her snatching the door open didn't bother me. She would walk in the bathroom while I was changing a tampon like it was nothing. I told her what Dee Dee and her friends were saying as I wiped myself. Brash took her bottle of water and poured it on my hands. I then took some hand sanitizer from her to clean my hands as best I could.

"Oh, I can't stand a ol' two-faced bitch," Brash fumed. "But I knew that bitch ain't really like me like that. Paul and his brother was telling me some shit they was saying, too. I got something for that ass."

"Brash, please don't start a fight, okay? You know how Laylah is, too. You fight and she's fighting. Then Marsha and Brandy," I pleaded. "And I'm not even supposed to be over here. I can't get in a fight!"

Quiet as kept, Brash should have been worried about the same thing. Our parents were an elite part of Roanoke. Anything we did reflected on them.

Brash shook her head. "I don't even know why you tell me that if you didn't want me to say shit," she snapped.

As she wrapped her ponytail into a ball, I knew she was preparing to fight no matter what I said. I got a sinking feeling in the pit of my stomach.

"Brash, I told—" Just as I got ready to defend myself a ruckus broke out.

"Get down! Get down," I heard male voices yelling. "Guerillas in the mist!"

Next thing I knew, shots rang out like the Fourth of July. I screamed out. Brash reached out to grab me, slinging me to the ground. I didn't know who was shooting or why. Both Brash and I screamed while we hid in the back. Other yells and screams blended in with ours, as screeching tires faded into the distance. Just as quick as it had started, it all ended.

I jumped up and so did Brash.

"Shit, we gotta get out of here," Brash yelled. "Cops coming soon," she said.

We both knew there was no way we could get caught over here. We rushed inside, screaming for Laylah, Marsha, and Brandy. Lucky for us, they were already running to the car yelling for us. I didn't care about anything or anyone else. I knew we had to get out of there as quick as possible. While chaos ensued around us, the gods were good to me. Nobody had blocked me in and all my friends were safe. People were scattering like roaches. Once we all got in the car, I cranked up, and backed out, almost hitting a dude who was moving too slow.

"Don't go that way, cousin," Laylah yelled. "Cops will be coming in that way. Turn around, turn around," she urged, patting me on the shoulder.

I put the car in reverse like I'd been cast in *The Fast and the Furious,* whipped it around, and sped away like a demon out of hell. I didn't breathe until that party was so far in my rearview I couldn't see the house anymore.

I finally let out a breath once I knew we were safe. "Oh, my God. What the fuck just happened?" I yelled.

"I don't know," Laylah said. "I think Guerilla sent somebody."

"Who?"

"Guerilla, that nigga who runs the other side of the hood. Shit! Damn. Blanket 'bout to have my whole hood shut down."

"Who is Blanket?" I asked.

Laylah sighed. "Brash, fill my white bread–ass cousin in when you get the chance please. A bitch too shook up to be answering all her damn questions. Y'all a'ight?" she asked around.

We all nodded and agreed we were.

"Nobody shot or hurt?" she asked. "Gotdamn. Can't believe them niggas shot up the party. I hope ain't nobody die."

"Me either. Fuck, and I was about to get my pussy ate by that nigga Lank, too," Marsha quipped.

Brash whipped her neck around to look at her. Through the rearview mirror I could see Brandy and Laylah staring her down too.

"What? Shit, I'm backed up. I need that shit," Marsha defended.

"There was a drive-by at the party we were at," I reminded her.

"Sure as fuck wish they had started shooting after that nigga broke me off," she mumbled.

We all laughed. I thought it was more so because we were happy and relieved to have made it out alive. However, like Laylah said, I hoped no one died or got seriously injured. Just as I was about to say so, a loud pop scared the shit out of me. There was a rumbling noise that shook my eardrums. The car swerved and we all screamed as I lost control of the car. We whipped and jerked until the car came to a complete stop, with my feet pressing the brake down so hard I feared it was broken.

"Oh, shit," Brash whispered.

For a few moments we all sat quietly. The breathing was heavy in the car as we all knew we had escaped death or serious injury yet again. I hopped out the car to see if what I was fearing was true. It was. My damn tire had popped.

"Gotdamn it," I mumbled. I ran a hand through my hair. If it wasn't one thing it was a-fucking-nother, I mused.

Brash and Laylah got out to examine the car with me. My cousin knew me and she knew I was about to panic. "Calm down, London. Let me call the tow truck," she said.

I didn't even argue. At this point, I just wanted to get home and pretend none of it had ever happened. Fifteen minutes later, a tow truck with the name BLACK TOWING AND RENTALS painted on the side with red and black letters showed up. I waited patiently as the truck drove a few yards ahead of my car, then backed up with the flatbed facing the front of my car. I was all set to get out my car and meet the man, but I stopped.

"Damn, who is that?" Brandy asked before I could.

He was tall and athletically built, and his red hair glowed in the glare of my headlights. Tattoos were visible on his neck and shoulder and he walked like everything belonged to him. There was something about the way he moved that intrigued me. The top of his overalls was tied around his waist, yet he pulled them up with the clipboard still in the left hand. A pen was stuck behind his right ear. That strong, chiseled face screamed that he was all male, but the way he bit down into his bottom lip before licking both made me feel some things between my legs.

I wanted to get out the car to introduce myself, but I couldn't move. He walked up to the driver side window, laid the clipboard on top of the car, then bent down. He was almost face to face with me.

"You called for the tow truck, mama?" he asked.

Gotdamn, his voice. "I, ah . . . I mean . . ." I was stammering all over myself. I heard Brash and Laylah giggle.

"What up, Saint?" Laylah said from the back seat.

He cast a glance behind me then gave a head nod. "Oh, wassup, Lay?"

"Shit. Cousin tire popped. You gon' help her out?"

"It's what I do, mama."

"Think she need a new tire. Oh, that's her friend, Brash. These two fat bitches Marsha and Brandy," she added.

He chuckled lightly, spoke to everyone, then looked back at me. There was no doubt in my mind he was the Saint Dee Dee had been talking about. It made me wonder where the Sinner was. Saint's brown eyes found mine and I think I blushed. I hoped like hell I didn't.

"Get out the car, mama. Come talk to me," he said.

It was almost a demand, but something in me made me move. I opened the door then stepped out. He walked to the back of the car where the tire had blown out.

"How this happen?" he asked, nodding at the tire then writing on the clipboard.

I shrugged. "I don't know. We were leaving this party and then, all of a sudden, my tire blew out."

"Party at Dee Dee's?" he asked me. I nodded, wondering how he knew. "Somebody was shooting over there, right?" he asked.

I thought it was weird that he asked or that he knew, but remembered it was the hood where good news traveled fast and bad news traveled faster. "Yeah," I answered.

He licked his lips then stopped writing as he looked up at me. "You see anything?"

I shook my head then gave a light frown. "No."

"Just asking. Wanted to make sure everybody was okay is all," he responded with a warm smile on his face.

"I really don't know. I was scared so I left."

"It's cool. You got ID?" he asked.

"Yeah." I went to my purse then grabbed my wallet. I gave him what he asked for.

He paused when he looked at my ID for a second. "London Royal?"

I gave a shy smile. "That's me."

"You stay over there. The hell you doing over here?" he asked.

I didn't know why his question made me uncomfortable. I knew by "over there" he meant Roanoke. I shrugged. "Hanging with friends and my cousin."

He studied me up and down, then said a simple, "Oh."

It's like his cheery disposition had left and coldness swept through between us. I ran a hand through my hair again, hoping this night would be over soon.

Chapter 5

Saint

On the corner of Shit and Ass Boulevards, little mama's car was right in the middle of downtown and near the Crack, parked near the cracked brick and asphalt sidewalk. Ahead of us was Goodman's old town area, which was nothing but abandoned old school brick buildings, a daycare where my younger cousins worked, a hot wings/gyros/pizza and more restaurant, our local Chinese food joint, a Rainbow clothing store, and that's about it. Oh, yeah, and of course a liquor store and gas station right around the corner, owned by black folks funny enough. Anyway, where we were at, the street was saturated with water from an overflowing rain gutter, and the scent of piss and liquor traveled on the hot summer air.

Behind us were open weed-infested lots with ragged and bent wire fences, broken bottles, trash bags, fast food bags, cigarette butts, used condoms, and the ideal tumble weave, stuck wherever they lay. In another empty lot stayed our resident homeless, nestled up behind a worn building that was used by the ATL Metro's outreach program. Some of them were shuffling down the street, scratching their nuts, talking to the sky or whatever they were holding in their hand, and going about their business.

Focusing back on the important things, I stood outside prepping to do my job. I couldn't help myself in thinking, *here we go with this shit. Snobby-ass Roanoke broads coming through Goodman to use our hood as some sort of initiation spot to say they racked up some hood points.* Or, in the case of the females, white, black, whatever, coming through there just to feel like they the shit and feel like they were owed the world, so they used us for their shits and giggles.

My eyes narrowed at the thought and at the name London Royal staring back at me.

Fuck outta here.

When I pulled up to handle my job, I sat in the truck listening to my uncle Red give me the location of where the Audi had broken down. Pac with Jodeci played in the background and I could hear my baby cousin cooing while my uncle Red spoke to me.

"Ey, nephew. The client is a group of females stuck on Dunham Street. Make sure you get out there quickly so we can get them up outta here quickly and without ya mom's knowing," Uncle Red said over the speakers of my ride.

"Why, something up?"

Now, when my uncle chuckled in the same mischievous manner my twin did, I knew he was up to some shit.

"Nah, but you'll find out when you get there. I'm going to charge this account down on my own, because we don't need the drama," he explained. "You know ya mom is still pissed about you chilling in the zone."

Here we go. I ran a hand through my hair and kept it pushing in the truck. My uncle knew what Sin and I did when we weren't either in class or working at the shop, so it didn't faze him when I told him that I was on the other side of Goodman and that I'd be a minute.

"You know why, though," I said.

"That I do, nephew, but like I told you, you keep that shit basic. You're making too many moves that should be left by me. If we going to keep Blanket off our asses and out of our neighborhood, we gotta move with ease, nephew."

Yeah, my uncle Red was my contact guy for Blanket. Back in the day when Blanket started appearing in the streets, it was my uncle who stepped to the mysterious cat and garnered a contract that stated that the nigga never sold anything on our block, by our business, or near or around the churches and community center. In order to appeal to Blanket with such a deal, my uncle had to become the dude's partner in crime. As a means to help keep heat off my uncle, Sin and I linked up and started working as runners to keep my uncle safe and to make some extra dough, all of it going back into the community on the low.

"I understand. It's still all protocol. We're doing a sniff out and sweeping up whatever comes out and it'll be smooth. As for Mama, I'll talk to her and keep her level. Sunday dinner coming up anyway and I know she wants us all there," I explained.

Cooing started again and it made me chuckle. My uncle was shifting the phone on his ear and talking to his three-month-old daughter. Red was a savvy businessman and co-owner of the family business. Everyone in Goodman knew him like they used to know my grandpops. Partially, the reason for that was because he was an all-out thirst-trappin' nigga. That's all I can think to call him. Nigga had four women in different area codes: one in Roanoke, and three in Goodman. Out of all of them only one woman had his child and, because of it, my uncle's life stayed filled with female drama.

Spitting out a Pac verse about not being a villain and revenge being the next best thing to pussy, my uncle laughed, then cleared his throat. "Make sure you handle the exchange quickly and break them off with a staked price. You'll know why when you get there. If work needs to be done, pull it up in your garage in the back and we'll work on it, a'ight? No doubt if Maya find out I'll take the hit . . ." He cut off his comment after that.

I heard gnawing and cooing on the phone as my cousin, Sunny, named after my grandpa, played with the phone then hung up on me. While heading to my destination, I wondered what exactly it was about this client that would have my mom heated. Whenever she got into her moods, everyone tried to steer clear of her. If we didn't we'd be spending hours listening to her going off and clapping with her hands.

By the time I made it to the Audi and saw those familiar plates, my annoyance level was already jumping off. *Roanoke residents.* When I made my way to the car and I laid eyes on the driver, and I saw it was the same female I was scoping when my brother and I rode by Dee Dee's, that spark of annoyance seemed to disappear. Shit, I couldn't lie. To me, London was sexy up close and personal. I wanted to make her laugh, just to see that gap up close too, but when she spat out that she was just here for shits and giggles, I returned to being annoyed.

Writing down her name, I walked toward her car to check it out and see if I could tell off the bat what was up with the tire acting up. As I did that, I heard a slow shuffling sound coming our way. No doubt, I was strapped and ready for anything, but not wanting to alarm everyone in front of me, I kept my cool and moved quickly around the car.

A slow whistling drew my attention. It was a song, one everyone in the block was used to hearing. The flicking of a streetlight washed over the approaching shape of an old man with a salt-and-pepper afro and knotty beard coming our way. At his side was a brown hound dog and in front of him was a huge shopping cart making a chiming noise.

"What'chu pretty thangs doin' out chea so late, huh? You ain't got no young bucks to cozy up to, huh?" he hollered.

When the females around me kept quiet, I said nothing because I knew the O.G. I checked how he tugged on his tattered shirt, looked down at himself with a frown as if something stunk, and said, "Am I invisible? Y'all young thangs don't see a brotha? See, see, that's what's wrong wit' ya young girls. None of y'all got respect fah ya elders. None."

"Sup, Mr. Jones," I said in respect with a nod of my head. "You know how these Ro-folks get, sir. These girls' car broke down and they are just anxious to get home, so don't worry about them, a'ight? See you around the Blacks, a'ight? You see anything while you've been out?"

Mr. Jones shuffled past us with his grocery cart full of black garbage bags and everything plus some animals. I stepped forward, dug in my pocket, and gave him a fifty spot. Mr. Jones used to be a sane man at one time, used to run a bookmobile bus with his wife Paula. When she died in her sleep, he took to the bottle, got his house repossessed and taken by Royal Realty, and now was on the streets. Whenever I saw him, I always gave him a grip, some fresh clothes, and food. Something I did outta habit because of my mom.

He flashed a conceited smile behind his tangled salt-and-pepper beard. Mr. Jones took the money, and then pressed his hands together as if praying with a partial bow. "Thank ya, Saint. You always looking out. That's why I love ya family. Nothing but good folk you are," he said.

After a while, he leaned to the side, arm slumped low; then he stared at me in sudden awkward silence. There was a far-off look on his face before he started aggressively scratching his jaw in thought. I felt bad for the old man. Mr. Jones shook his shoulders then pointed down the street. "Two monkeys in the shadows over on Paige Street talking 'bout shooting up Dee Dee's. Might want ta get 'em to stop throwing shit."

"Thank you, Mr. Jones. You be safe now."

Mr. Jones grabbed his cart then waved. "You know I will."

While he walked off, he started singing some old-school song about a woman with a crooked foot and how she loved to shimmy for her no-good man. I chuckled at that and saw Laylah laughing in the back of the car. I knew she was familiar with Mr. Jones too, so wasn't no explaining that I had to do about that.

I stretched my hand by the tire. I looked it over, kicked it, glanced at my watch, and then stood up. "A'ight, so clearly I need to work on your ride. You have two choices: take the late-night bus outta here, or rent a ride from me while I work on it."

"Wait, will it take that long to fix the tire?" London asked with side eyes.

Because I was a perfectionist, I looked over the ride again and gave a shrug, already knowing the standard price I was going to give them for being in our area. "It's up to you. If you wanna wait it out then a'ight. Or, as another option, you always can leave your ride here."

On my way back to my truck, I tossed my clipboard in the driver side then turned with crossed arms to stare down at little mama's frustrated face.

"Leave my car here? No, I'm not going to do that. Give me a second please." I watched her huff, step off, then turn to speak to her girls. "Look, I'm not going to leave my car out here and I'm not renting a car, but . . ." Her words trailed in and out, mixing in with the chattering of her friends.

I heard Laylah offer that they could stay at her place, but London shook her head. London spoke some stuff about her father being upset if he found out about where they were and possibly taking her car away.

That's when some female I heard her call Brash spoke up. "Girl, stop tripping. Breathe then let him take the car to his shop. We'll go with you of course and I'll rent the car."

"I'm not leaving my car in Goodman. They might steal parts or something," she said, glancing my way as if I couldn't hear her.

Sexy as she was, she was a typical Ro-girl and that annoyed me, but didn't surprise me.

"Cousin! You're so spoiled I swear. Get in the car and let him take it, damn," Laylah huffed.

As if defeated, London came back to me and shifted on her kicks. "Take the car, but we're sitting at your shop as you work on it. Can it be done by tonight?"

Leaning to look at her car and do a once-over again, I gave a shrug. "Possibly. I'll know when I get a better look."

"Ah. Okay, we'll do that please. I appreciate the help," she said, playing with the ends of her crinkly kinky hair.

Something about her made me chuckle. I wasn't sure if it was how her eyes kept darting around where we were as if something was going to jump out from the bushes, or if it was something else hidden behind her big doe eyes. Whatever the case, it amused me.

I opened the side of my truck, then gave her a nod. "It's no issue. You called me. I'll hook up everything and y'all wait."

London mumbled another mouse-like thank-you then quickly got into her car. As she slightly brushed me, I smelled her perfume. It was light with a hint of vanilla. I liked it and liked how soft she felt when she walked past me. While I moved around my truck, I swore I heard her say in an embarrassed tone, “Oh, my God,” as other whispers of, “He’s so fine,” echoed behind me. Whatever the case, my mind was on a lot of things, especially the fact that I was helping some Roanoke chicks. Getting in the mode, I backed my truck up, added the car to the back of my caddy, then drove them through Goodman

Once we arrived at my family’s towing yard, I went to the back where the entrance was to the yard, hit the remote in my truck to open the gate, and drove through. Out of habit, I glanced for my Yukon and saw it near the upper back way to my apartment. The sound of my truck beeping as I moved London’s car into the private garage that was mine drowned out the music playing in the truck. I hopped out, motioned for them to drive the car off the ramp, and waited as they did so.

Everything went smoothly after that. I put the truck away, grabbed my clipboard, and then walked up to the group of females who stood huddled together.

“So like yeah, I’m going to check out the car. Once I’m done with that, I’ll come back to you with the estimated time it’ll take and price,” I said, approaching London.

When she gave me the go, I went to her car and began my inspection. I figured that the trumped-up cost for fixing her car could come to my service fees, but as I began working on it, I noticed additional simple issues with the tire, such as needing a realignment. I could tell from the slight damage that something had hit it when she pulled over. It was simple, nothing stressful and something I could easily fix on my own, so I did.

“So, Saint, why weren’t you and Sinner at Dee Dee’s party?” I heard while I was under London’s car.

Flashlight in my mouth, I shifted and took it out my mouth. From the familiar voice I knew who it was. “I was busy here working, Lay.”

"Oh, well. Be happy that you didn't come," she said.

"Why'd you say that? What went down?" I curiously asked.

I watched her hi-tops shift back and forth. Then they were joined by a matching pair that I knew were London's. As I waited for her to give me the details, I heard London ask, "Is it bad? I hope it's not bad."

Coming out from under the car, I found myself surrounded by hella females. Pursing my lips, I shook my head at it all and got up, keeping it professional. Wiping my hands, I focused on London's worried face. "Nah, actually it's not. I'm going to set you up with a replacement tire, realign you, and then you can go home. It should take me maybe an hour and a half. I know it's late, so if you don't want to chill here, like I said, we offer rental cars and you can pick your ride up first thing in the morning."

I could see the wheels churning in London's head. She was clearly uncomfortable being here and so was I. I didn't like the idea of a Royal being here or a Ro-chick, but it was what it was and money was money. I stood there wasting time, watching her battle with whatever internal voices little mama was speaking to.

As I turned to go back to the car, I heard quick steps following. "Just fix it. I'll . . . we'll stay."

While staring down into London's big brown eyes, I checked out how she nibbled on her lip. I took in the way she played with the ends of her multi-toned hair and it made me inwardly frown. Her hair was black at the roots and sandy brown toward the ends. Whatever nerves she had going on was making me anxious.

"Well, the waiting room is locked up, since this is late-night hours. I won't bite, unless you want me to, a'ight? It's pretty quiet over here, so you don't have to duck and cover, so relax. Nothing is jumping out to take your money but me," I said lightheartedly just to get her to calm down.

London gave a light little laugh then glanced at her car. "I just want my car to work, that's all."

"I get that, mama, and I promise your car is in good hands. Why don't you go sit on some of those big monster tires on the side of the garage?" I motioned with my chin, and London then gave me a half smile.

"Don't have any chairs for you all to sit on, but find a spot and chill. If ya need some drinks or something, we have a pop machine outside the front of the shop." Kneeling by the tire, I picked up my work again. "Lay, come see me at the car and tell me what happened."

When Laylah came forward, all of the girls came forward, including London. I shook my head at their hive mentality and chuckled. I respected how they kept each other protected.

"Ooo, so," Laylah started. She explained everything that happened at the party while I changed the tire.

Time slowly passed. When she told me that Dee Dee's was shot up, I stopped what I was doing and looked at shawty. "So, none of y'all saw a thing? No one knows who it was exactly?" I asked, stepping back.

Everyone shook their head and I chalked it up to them being scared and not being from here. I was somewhat salty about that. "Guess this will be the last time y'all show up on our side of the fence. You got to experience the hood, so you good, right?" I asked, glancing at the other four girls.

"This isn't our first time coming here," London said with a tinge of annoyance in her voice. "And we're not trying to experience a thing. We were just going to a party and that's it. You all do the most sometimes and are just rude to us for no reason."

I gave slight laugh while watching her. There was some fire to her and annoyance, too.

"Can you blame us? All you Ro-folk do is come down here to either look at us like charity, use us for an after-school special, rip us off, eat at our soul food joints, or use us as entertainment. Y'all don't really do much."

"You're lying. My dad helps Goodman all the time," London quipped with her nose wrinkling up in her irritation.

I flashed my teeth in an amused smile and tilted my head in surprise. "Who? Mr. Royal?"

"Yes, Mr. Royal! He's been working for years to build up Goodman, Jonesboro period, and clear out the drama that comes with living here. I say that's helping."

Hunching my shoulders, I continued working on her ride. "Yeah, like I said, use us for charity and that's it—"

"We, the people of Goodman and other 'needy' areas of Jonesboro, make him look good, that's it. Devon Royal doesn't do a thing for us but take our homes. Like always, Devon has felt entitled to the world since he was in high school; and I'm curious as to who these young ladies are, Santana."

Oh, shit, ran in my mind as I heard that acid, angry, familiar tone. "Mom, you know Laylah, right? I'm helping her with something," I quickly threw out there, hoping my mom would accept that as peace.

In the middle of the open garage stood my mother in all her might. Black Capri leggings showed off her curves and ample hips. She wore a red, yellow, and gold dashiki dress that had a plunging neckline. Curly black natural hair lay over her breasts, her almond-shaped brown eyes were narrowed, and one hand was on her hip as it held a sling bag that I knew had food in it.

Maya Black was in the house with my brother standing behind her giving me the "I'm sorry" look. Frustrated once again, I wiped my hands, put my rag in my pocket, then sighed. I had some explaining to do. Damn, it was too late for this shit.

Chapter 6

London

"I'm Brashanay McCullen," Brash said as she sashayed over to the woman who reminded me of a Black Power fighter, a Black Panther in other words.

My best friend held her hand out to the woman and acted as if she wasn't fazed by anything that boy, Saint, had just said. People always had something to say about us over in this place. Everyone I met always thought the worst of us. I was not some rich, spoiled bitch of brat. I mean, I was spoiled, but I wasn't; I didn't think too much of myself. Not since that time Mama beat the crap out of me, and not since spending those days with Auntie Nikki.

Did some of the things that happened in Goodman scare me? Yes, they did, but who wouldn't be afraid of people shooting and killing one another all the time?

"Hey, Ms. Maya," Laylah said as she waved.

After shaking Brash's hand, the woman smiled at Laylah and greeted her in kind. Brandy and Marsha spoke as well. Me, however, I stood frowning at the woman who spoke about my father as if she knew him. I looked her up and down, wondering just how well she knew him.

"And who are you?" Ms. Maya asked when she realized I wasn't speaking.

"I'm London Royal," I said, enunciating my last name so she would know my kin.

That was all I said as I stared the woman down. She had better not be one of those tricks my mama was always fussing about that Daddy had been with. Daddy was a good man, but like every man with power and money, the whores were on him thick. And even so, how dare she speak about my father with such disdain? I stared the woman down so long, she tilted her head and gave me a pointed look. I swore she reminded me of my mother when she did that. Mama did that same shit when I thought I was too grown to adhere to her rules or tried to stare her down even. It was a look that told me I was seconds away from a beat down.

While the look kind of shook me, that woman wasn't my mother; and if she was thinking about running up on me she had another think coming.

"Yo, chill, London. Damn, I swear you always ready to rumble about Uncle Dev with anybody," Laylah said. "Ms. Maya, she don't know no better," she said, looking at the older woman.

I ignored Laylah. She hadn't grown up with her father around so she didn't understand my plight.

"I see being rich doesn't come with manners," Ms. Maya said as she dropped the bag of food on a nearby table. "Staring me down like you want to rumble won't change the fact your father's a scoundrel."

"I'm about sick of this shit," I spat out. I shocked myself, so imagine Brash's eyes. "My daddy ain't did nothing to you, woman. So please spare me the theatrics. If it weren't for my daddy this piss poor–ass place would be a ghost town. Nothing would come through here if weren't for Daddy. Nobody over here is fighting for y'all, but my daddy does."

"London, chill, cuz," Laylah said as she grabbed my arm. I hadn't even realized I'd moved and had been talking with my hands. "You can't talk to Ms. Maya like that, girl. You fooling."

I turned to my cousin, frustrated and angry that she wasn't defending family. "How you just gon' stand here and let these folk trash my daddy like that? If it weren't for Daddy Auntie Nikki's ass would be on the fucking street! And you wouldn't have nowhere for you and Chance to lay your fucking heads."

Laylah took a deep inhale then snapped her mouth shut. Her eyes narrowed and she huffed. "Oh, bitch don't get cute. Uncle Dev ain't never done shit for me, okay? He only help my mama because if he don't folks gon' know he let his sister be homeless, and Uncle Dev always about image so we can cut that shit at the pass. Everything me and CJ got I worked for. I know working at the wing shop may not mean shit to you, but it's a fucking job and I ain't never asked you, your mama, your uppity-ass brother, or Uncle Dev for shit," she said emphatically.

When she mentioned my brother, Brash frowned and shook her head. I didn't want to argue with my cousin in front of everybody. I hadn't meant for what I said to come out so harsh, but people didn't understand what it was like always having to defend your family's name.

I was about to say something else when Laylah cut me off. "And don't be coming over here acting like you the Queen of England or some shit. Stop talking to folk like you stupid, Lon. Ms. Maya ain't done nothing to you. But you can't be mad if folk don't like Uncle Dev. You need to start asking why so many people speak ill of that nigga. Shit."

Laylah shook her head and huffed. Brash had a smirk on her face. I knew the scene just made her night. Anytime somebody spoke badly about my daddy it made her day. Marsha and Brandy stood wide-eyed with silly expressions on their faces. They looked like they had been placed in an awkward situation.

I was embarrassed as I looked at Saint who had an expression on his face I couldn't read. He was standing wide-legged with arms folded across his chest. The young man standing by Ms. Maya had to be Sinner, as he had red hair and almost looked like Saint, but there was a distinct difference between the two. Sinner kept a smirk on his face and Saint always looked serious, like he was in deep thought.

"Whatever, man. Just fix my car so I can pay and go home," I said.

My patience was gone. I'd been in a drive-by shooting, my tire had blown out, and now I got folk, even family, wanting to talk bad about my daddy. The night couldn't get any worse.

"Won't be any work on your car tonight. Come back tomorrow to get it," Ms. Maya said.

Now it was time for my eyes to widen. "Excuse me?" I turned to look at Saint. "You said you could fix my car tonight," I said.

He shrugged. "Her shop," he said nonchalantly. "Besides, us piss-poor folk need rest in order to get to our nothing-ass jobs tomorrow."

My heart sank to the pit of my stomach. God knew I hadn't meant for the words to come out of my mouth like they sounded, but I was so damn angry and annoyed. I wasn't the kind of person they thought I was, but nobody wanted to give me a chance to prove that. From the girls at the party to Saint, everyone saw a girl from Roanoke and thought the worst!

"You have got to be shitting me," I yelled.

"I assure you I'm not," Ms. Maya said. "Want your car, come back tomorrow. Better be here by noon. We go to lunch at twelve-thirty and won't be back until three."

"What is wrong with you people?" I asked. I was beginning to think my father was right. These damn ghetto-ass people only cared about themselves. *Who would leave a car full of girls stranded like this?* my mind quipped.

As if he had read my mind, Saint said, "I offered you a rental, mama."

"I don't want a damn rental. I want my car!"

I was on the verge of tears I was so frustrated. I had no idea that my tantrum was further proving to Saint, his family, and my friends that I was indeed the spoiled rich brat I claimed I wasn't.

"London, chill, sis. I can rent the car. Your daddy won't know you were over here, I promise," Brash said.

As soon as the words left her mouth, bright headlights lit up the shop. Saint and Sin both flanked their mother, who reached underneath the table and pulled out a shotgun. Everything that made me human froze up. I prayed to the Lord I wasn't about to be caught up in a shootout again. Brash grabbed my arm and pulled me back. Laylah backed up with us while Marsha and Brandy did the same. We all ducked down as far as we could in the corner.

I made out the shape of three men as they walked up. One man pushed the garage door up farther and my heart fell out of my chest. Maya cocked her shotgun and raised it, while Saint and Sin had brandished guns and I didn't know where they had come from.

"That's far enough," she spat at the men.

"Daddy," I called out.

There stood Devon Royal, looking like he had just stepped out of a corporate business meeting. There was a grim look on his handsome dark-skinned face. Daddy's hair was cut low in a wavy fade. He was dressed in a cream-colored suit and a black dress shirt, with a cream-colored tie laid against his chest. Standing at an even six feet, Daddy's broad shoulders gave definition to his athletic frame. His coffee bean–colored eyes scanned the room until they settled on me.

"London Royal, get over here, now," he ordered.

The bass in Daddy's voice chilled me to the bone as I stood timidly. At that moment I was no longer a nineteen-year-old young woman. I was back to being that twelve-year-old who got caught with a boy in her room when he wasn't supposed to be there. Daddy took his eyes off me and laid a hard scowl at Maya.

The woman didn't flinch. "Feeling's still mutual, Devon," the woman said calmly.

I didn't care how calm she seemed. The fact that she had the shotgun aimed at my father's heart scared the life out of me. Daddy's upper lip twitched as he glanced around the place. His eyes settled on Brash and he grunted low in his throat. Someone smacked their lips and huffed. I didn't have to turn around to know it was Brash.

"How did you know I was here?" I asked.

"Your phone called me and I assume you didn't know that," he said coolly.

I groaned low in my throat. I had a bad habit of butt-dialing people and not knowing it. I'd done it to my brother a couple of times.

"The hell are you doing over here?" Daddy wanted to know. I was about to answer but he held up a hand to stop me. "I don't even care. Darryl, hook up her car and bring it to your shop."

"Ain't nobody taking shit out my shop," Maya cut in. "She can come back to pick it up tomorrow as I said."

Daddy frowned harder as he turned back around to face Maya. Uncle Darryl, Daddy's youngest brother, stepped forward, but Saint's gun to his left temple stopped him.

"Please do it. Please do so I can spill some Royal blood tonight," Saint said contemptuously through gritted teeth.

I didn't know if Saint was being funny by saying "royal blood." Tap, Daddy's other guard, went to make a move but Sin caught him with a warning shot by his feet. I screamed. Somebody squealed behind me.

"Next shot won't be so friendly, my nigga," Sin said, still smirking.

"And keep looking at my mama like that and I'ma rock your ass to sleep, nigga," Saint told my father.

He and my father locked eyes. Daddy blinked once then something akin to a slow and easy smirk adorned his lips.

"Come on, London. Brashanay, if you need a ride home, you're welcome to join us. Same to you, Marsha and Brandy. Laylah, I would offer you a ride, but you seem to be most comfortable where you belong."

I glanced over my shoulder to see Laylah shaking her head. For as much as we fought, I loved my cousin and I knew Daddy's words stung.

"Nah, I'm cool. I'll find a way," Brash said.

"We're cool, Mr. Royal," Marsha added.

Daddy didn't respond as he opened the passenger side door for me. He helped me up then closed the door after I got in.

"Darryl, Tap, let's move out. See you around, Saint," Daddy said with a smile, but there was something in his eyes that unsettled me. He nodded at Sin. "You too, Sin." Then to Ms. Maya, he said, "Good boys you raised there, Maya. I'm sure Rooster would be real proud."

Maya's face turned down and she moved forward, but Saint stopped her. Daddy chuckled as he got in his truck. Darryl and Tap got into the big Ford F-150 behind us. I already knew Daddy was going to read me the riot act so I said nothing the whole ride home. The tension in the truck was thick. Daddy turned on some Boney James, but said nothing to me as I crossed the tracks into Roanoke.

There was a vast difference between the two neighborhoods. Streetlights lit up the way as we passed Macy's, Nordstrom, and other upscale stores and boutiques. There were no Walmarts or mom-and-pop stores in our city. All the storefronts were clean and inviting. Police in new-model Chargers cruised the streets keeping an eye on things. The big AMC 24 movie theater was crowded. Local bars and pubs didn't look as intimidating as the ones in Goodman. Immaculately designed buildings made up downtown Roanoke. Citizens were friendly. People sat outside coffee shops chatting with their friends as if nothing was wrong in the world. I wondered if any of them cared that a house had just been shot up in Goodman.

As soon as we pulled into the cobblestone cul-de-sac in front of Daddy's mansion, my mother rushed out of the house in her expensive kitten heels and came right over to me.

Tamika Royal was still beautiful at forty-three. Her short-cropped haircut made her look like Toni Braxton even though she was lighter than the singer. Mama was clutching her silk blouse at the top as the wind seemed to have picked up on our side of town. It had just been hot as hell in Roanoke. It seemed as if even the weather favored us more on this side. There had been times it was literally storming in Goodman, but we could stand in Roanoke and feel the sun.

"You scared the crap out of us, London. What were you doing over there? Just saw the news about a shooting and everything. Two boys were killed and more people injured," Mama fussed as she ushered me in the house.

Oh, God, my mind screamed. So someone had been killed at the party. I walked in to find DJ, my older brother, standing in the foyer with a frown on his face.

"You a'ight, sis?" he asked.

I nodded. "Yeah, my car, the tire popped."

"While you were in Goodman?" Mama cut in.

I nodded. "Went to a party with Brash and Laylah."

"Was that the party that got shot up? Where's Brash?" DJ asked.

"Brash stayed behind. We left the party before the shots rang out," I lied.

The last thing I wanted was to hear Daddy's mouth. To my surprise, he hadn't said a word. So I decided to say something first. "Daddy, I—"

He cut me off. "I don't have time to deal with you tonight, London. It seems that for as hard as I tried to keep you away from that life, you let people like Brash and Laylah talk you into it anyway. I don't know what else to do. Don't really have anything to say about it tonight either."

I watched as Daddy walked into the front room then came back out with a tumbler in his hand. In the tumbler was an amber-colored liquid with four cubes of ice.

"DJ, follow me in my office. Got some things I need to run by you. Tammy, talk to your daughter," was all Daddy said before he walked off. I was disappointed that he didn't want to say anything more to me.

DJ laid a hand on my shoulder. "Glad you're okay, sis. We'll talk tomorrow. I'll go with you to get your car, cool?" DJ asked.

I nodded. Mama took my hand and walked me into the front room. She asked me to tell her what happened. I did, keeping out the part about the gunshots at the party. It was only when I mentioned Maya that Mama's facial expression changed.

"That woman doesn't care about anybody but herself. She never has, but I tell you what, she pull a gun on my husband again and I'm crossing the tracks my damn self. Tuh. Fucking classless cunt," Mama said.

"You know her?" I asked, now more curious than ever.

All Mama did was shake her head then pour herself a drink. She walked over to the large bay window and looked out, glass in her hand. She didn't answer me, though. I called her a good three times before she turned around.

"Huh?" she asked.

"I asked if you knew that Maya woman," I said.

Mama shook her head. "It's a long story. One I'll tell you later."

That was the end of that conversation.

Chapter 7

Saint

I stood in thought, in a rigid wide-legged position with a locked jaw. The nerve in the side of my face twitched while the gun in my hand conformed to my squeezing grip. I didn't like Mr. Royal. On some "fuck that nigga" level, I didn't like that dude at all. Nigga taunted my mom and I guessed he thought no one would say shit? Maybe he thought that she was by herself in the world and that family wouldn't be by her side to hold her down when disrespected?

Nah.

That nigga had the wrong ones. Now that I got to meet the man whose face was on every billboard in Jonesboro, I came to the conclusion that I didn't like that nigga. I checked how he looked at me and my brother and how he made a point to let us know that he knew us. Intimately. I caught that shit clearly and it bothered me.

He was low-key flexing on us and I caught the street behind those eyes immediately. In that, I guessed my mom was right all this time: Mr. Royal was a chameleon. When the lights faded on the back of that Yukon Denali, my thoughts shifted and I was already in my head counting until doomsday decided to kick off from my mother's mouth.

Luckily, I could see her pacing, gripping her hands, and signaling for me to deal with Brash, Laylah, and their two friends. Out of all four of them, only two of them were watching on the sidelines, wide-eyed. Laylah stood by Brash's side unimpressed, while Brash watched with a quirked eyebrow, whispering to Laylah.

As if on cue, while I strapped my Glock, all I heard was a loud clamor of something metal with the sound of someone spitting. I then heard my mother start going off in a low, calm tone with a slight, sarcastic laugh. "Slick, arrogant bastard struts up in here as if he owns this shit. As if he owns me! I own this! Our name is out there on the sign of the shit. This is mine!"

My mother strolled back and forth in a fit, the bottom of her sandals slapping on the concrete flooring. As was typical of her, she had one hand on her hip, and the other slapped the top of her ample breasts in anger.

Embarrassed as fuck, I made my way to the girls. Brash watched my mom in shock then grinned in something like approval. I leaned in toward Laylah and heard Brash whisper, "I so don't like him. I know that's my girl's father, but fuck him really."

A part of me wanted to speak up on that and agree with her, but the part that was upset that they had to see my family in that light kept me quiet.

"He's always been that fucking way. Ms. Maya was right about that shit. He is arrogant," Laylah whispered back, crossing her arms over her chest and twisting her face up.

With a sharp exhale of breath, I quickly headed toward them at the same time as Sin. They needed to go, like right now. My mom was a growing volcano, and I was not about to have her look crazy in front of strangers.

"Sorry you all had to see that. Sin . . . Will can set up a rental car with whoever is going to handle that," I explained.

My twin flashed a flirty smile and low-key ran his eyes on all the girls in front of him, until his gaze settled on the pretty, light-skinned, curvy girl. I watched Sin position himself in her way and I was about to blast him for it, but when my mother kicked something else in the garage, I turned to make sure that she wasn't scratching up the car or something.

"Then he has the gall to gloat? That bastard was gloating! I need y'all to know that," she spat out in fury to us and to the imaginary jury I assumed she was speaking to in her mind.

Whenever my mother was in beast mode, all of us tried to find a way to ghost out. From the corner of my eye, I saw Sin snatch the bag of food and glide out the back of the garage, escorting the girls. That nigga, as usual, was leaving me to our mother's wrath. I guessed I'd take that, but I didn't like the shit. When he chucked me the deuces at the same time with a huge grin, my eyes narrowed in thought. I hated that soft-foot motherfucker.

Since Sin had slickly exited from the back, I knew that I had to find another exit plan. Taking a look at my mother, I saw that she was walking vertical in the garage, meaning she was sideways in front of me. I figured that if I moved quickly but quietly, I could dip before she even realized it. Which was what I chose to do. Going off what she said earlier about that nigga Mr. Royal coming up in here, I headed toward the front of my garage.

"Santana Sonny Black."

Inwardly cursing, I gritted my teeth then tried to keep a cool face as I pointed ahead of me. "Ah, yes, ma'am? I was just gonna check out the gate 'n' stuff. You know, make sure everything is clear." That was my best and quickest excuse, because outside of breaking lock on the gates, no one could get in unless they climbed it.

"William Jr.!"

Flexing my hands, I frowned at my mother's shrill yell.

"Yes, ma'am!" Sin yelled back. Nigga was on the steps to my apartment, being nosy, no doubt. That's the only way he could hear her.

"Go clear the area and lock down the gate. I had it open when I came in. Thought I had locked it back but clearly I didn't, thanks to your brother," she said, narrowing her amber eyes at me.

Okay, see what she said ticked me off. I didn't do a damn thing but my job. Yet, she was coming foul at me. Damn. Sometimes she got on my last nerve. But like any black mother who flexed an iron will, there was only so much testing her boundaries that a child was allowed. I had used up maybe one talk-back card with her already. I had two more left.

However, she hit a nerve and I was becoming pissed off. My face reflected that as I stood there, arms up with a "what the fuck" smile on my face. "Mama, come on now! That wasn't my fault at all."

"Ah yeah?" she asked with a sassy head tilt. She pointed around the room with her black outline-tipped fingernails. She gave me the death look of a mother and said, "So, all these Royals up in our house isn't your fault?"

Inwardly in angst, I rubbed the back of my neck and let out a sigh. "Here you go," I muttered.

"Excuse me? Damn right here I go. So you forget my feelings about that family, huh?" she hissed.

Welp, I just ran out of cards. "No, ma'am. I was just doing my job. I got the call and picked up the ride. I didn't know who they were until I got here," I lied.

"You didn't follow the Black standard? Something you train the rest of our team that works here? You didn't follow that?" she stated, inching my way.

Gotdamn it. From how she was approaching me, I knew to keep a distance or those sharp nails of hers would be poking me in the chest.

Scratching the side of my jaw, I tried to quickly think. "Ah, I mean I did, but I didn't even realize that her last name was Royal. I was just doing my job, Mama. Come on, Mama! It's late. I know you're sleepy. You know you always need that beauty rest of yours." I flashed a smile trying to soften my mom's temper like I sometimes could.

Of course, it wasn't working this time.

Had Mr. Royal not shown up, my mom's anger might have just been chill, but because he came through as he did, hell was opening up in the middle of the garage. I knew one thing, though: I wished she would just tell us why she hated Mr. Royal so much. It might make things easier.

"So what were you going to do, Santana? Secretly work on the car and not charge? Give people something free that they don't deserve?"

Quickly, I let her know that wasn't the case. "No, ma'am. She was going to get the same Ro charge that we give to all Roanoke people. Trust me, Mama. I had it handled."

"Did you? Doesn't look like you did because that man strolled up in here, I say again, like he was some-damn-body! I just . . . I just . . ." Becoming rigid with anger, my mother took a deep breath, ran her tongue over her lips with a cold snarl, and sucked her teeth.

"I'm going to go home now, baby boy." She walked toward the exit door and spoke to me without looking at me. "I brought you some late-night food because I know you were in these streets doing shit you have no gotdamn business doing. But, my anger right now is on other things so I'll let that slide. With you too, William Jr.!"

"Yes, Mama," Sin faintly yelled back.

It felt as if I was letting her down, so I jogged to her and turned her around to hug her. I then gave her a loving kiss on the cheek as an adoring son does for the woman who cares about and birthed him. “I’m sorry, Mama. I really didn’t know who she was until I agreed to help her.”

I held her hands against my chest and pulled away. My mother’s shoulders slumped in a solemn manner. She gave a light exhale while tightly hugging me back. Somewhere in the back of my mind, I knew that she was hugging me, like she always did, as if it was going to be the last hug for us. It was her way of making us feel her protection, respect, and love.

“I love you, baby,” she warmly said. “You and your bad-ass brother. I just am trying to keep you both safe and from—”

“Mama, you’re going to have to tell us why you’re so angry at him for real. You have no issue with Laylah coming by, but—”

“Don’t go there, Santana, not right now,” my mother said with all seriousness in her voice. She reached up and endearingly tugged on my chin beard. “One day I’ll speak on it, but it won’t be tonight. I just can’t.”

She kissed my cheek and then stepped away from me. “Don’t tell your uncle about him being here or the guns being drawn, okay?”

I knew my uncle wasn’t wrapped tight, but I didn’t think he’d jump off the deep end, considering he was the one to tell me to hide London being at the shop. But, since my mom asked and didn’t order me not to tell him, I decided that I’d keep it to myself for now. There was something in her eyes that I didn’t like, which was what added to me not saying anything.

“Yes, ma’am,” was all I said while watching my mother in concern. When she slowly walked out and I heard her slam the door of her car, I noticed that she never answered my question about Laylah. Shaking my head, I stepped out in the night heat, and looked at Sin.

He stood up and gave me a familiar shrug. "One day she'll speak on it, brah."

"Yeah, I know. I just hate seeing how much pain she's in," I said, locking up my garage, then heading upstairs to my apartment. Sin threw an arm over my shoulder and followed.

With a pause in our step, I gave him a look. "Where's Laylah and the others?" I asked in curiosity.

"Ah, see," he started. I immediately knew he was up to some shit when he said that. "The keys to the main building were with you and in the garage. So, I took them upstairs to wait."

This mother! I punched my twin hard in the shoulder and moved away from him. "Man, you stay plotting. Fuck! Get them out my place! Uncle Red was in the front. More than likely he's still fucking there, just clueless about everything that popped off. All you had to do was take them there, shit."

"What had happened was I was busy watching that brown redbone's ass. Learned her name is Brandy. I like how she sports that red lipstick," he said, looking at the door of my place.

"Man." Thumping him upside the head, I headed into the apartment. When I stepped in my place I saw Brash walking around my living room, picking up books and things. Laylah was looking at pictures with a big smile on her face, probably because she saw some old high school pictures. Brandy and Marsha were the only ones who had some damn respect by sitting on the edge of my black couch.

"Ladies, welcome to my crib, but this is not a waiting room. Why don't y'all follow me out to get that rental car of yours and we'll get you home in no time, on my word," I said, motioning for them to leave.

Everyone walked past me, but it was Brash who paused. "You have a nice place, Saint," she said then gave me a cute grin. "I like that you're very well learned. It means you're not just about the streets."

I got ready to say something smart about her stupid-ass comment, but instead, I followed where she glanced at the books on my coffee table and I let her nosy ass talk. "Management? Hmm. Who would have thought?" She gave me a cute wink, giggled, then walked out to meet up with her friends.

This was exactly why I hated strangers in my home. I was going to kill my messy-ass brother. Mean mugging my twin, I pushed him down the stairs and slammed the door to my place. Setting them up with a rental was no issue. Like I thought, my uncle was inside with his bottle-feeding son strapped to his chest. He gave us both a look and I held my hands up as if to surrender.

Sin walked past me to whisper in my ear. "Had I not had Jamal with me . . ." He trailed off.

The tension in my body began to turn into slight annoyance. I reached up and pinched between my eyes with a nod. I figured that he was paying attention and watching the monitors back in the front office. In my mother's anger, I gathered, she didn't know that he was still in the office. Now, because of that, I had to worry about what he was going to do.

"What are you going to do?" I muttered, keeping all emotion from my face.

"Me? Nothing for now, nephew. Jamal has me chill and we all are blessed for that." Reaching behind me, my uncle grabbed some keys and tossed them to Sin. Sin exited, then came back a minute later, honking.

"Ladies, thank you for doing business with Black Towing and Rentals. Miss Brandy Williams? The white Dodge Charger is yours for the night. For the difficulties, we upgraded you," my uncle said with a smile.

"Ooo really? Thank you so much!" Brandy said with a squeal.

As the girls left, one of them whispered, "Damn, he's just as fine, too, just older."

From the geeked grin on my uncle's face, I knew that he had heard them.

I narrowed my eyes at my uncle in a territorial manner while I spoke through gritted teeth. "That's my ride."

He chuckled with a lopsided smirk. "And I'm sure they'll take care of it. Call it a consolation for stressing your mother out."

"But—" I started but by then my uncle walked out.

Fist slamming on the counter in front of me in annoyance, I growled low and went to my apartment. "Fuck shit."

Late to bed, but early to rise, Sin stayed his ass on my couch that night and, in the morning, stole more of my clothes. I used the energy from last night on fixing London's ride and was happy when my uncle picked up my car from the Roanoke side. The removal and alignment, since I had Sin working on it with me, didn't take long, but as was the rule with Roanoke folk that was something I wasn't going to let London know. After moving the car to the front service garage, I pretty much chilled waiting for noon to come through.

Chapter 8

London

I was up at seven sharp. I had to sleep in my old room as no one volunteered to take me home. I was going to get my car even if I had to walk to get it. I called Laylah but she didn't answer; called Brash and she didn't pick up either. I wouldn't even attempt to call Marsha and Brandy. I knew their parents were probably somewhere hovering around them like vultures.

Luckily for me, I didn't have to walk. My brother, DJ, was waiting for me by his truck when I walked outside. Brash always talked about how my brother was a sexy nerd and was one of the only guys she found attractive on our side of town. DJ had on his black-framed glasses, khaki slacks, dark brown loafers, and a black button-down shirt. He had the sleeves rolled up to his elbows. DJ worked out faithfully. He was an inch or so taller than Dad. His hair was cut in a low fade like Daddy's as well.

His sandy brown skin glowed in the morning sunlight. He smiled as he looked at me. "I called the shop already. Dude named Saint said your car would be ready when we get there," DJ said. He held his arms open to hug me before he walked around to open the passenger side door for me.

I smiled. I loved my big brother. Laylah could call him uppity all she wanted, but DJ was down to earth and he never turned his nose up at people.

He got in and we made our way to Goodman. "So Daddy told me what happened. I'm not going to browbeat you or nothing but, baby sis, you have to be careful, a'ight? Shit can happen to you over there," DJ said as we stopped at a light.

"Stuff can happen to me over here too, DJ," I said.

"Yeah, but there is a far less chance. Our crime is nowhere near the level of shit that goes on over in Goodman, baby sis. Quiet as kept, I know you were at that party when the shots rang out," he said.

I looked at him. "How?"

"B told me," he confessed.

By B, I knew he meant Brash. "When did you talk to Brash? She wouldn't even pick up for me," I quipped. I was a bit put off by the notion she would talk to my brother and not to me.

DJ chuckled and shook his head as we pulled into traffic. "That's neither here nor there," he said. "What's important is if you're going to be hanging out in the hood, you need to get a hood mentality. It's a different kind of jungle when you cross these tracks, baby girl."

I frowned a bit. DJ was talking like he hadn't grown up just as sheltered as I'd been. "And how would you know?" I asked.

"It's all about adapting, sis. You stick out like a sore thumb."

"I do?"

"Yeah, you do. And whether you want to admit it or not, you do come off like a spoiled brat."

"Oh, my God."

"I'm just saying. Just saying." DJ chuckled as we crossed over the tracks into Goodman.

My nerves got antsy as soon as we did and I was reminded of the fact that I was at a party where two people had died. Once we got into the center of Goodman, I figured DJ didn't know where he was going.

"You know where the shop is?" I asked.

He nodded. "Yeah, but need to make an important stop right quick."

I didn't question him. My mind was on what he had said to me. Did I really come off like a spoiled brat? I shook my head. And what the hell did DJ know about adapting to the hood? He was driving a 2015 Escalade, a Rolex was on his wrist, he was in line to get Daddy's real estate business, and he had never suffered a day in his life for anything. What the hell did Devon Jr. know about being hood?

We'd pulled up to Auntie Nikki's house when I finally realized we had stopped. I shook my head again. Auntie Nikki needed her ass whupped for the way her yard looked. Trash, toys, and only God knew what else littered the yard. My older cousin, Mudbuster—don't ask how he got that nickname, I didn't know and couldn't tell you—walked up to the truck.

"Whaddup, cuzzo?" he asked DJ as they slapped hands.

"It ain't nothing," DJ answered and my eyes widened at his vernacular.

"Wha's good, Lon?" Mudbuster greeted me.

He was twenty-five and still lived with his mama. Tall, dark brown with a Gumby haircut on his head, tattoos littered his body, and it always looked like he was wearing a colorful shirt even when he didn't have one on. He was lanky. Looked like he needed to be fed often.

"Hey, Leon. How are you?" I asked with a smile.

"I'm good. I'm good," he said with a gold-tooth smile and then looked back at DJ. "What'chu need?"

"You seen Laylah and Brash?" he asked.

"Yeah, they at some crib over on Paige Street. You 'bout to dip over there?"

DJ nodded. "Yeah, need to pick up something."

Mudbuster chuckled. "You taking her with you to get it?" he asked with an amused look in his eyes.

DJ shook his head. "Nah. It ain't nothing like that. I'ma hit you up later though so we can discuss some things. That nigga made a move yet?"

"Ain't heard shit. Ain't seen shit. No birds chirping or covers rustling today, kinfolk."

"Bet," DJ said. "Auntie Nikki cool? Y'all need anything?"

"Mama need a few things. I don't get paid until next week though."

DJ reached over in the glove compartment and pulled out two rolls of money, but it was the gun I saw that made me gasp.

"DJ, why you riding around with that thing in here?" I asked in a rushed whisper.

He shook his head. "Not now, baby sis," he answered then slapped the money in our cousin's hand. "Tell Auntie Nikki I love her and will be back to see her later on. Also, take that other stack and get somebody to clean up this fucking yard, nigga. I see you out here trying to clean it, but, nah. Get some of these fiends out here together and get it done. I may have some work for you over in Roanoke, too. We'll talk later, a'ight?"

Mudbuster stuffed a roll of money in his pocket and then nodded. "Fa'sho, cuzzo." He dapped my brother and then DJ backed out of the yard.

Meanwhile, I was staring at my brother like I was seeing him for the first time. I wanted to ask so many questions, but I couldn't. DJ pressed CALL on the OnStar button in his dash. The phone rang about three times before Brash's voice came through.

"Where are you?" DJ asked her.

I heard Brash smack her lips. "With Laylah," she then answered.

"With Laylah where? You got her in the crib?"

I heard Chance, Laylah's son, crying in the background so Brash couldn't lie.

"DJ, chill out, okay?"

"Nah," was all he said before he pressed the END CALL button.

DJ pressed the gas and made a right turn off Auntie Nikki's street. About ten minutes later, we turned onto Paige Street. It was still early in the morning so hardly anyone was outside. Just the homeless and what looked to be a few drug addicts. I swore, even the houses that had clean yards looked dirty. Nothing about this place was clean to me. But the house DJ pulled up to stood out. The ranch-style house had cream-colored paneling with red shutters on the windows. The yard was manicured and nothing was out of place. DJ parked on the street and then walked up to the door. Before he could get to the door Brash came out.

I had no idea what the hell was going on. I felt as if I was in the Twilight Zone.

Brash had on yoga shorts and a sports bra. Her shapely body was on display as she stepped in front of DJ to stop him from going in the house. "DJ, stop," Brash said as she shoved him back.

My brother looked down at her. "No, B, Laylah is disrespectful."

Just then Laylah shoved the screen door open. She had on sweats, tennis shoes, and a white wife beater. If I didn't know anything else, I knew that was fighting gear. I hopped out of the truck, more than a little confused.

"Laylah, go back in the house," Brash yelled.

"I'm disrespectful? Nigga, fuck you. You think just because you got a dick and money—"

DJ didn't spare Laylah a second glance. "Get her away from me," he said to Brash.

"What's going on?" I asked. Nobody paid me any attention.

"Get her away from me and get in the car, B," DJ continued.

Before I could wrap my mind around anything, Laylah reached around Brash and swung at DJ, barely missing his face. While Brash was trying to hold Laylah back, DJ reached over her head and slung Laylah to the ground by her hair.

"I told you the last time you put your hands on me I was going to forget you were my cousin, Lay. I told your ass, didn't I?" he barked out.

Laylah hit the ground so hard, I was sure I heard her hip crack. She tumbled then rolled. Brash turned around and shoved DJ.

"Stop," she screamed with tears in her eyes.

I grabbed DJ's arm as I didn't understand what was going on, but I didn't ever want to see my brother handle family like that.

"Get in the truck, B," DJ told her.

I knew he was angry if he didn't display any aggression on his face. My brother was like my father in that aspect; no one could tell what emotions were going on with them if they didn't know them personally. DJ and Daddy could be laughing but be so angry inside I knew smoke was coming from their ears.

Brash was busy trying to hold Laylah back, who was fighting mad. Brash was damn near tearing the shirt off my cousin to hold her back. Laylah's face was red and tears stained her face.

"I'ma kill this nigga. Let me go, Brashanay," she screamed.

By now we had an audience. Cell phones were out. DJ's face would be all over the Net and Daddy would be livid. Brash was still trying to keep Laylah back while I was pushing DJ toward his truck.

"Get in the truck, B, or I swear to God, all this shit disappears and that clown will be back at Auntie Nikki's crib. At this point, I don't give a fuck," he said.

"DJ, stop, please! Don't do this," my best friend pleaded.

"If I get in my truck and pull off, I'm done."

With that my brother turned and made his way back to his truck. Brash lost control of Laylah and she came charging toward the truck. I stopped her while Brash ran into the house.

"Laylah, stop this and go into the house. Your son is crying!" I pleaded, but she was like a rabid animal.

She was foaming at the mouth trying to get to DJ. She didn't hear me or her son wailing from the house. She didn't notice Brash as she ran into the house, grabbed her purse and shoes, and rushed back out of the house. When Laylah realized Brash was leaving, her eyes widened. Something akin to hurt and sadness washed over her face. I'd never seen Laylah look so downtrodden.

"So you leaving?" she squeaked out like all the fight had left her. "You gon' leave with this nigga?" she asked Brash.

"I'll be back, Laylah," Brash responded.

"No, you won't," DJ said from the front seat.

Brash whipped her head around at him as she had one foot in the truck and one foot out. "DJ, please."

"Get in the fucking truck, B!" he yelled in response.

I didn't know what to do or say. Had no idea what had been going on. By the time I figured out Brash and DJ had something going on, just as Brash and Laylah did, Laylah came out of her shirt, ran around me, and started punching Brash in her face. The hits were so rapid and hard they caught Brash completely off guard. She started flailing her arms as Laylah snatched her out of the truck by her hair. Brash fell to the ground. DJ jumped out of the truck and rushed around. I tried to pull Laylah off Brash, who by now had gotten up and started fighting back. DJ grabbed Laylah up like she weighed nothing and he tossed her in the grass behind him.

He pointed to one of the dudes who were standing around. "Grab her," he said. "And I better not see any of this shit on any social media site."

The boy rushed over like there was a fire lit under him. He grabbed Laylah in a bear hug while DJ grabbed up Brash. He pushed her in the truck then yelled for me to get in. Laylah was screaming for Brash as the guy dragged her back into the house. DJ sped off seconds later while my best friend cried in the front seat.

We made it to Black Towing and Rentals about twenty minutes later. Brash was covering her face; sniffles could be heard from behind her hand.

"Somebody want to tell me what's going on?" I asked.

DJ sighed heavily. "Go get your car, baby sis. Let me take her somewhere right quick," was all he said.

I knew I wasn't about to get anything else out of him.

"Brash, you okay?" I asked after I got out of the truck and walked to the passenger side window.

When she looked up at me, I saw that Laylah had left her mark. Brash's lips were busted. Right eye was swollen and there were scratches on her face and neck. Her green eyes were puffy and red. "I'm cool," she said.

"Get your car, London. Let me handle this," DJ said.

"You're going to leave me by myself?"

"You'll be fine, London. Call Mudbuster if you need some help."

I didn't have anything else to say so I backed up and he pulled out. I knew that he and Brash had a lot of explaining to do. But right now wasn't the time since they seemed hell bent on getting away.

I stared after my brother's truck for a long time. I realized I didn't know DJ as well as I thought I did. It was like he had been two different people. He was the well-spoken and well-respected Devon Royal Jr. on the Roanoke side of the tracks. Over here, I didn't know who the hell he was. Not to mention, I had no idea he and Brash had ever had anything going on. I felt lost. I shook my head, turned around, and ran smack into a wall.

I stumbled, looked up, and found Saint standing there.

Chapter 9

Saint

Gotdamn, ran in my mind.

I stumbled back, dropping my bag of chips—I was on lunch break and was hungry as fuck—and I held London's shoulders as she looked up at me. I had checked her stepping out of the truck while I was at the front desk. After having a slow day with customers, Sin and I had decided to do some hood workouts with our uncle Red, you know, crunches, pull/push-ups, and more. Sweating like beasts, we ended with breaking for lunch.

Eating a foot-long from Subway and some veggie chips with Sin, we both saw when London pulled up. Uncle had been speaking to us about what he learned from having my boy Choppa go through Marvin's place, and secret hideouts that he didn't think we knew about. From what he learned, Marvin had been skimming product we gave him to sell. Talking with people he sold to on the block, we learned that he was charging them double what we typically charged.

Uncle Red cut his eyes at us all as he spoke low and curled a lip. "This accounts for two things, nephews. This shows us where some of our product was going and why our money kept coming up cut. Nigga was padding the price to make up for what he'd take."

Making doodles on his notepad, Sin shook he head and clicked on the computer at the same time. “He’s sloppy. That’s why we were watching him anyway. Since he was padding, it should have come even but it didn’t.”

“Right,” Uncle Red said, glancing my way. “It never came even. Why? Because he was trading some of our product with Guerrilla’s crew and undercutting us, all to get high and make profit as the same time.”

I stood, leaning with my arms against the desk while I ate. “He could have been doing this to build up their turf and split on us. He kept spitting nonsense about them making him do it, but that shit doesn’t make sense, unless they were trying to convince him to give up his turf we assigned to him.”

Uncle Red scraped sweet red slushy ice from his white Styrofoam cup. He slid the spoon in his mouth with a contemplative gaze then licked his lips. “Yeah. Y’all keep your ear to the street. Whatever you find out, report. Blanket isn’t going to like this shit, so I need to do whatever I can to keep all ties straight. If it’s some warfare shit ready to go down and thief, I need to know immediately,” he said, reaching over to give my baby cousin Jamal his small baby bottle.

He lay chilling like a three-month-old does, watching us and the invisible angels around him, as my mom called it. After that we spoke on everything and nothing. We watched the Escalade and heard loud voices popping off. Because it was my responsibility with the car, I stepped from the desk and stood by the open door, feeling the heat on my skin.

The Georgia sun was blazing so we both had our suits tied around our waists. My beater was pulled behind my neck whereas Sin still wore his. Uncle Red was shirtless all together but had just the front of his suit unzipped. My mom believed in using air, so we had our AC on full blast, and it was rattling loudly. Guessed it meant it was time for Uncle Red to work on it again.

People from the neighborhood occasionally stopped by to buy bottled water, soda, and freezer pops from our side store my mom had opened back up because of the weather. Music was on blast. Kids played ball in the street; some used water hoses that my mom propped up for them. Others played in plastic pools she set up. Hot as it was, the block was somewhat active and the energy was banging.

When London stepped out the truck still talking to whoever, I had stepped back to the desk to cop her keys to her car. Snatching my chips from my brother, I ended up walking toward her, and was just about to call her name when she backed up and rammed into me. I knew it wasn't on purpose by far but girly hit me almost like a linebacker. The thought of that in my mind made me chuckle as I looked over her head at the departing truck.

That Escalade was familiar to me. Everyone knew it belonged to DJ Royal. Whenever he was on our side of the tracks, you could see him around Goodman parked in front of the abandoned houses or foreclosed houses his family now owned, with a crew of people working. Back in the day, I had some homies work for the Royals just for quick summer money. I heard all types of shit about how well they took care of the work crew, and how particular they were about rehabbing houses.

At one time or another, I used to be jealous about not being allowed to work for them. It was easy money to me, and I was good with my hands. Back when I was younger, I knew that I didn't like how the Royals were taking people's houses. But I reasoned it away as just part of the game of business.

I knew back then that my friends were getting dough and I wanted in on it. Those thoughts were before I realized how deep my mom's dislike for them ran and it was why my mom dropped me in jobs with the towing company. She felt like if I needed money that bad, then I should have no problem working for family. For a while it pissed me off but, eventually, I got over it and ended up loving what I did for the towing company.

While I was stepping up to London, I heard them fighting about something. For the life of me, I kept being distracted by several things. One: that this was the most Royal blood we'd had in my area of the hood; and two: London had on these shorts that let me see how nice her legs and ass were. It made my head tilt to the side as I watched her.

She had a petite build. Everything was proportioned right for her. Yeah, I loved a big ass like every other nigga, and breasts, but I could also appreciate the small onion booties out there as well. London had that type of build. But, she also was stronger than she appeared.

I rubbed the center of my chest where she rammed into me, then I chuckled. Sun glaring in my eyes, I squinted while giving her a look. "Damn, mama. You good?" I asked while dropping the hand that held her shoulder.

A brown caddy bumping Fetty Wap rode by, honking its horn. I gave a "what up" nod, recognizing the people inside while watching them drive past.

"Sorry, I didn't see you there," London said and I noticed that she seemed to fluster and turn a slight soft red. Wide-eyed, girly quickly stepped back on my bag of chips and spun around to see who was honking.

"Don't worry about it, and you're safe. No one doing a drive-by," I said, bending down to grab the bag. Crumpling it in my hand, I tossed it in a sharp curve into a big blue plastic circular trash bin, then motioned with my chin.

"Why do you all do that, huh?" London firmly asked.

"Do what?"

"You know what." She glared at me then shook her head before scoffing. "All you people do is judge us as if we're fucking up your world."

For a second there I didn't know what she was talking about; then it dawned on me. I remembered all the shit she said last night, too, and I quickly got annoyed.

I kept my chill with a slight roll of my shoulders and brush of my thumb against my nose. "Shit, I mean, look. It's the same y'all do with us, let's be real about it."

"Whatever, that's not true," London said, walking away from me.

Like shit it wasn't, I was about to say, but that thought was dropped when I got lost in the sass of her switch. Following her, I chuckled. "Look, you don't even know where to go. The main office is on your right. Walk in there and look over your forms. Sin handles that."

London turned back my way and I noticed that she would occasionally drop her eyes. I wasn't sure what that was about, but I waited to see what she was about to say.

"I wanted to say sorry for how I acted last night. It really came off bad but, I'm not mad about my temper because I don't appreciate how you all around here discuss my father. But, I am sorry about my words. I didn't mean it like that," she said, speaking with her hands.

Hands in my pockets, I looked toward the garage with a shrug. "It's hard to accept that apology when you use words like 'you people' and you always are jumpy."

"I'm not jumpy," she said with narrowed eyes.

"Nah, you are. This is only my second time meeting you, mama, and yet again, you look like you're ready to jump out ya skin," I said with humor in my voice.

It seemed that I was getting under London's skin because she rolled her eyes at me and wrinkled her nose. "That's your view and I disagree with that. You don't know nothing about me, for if you did, you'd know that I got family in Goodman. I've stayed at Laylah's house a lot of times," she started.

Waving her off, I laughed out loud again. "Fuck! What does that have to do with anything? You're still scary. Like now, you for damn sure look like you're ready to ride out of Goodman as quickly as possible. So . . ." Kicking a chip out the way with my boot, I shrugged again, teasing her.

"It's hot is all," she said, trying to act relaxed. "Laylah took me around with Brash. We went—"

"To her front yard, maybe to the start of her street and back." Laughing, I walked up to where we parked finished cars in the front garage. "Like I said. A lot of Ro-folk do us like you feel we do you. I can't make you see that perception right now, but I bet you money that you wouldn't walk around Goodman with me and not be ready to call Daddy for help. That's just my view on it," I said, then gave a slick grin.

A part of me felt like testing her to see if she'd accept my challenge. I wasn't sure what it was about her, but I didn't dislike her or hate her, like I didn't like her father. There was something about it and it made me curious about her.

"Look, I came here for my car," she began.

Laughing, I paused at the garage door. "Ah huh, I knew that shit. You're ready to run back to the golden gates of heaven. We poor Goodman residents are only good to look down on. I got it."

"Oh, my God! You didn't even let me finish! Stop being an asshole, Saint," London whined, stepping to me. "I was going to say"—she stressed the "say"—"I came here for my car, but I'm going to prove to you that I'm not scared because I want to see your face break. I'm not like other Roanoke people."

I smirked while checking her out with a nod. "Prove it then." With a grin, I pushed up the door to the garage and showed her her car. "Your ride is back to normal. Like I said, tire is fixed and we gave you an alignment. We also checked your oil and cleaned that."

"I didn't ask you to do that though," she said with a frown.

"Well, we did and she shouldn't cause you any issues," I added. "Head inside and sign off. I'll keep your ride in here. I know you're scared that someone might take your precious Audi, since all we Goodman people drive are hood rides." A teasing smile spread across my face and I watched her scowl at me and storm off talking to herself.

I heard her say, "Ooo you get on my last nerve, you ol' big head red Kool-Aid-looking asshole! No one was going to say shit about my car being stolen!"

When she said that, I laughed so hard that tears lined my head. Clearly she was annoyed and it amused me. Hopping in her ride, I played with her radio as I drove forward and parked it in our ready carport. From what her saved stations were on her radio, London had a varied taste in music, classical being one of them. I sat listening as a piano strummed keys and blended with harps and violins. I tried to get into it but London was stomping out of the office with a paper in her hand looking like Ms. Sophia.

I turned off her car, climbed out, and looked at her over the roof of her Audi. “Everything good?”

“I feel like you all are too expensive,” she said, folding the paper up then reaching out to open the passenger door and toss the paperwork inside.

“Well, you did ask for service late at night on our emergency line.” When she gave me a look, I stopped joking and headed to the office. “I’ll be back,” was all I said.

Quickly, I took off my workman jumper, and grabbed two iced bottled waters from our freezer. I passed Sin, who sat at the front desk.

As he scrolled through Facebook, he glanced my way and asked, “Where you going, turtle face?”

I hated when Sin called me that. Nigga played a joke on me when we were ten where he sat a turtle on my face when I was asleep. Suffice to say, I fell out of bed crying and screaming for our mom before realizing I wasn’t having a nightmare. After that, I had been turtle face ever since.

“Going around the block and back up to deez nuts. Get out my business, hamster dick,” I threw back at him.

Sin leaned over the desk then chuckled to himself. “You really about to walk around with a Royal? You sniff too many gas fumes, my brotha?”

I literally stood there wondering the same thing. I didn’t know what the fuck was going on in my dome with walking her around, outside of the fact that I was getting a kick out of testing her. I knew what my mom would say. I knew that she’d dig in my ass, but at the end of the day, she knew I was twenty-one so there wasn’t shit she could really do about it.

Which was why I gave my brother a shrug and a smirk. “Nah, but I enjoy doing things I got no business doing.”

“See, that’s why you should have been Sinner. You do more crap than I do,” Sin said with a laugh. “While y’all out, ask her about her girl Brandy. I was this close to getting her number, but that blond chick blocked it."

"Man," was all I said as I walked out to London. Tossing her a water bottle, I walked a little past her. "You ready?"

London rolled her eyes at me and stepped to the street corner.

"Ah, so you know where we going then?" I asked, walking up on her.

"You know I don't," London said with sass.

I inwardly laughed and stopped in front of the bus stop. "Then you might want to stay by my side and act like you know me. I'm just saying."

London crossed her arms, stepping backward to end up at my side.

I pointed with my thumb while chuckling. "You ever ride a bus?"

"No. I've never had to," she explained.

My head shook in response. "So, check it, we're getting on the bus."

"Wait, why?" she said with slight panic.

"Because I said so," I added, digging in my pocket. "But nah, because it's the best way to experience Goodman people."

London gave me a look and held a hand out with the "what the hell" face. "But you said we were walking the block. I thought that was the point of all of that."

I held a hand up as a huge MARTA bus turned our way and I smiled. "Yeah, but I thought about it. We'll ride up the block, get off, and then walk back. Besides, you're sweating. We need a little air."

"See, you're being extra now," she said.

I guided her forward with my hand against the small of her back. I then pushed her on the bus, flashed my bus card, and paid her fare while following her. "Maybe."

Since it was lunchtime, the bus wasn't that bad; however, I chuckled when London took the first seat she could find, which was the front aisle seat on the side. I spoke to the bus driver who was my old babysitter, Mrs. Jennings. She told me about her grandbabies and church then I moved to take a seat.

Purposely sitting across from London, I rested my arms on my legs and checked her nervousness. "Look at you, not dying because you're on a bus, mama," I said, watching her.

"Whatever. There was no point in me being on a bus in Roanoke. I have a car," she said matter-of-factly.

"Since how old? Because I've been riding the bus since forever, mama, and I have two cars now, one I share with Sin, and we still ride the bus," I said back, not understanding her world.

The bus came to a halt. Several people boarded and a tall, lanky dude with ratty, short dreadlocks, black jeans that showed his Hanes boxers, and a dingy black tank, sat by London. I knew the dude as Rabbit. He was one of my contact dudes. The fact that he had seen me on the bus and got on let me know he had some business to do with me.

Reaching out, we clapped hands as he said, "What's up," to me before relaxing in his seat. I watched her tense up as he widened his legs and gave her the once-over with a gold-plated grin.

"Damn you sexy, gal. Where you going? 'Cause I need to go there with you, shawty," he sleazily said.

London sat quiet, acting like she didn't hear him.

"Sup, mama, I'm Rabbit. You must not be from around here," he said, eying her.

"Nah, she not. She's with me, homie," I explained, looking at the paper in my hand. Unfolding it on the low, I peeped that it said to meet at Silky's about Marvin's old lady. More info was coming our way with Marvin's dealings. My uncle would be happy about that. Tugging the stop rope, I stood, clapped hands with Rabbit again, handed him money on the low, and I motioned to London.

Quickly, London stood. "Nice to meet you, ah, Rabbit."

I watched her rush off the bus and I laughed. "You be safe, man."

"Damn, she's kinda rude, but she's still cute," Rabbit said, watching. "You be good too, man."

Back in the heat, we stood in front of one of my favorite wing spots. It also happened to be where my boy Silky worked, G-Town Grill. "Want some ice cream?" I asked London as we stood across the street.

"Oh, my God, like I'm sorry, but your boy's nails were so dirty and he was straight all up in my face," London said, glancing at me.

Frowning, I gave a nonchalant shrug. "I mean, shit. Nigga does how he does and he found you cute, so yeah, he was in your face."

"I know but, that's not how you talk to a woman though," London explained.

My eyebrow rose up slowly, and I turned my attention across the street. "I'm getting some ice cream. They have mad good wings and ice cream here, so come on. You get to see more of Goodman again."

London hurried to my side and we crossed the street. "I think I'm seeing enough though," she said.

"So you're ready to go?"

London gave a deflated look and walked ahead. "Boy, let's get the ice cream. I'm good. Not scared or anything."

"Good," was all I said.

Once inside, I signaled Silky, a tall red-bone dude all the females on the block wanted because he was so pretty. Nigga had so many females it was crazy. He was the one who always made the parties popping because he deejayed part time and brought pussy galore. With London by my side, I watched how she seemed to be a little more relaxed this go-round. We found a table, I had her chill, and I went to the back to get my info for my uncle. I figured London would make plenty of friends in here now. Especially, when I heard her sigh and say, "Oh my God," as I walked to the back. I stopped then turned around.

Around London's booth were several niggas who I didn't really care for. Four niggas hovered over her, thirsting. One bucktooth nigga flipped London's hair talking about why she didn't perm it. Another tried to grab her waist, talking about why was she being rude and not giving her number. And another sat across from her licking his lips and talking about eating her out.

Pissed, I glanced at Silky.

He came from the back of the kitchen in his white smock. "Niggas crossing a boundary?" Silky asked me in a low bass.

"Yeah," was all I said.

When London said, "I don't even know you. Get the hell up out my face with all that," I walked forward and pushed in between the group of niggas.

"Oh, shit, a Black! What up, nigga?" one of the dudes asked.

Thumbing my nose, my eyes darting back and forth, I moved to block London. The nigga who was simulating oral sex with his fingers tried to touch London's hand, ignored her, and said, "Why you tripping, huh? Let me taste them panties, sexy."

I snatched that nigga by the side of his Kermit-looking face and slammed his head against the wall of the booth. "What up, bitch?" was all I said.

Behind me Silky jumped forward and pulled one of the niggas back, making him fall into tables, and all hell broke loose, all with London watching in shock.

Chapter 10

London

I didn't know what I'd gotten myself into, but I wanted to get out of it. So what I'd lied when I told Saint I had been to Goodman more than once before the party? I hadn't, but he didn't need to know that. Well, if you counted the fact that I was there now then, technically, I wasn't lying. He didn't need to know anything more about me than he already assumed. That was neither here nor there because at the moment I was watching him and the guy he called Silky take on four guys alone. Apparently there was more to Saint than met the eye just like it was obvious the Black name had pull around these parts.

"Fuck niggas got no manners. The lady said she wasn't up for your bullshit. Shoulda let her be," Saint snapped as he stomped a dude into the floor.

That would make the second fight I'd been at in less than an hour. Quiet as kept, I hadn't seen an up-close fight since high school. In Roanoke these kinds of things didn't happen regularly. I screamed out at the horror of seeing another human get their face stomped in up close. Saint was vicious and he had attacked with ruthless aggression. Every hit to someone's face sounded off like it was the Fourth of July.

"Saint," I called out, not sure what calling him would do.

I had backed into the booth with my feet on the seat, trying to shelter myself from the melee. Silky was no better. While the man was heavenly on the eyes, he was hell in the fight. He picked one dude up and slammed him so hard that Silky didn't have to hit him. Dude was out from the slam. One man was out on the floor. Two had run off after getting their asses handed to them and one was in the corner moaning while holding his bloody face.

"Yo, homeboy, get'cho folk and dip up out my place of bidness, you feel me?" Silky said.

The dude moaning crawled over while trying to keep blood from falling through his fingers. He grabbed his friend up as best he could and got him out the door.

"Sandra, ma, can you come out here and clean this up for me?" Saint yelled as he ran a hand down his face. He then looked to Silky. "Sorry about that. Call to the shop and Unk will take care of the damages."

"It ain't nothing, big homie. What can I get for you and your lady while you wait?" Silky asked.

"I'm not his anything," I quickly corrected.

Silky flashed a lopsided lady-killer smile and then tilted his chin up while pointing at me and looking at Saint. "Ro-girl, right?"

Saint smirked and nodded once. "You know it."

"It's all good, li'l lady. What can I get started for you?"

Saint slid me a menu and I quickly glanced at it. I didn't need it, but I asked for a ten-piece lemon-pepper wing plate with fries on the side. Saint ordered the same then asked for two Coronas. We decided to order the ice cream after we were done with the food. I thought Silky would have asked for my ID but he didn't.

"You know I'm only nineteen, right?" I asked Saint when Silky walked off.

"Yeah, it's cool. No cops gon' run in here and snatch your drink from you," he answered.

I noticed he was bleeding a bit by his eye so I picked up a napkin, touched his chin, then dabbed at the injury. I was well aware that his gaze was on me as I did so, but I refused to look into those brown eyes of his. I felt my stomach muscles coil and my pressure points heat up.

"It's good now. Probably need to put some alcohol or something on it when you get home," I told him.

"You can come home and do it for me," he countered.

I rolled my eyes, trying to act like his words didn't rattle me. "Whatever."

"So tell me something about yourself, London. Who are you other than a Royal, since you want me to see you in a different light and shit?"

I shrugged. "Not much to tell. Ask me what you want to know."

"You in school?" he asked.

"Yeah, engineering. Chemical. Going to med school afterward."

As we talked, a small woman with the nametag that read SANDRA came out and started straightening up the mess that had been made. She had on black khakis, a hairnet, and a shirt that read G-TOWN GRILL on the front. She never looked at me or Saint. She had an eye patch over her right eye and only two fingers on her left hand. She had a bucket full of soapy water, a mop, and a broom.

"Oh, so a doctor? That's dope."

"What about you?" I asked.

"Yeah, going to school online for business," he answered.

"Why online?"

"I work. Help with the family business; and a nigga ain't trying to be sitting up in no classroom all day and shit, either."

"Understandable. So, do you know why your mother hates my daddy so much?"

I was surprised when Saint sighed and shook his head. "No, I don't. Been trying to figure that out myself. But your pops has taken a lot of cribs from people over here. Good people, too."

"So, it's his fault people can't pay their rent? Shouldn't y'all be blaming the banks and stuff for that?"

Saint shook his head as if I didn't understand. "Your pops, man, he could do a lot more for people than just come and take their houses from under them. You do realize your pops owns Goodman Community Bank right? One of the banks that so many people on the Goodman side of Jonesboro got home loans and shit from, right?"

I swallowed and looked around. I knew Daddy owned a lot of property, but had no idea he owned a bank over here. Why wouldn't he tell me that? Did DJ know? Did Mom know? While I was trying to figure that out, our food was placed on the table. My stomach growled so loud it embarrassed me. Saint chuckled but didn't say anything. We both dug into our wings and fries. Saint swallowed all his fries down in one bite, it seemed, so he started eating them off my plate. I swatted his hand a few times, but that didn't stop him. I took a sip of the Corona and blanched at the unusual taste of it going down. Didn't want to tell Saint I'd never had an alcoholic drink a day before in my life.

We talked about different things. I asked him how many times he had been to the Roanoke neighborhood and when he said never, I cocked my head back and looked at him.

"What?" he asked as he swiped one of my wings.

"Damn it, boy, stop eating my food," I snapped playfully. "Give me my wing back."

Saint put the wing in his mouth between his teeth then said, "Come get it."

I tried to hide a blush, but couldn't. I stared at him for a long time and even with the wing in his mouth I could tell he was smirking. The mischievous glare in his eyes intrigued me. I hadn't been kissed in a long time and there was something about Saint that appealed to me. I'd forgotten all about asking him why he hadn't stepped foot in Roanoke. I'd just met the boy last night. I didn't know his age or nothing. And, yet, I wanted to kiss him. I wanted his hands on me. He took the wing out of his mouth then licked his lips. One arm was behind me since we were sitting side by side in the booth.

"I told you last night, I don't bite unless you want me to," he said.

God knew I thought I wanted him to, but God must have also known I wasn't ready to go there yet. The door to the wing spot opened and in walked a pretty white girl. Her long blond hair cascaded down to her ass and she was black-girl thick. With skinny jeans that looked to be painted on, a half shirt, and tall stiletto heels, the girl walked like she was the be all and end all. She was all smiles until she saw Saint. She looked like she saw a ghost and turned to make a quick dash from the building until Sin walked in the door to stop her. She tripped, twisted her ankle, and then stumbled to fall onto her big, round ass. She kept trying to get up to no avail. Sin stalked in. The closer he got to her the more she frantically tried to get away.

Damn, Sin was fine to look at. That beard on his face was immaculate. I didn't know why that had just occurred to me. Before he'd had a smirk on his face every time I'd seen him. This time, he looked to mean business.

Saint stopped gazing at me and sat upright. Silky came from the kitchen and the white girl backed right into his legs.

"What up, Mellie?" Saint said without looking at the girl.

"Fuck, man! Fuck, I swear! I swear I don't know nothing. I don't. I don't. Oh, God," she cried.

"Know nothing about what?" Saint asked as he cleaned a drumette with one bite. He chewed slowly and licked his lips from time to time before taking a napkin to wipe his mouth then drinking the last of my Corona.

Mellie looked like she had pissed herself.

The hairs on the back of my neck stood up. I may not have been from the hood, but I knew some shit was going down.

"I told him . . . I told Marvin not to do it. I did, Saint. I swear."

Sin reached out to snatch Mellie up by her hair. The shrill cry she let out as she grabbed his wrists chilled me. I had no idea why she had grabbed his wrists, but Sin seemed to be amused by it.

"Let's discuss this in the kitchen, shall we?" Saint asked. Well, it was more like a command than a question.

"Ahhh, oh, God. I swearrrrrrrrr, I didn't have nothing to do with it," she squealed.

That didn't stop Sin from dragging her to the kitchen, though. I was nervous as shit as they all disappeared into the back. Wasn't sure what was going on, but I knew this kind of fare made my skin crawl and I was desperate to leave.

For about five minutes, I just sat there, then decided to head to the bathroom. I prayed no cops or anything showed up now. I wouldn't know what to do if they did. I was tempted to walk back to the shop and, to be honest, I was afraid to walk alone. I was out of my element and I was sure the last name would do me more harm than good in these parts.

As I walked around the corner, I heard Sin say, "Thought you didn't know nothing about nothing."

The double doors were closed but there were two small windows in each that I could clearly see into.

"I'm sorry. I'm sorry. I'm scared," Mellie whimpered.

Saint frowned and finally turned to look at the woman. "Of what, exactly?"

The kitchen was cleaner than any one I'd ever seen. Saint sat regally on a stool, both arms folded across his sculpted chest. His look was unmoving as the white girl trembled where she stood.

"I . . . I told Marvin he was doing wrong."

"Why didn't you come and tell me or my twin?" Sin asked.

"Marvin beat me."

"You look fine to me," Silky chimed in.

"I can take my pants off to show you. He won't hit me in my face or upper body. Only my legs, thighs, and ass. I can't make no money if he do anything else. Please. Please . . ."

Mellie was slobbering from the mouth. Her whole face was blood red; and I didn't know what to do or say so I remained silent and uncomfortable. Maybe she stole some money from them or something, I rationalized. Or maybe she did something to their mother, she and whoever Marvin was. I glanced around behind me to make sure no one would catch me eavesdropping before turning back to the window.

Saint studied the woman. "Who was his connect? Was it somebody from Guerilla's camp?"

"Yeah, some dude with a funny name and lots of tattoos."

"You can point him out to me?"

Mellie started crying harder. "I don't . . . I don't know where he is."

Sin grunted as he reached in his pocket. Out came a pocket knife.

Mellie's eyes widened. "Sin, I swear I don't knowwww where he is. He was driving a truck. A white truck with Roanoke tags. That's all I know. That's all I know. Please, my kids, Sin. Please don't take me from my babies. I'm all they got."

Sin popped the knife open and shoved the pointy end into the woman's cheek until it drew blood. "You better tell us something useful or you're going to be walking around with a permanent smile," he threatened.

My eyes widened. I didn't belong here. I had no idea what I had just become an accomplice to. I felt as if I had just walked into a gangster or mob movie.

"I . . . I know a house. I know where a house is. A stash house," Mellie blurted out.

"Guerilla's?" Saint questioned.

Mellie nodded.

"Talk," Sin demanded.

"Paige Street. Two houses down from where Nikki Royal lives."

Saint frowned. "That nigga got a stash house in our hood?"

Silky frowned and scratched his head. "This bitch gotta be lying. No fucking way that nigga encroached on our territory like that."

"I ain't lying. They . . . they shot up a party last night! They came from that house. Marvin, he moved the dudes you put there to a new house, Saint. Moved Guerilla's men in—"

"Take her to the safe house, and leave her there with one of the niggas watching her. Meet me back here," Saint told Silky, cutting the woman off.

He stood and I hurried into the bathroom. I rushed into a stall, flushed the toilet, then came out and damn near jumped out of my skin to find Saint standing in the door. There was a questioning look in his eyes.

"What?" I asked like I hadn't been just listening to his whole conversation.

"What are you doing?"

"Um, it's a bathroom. So I was more than likely taking a piss if that's okay with you," I responded flippantly.

Saint grunted, but didn't move away from the door until I was finished washing my hands. He held his hand out for mine. I complied, nervously so.

"I'm sorry our day has to be cut short but, look, take my number, and call or text my phone so I can have your number, a'ight? I'll make this up to you," he said to me, passing me a business card.

He said all of that as he walked me outside. We made it to the corner just in time to see the bus. He flagged it down and swiped a card to pay my fare. "Take her to the shop," he told the driver.

The woman nodded. I hopped on the bus a little mad but more annoyed than anything, and scared out of my mind.

"And, London?" Saint called as he stepped off the bus.

"Yeah?" I answered.

"You didn't see or hear anything, right?"

I knew instinctively that my answer was to be no so I shook my head. "No, Saint. I saw or heard nothing."

He flashed a smile. "Good."

Ten minutes later, the bus pulled in front of the car shop. I didn't ask anybody anything. I jumped in my car and got the hell out of Goodman

Hours later, after I'd gotten home, showered, and sent Saint a text, which he didn't respond to, I called Brash.

I needed someone to talk to. Had to tell someone something about my day. For as much as I'd seen and should have been appalled by, I was more so intrigued. What was this power that Saint and Sin wielded? How did they have so much power? Who in hell was Guerilla? Not to mention, I needed to check on Brash and Laylah. One of them had to tell me what the heck was going on between the three.

Brash's phone rang three times before DJ picked up. "Hello?" he answered.

"Um, why are you answering Brash's phone?" I asked, clearly surprised to hear his voice.

"Where have you been? Pops was looking for you. Thought you were just picking up your car and coming right home," was his answer.

"I was out."

"In Goodman?"

"Why? Where is Brash?"

"You better stay the hell from over there, Lon, unless you going to see Auntie Nikki or something. You have to either learn to adapt or stay away. It's not safe over there and if Pops finds out, that's your ass," he warned.

"Shut up, DJ. You don't know that I was over there. Well, you don't know that I stayed over there. I could have been at home."

"You weren't, though. Pops went to your crib to drop you a line and he said you weren't there. So you better come up with a better excuse when you see him."

With that, DJ told Brash she had a phone call. I swore I heard covers rustling. I walked around my house trying to see if Daddy had left me some money since I was low on that, too. Shit, Saint charged me like they had fixed way more than he said they did. When I didn't find any money in Daddy's normal hiding spot, I checked my account, hoping he left something. When I saw he hadn't, I sighed and shook my head.

"Hello," Brash answered groggily.

"Hey, bestie. How are you?" I asked.

"I have a headache, but I'm cool. Where are you?"

"I'm home now. Are you at DJ's place?"

She groaned low then answered, "Yeah."

"Okay, somebody needs to tell me what the hell is going on."

There was a long pause on the other end of the phone. "Me and DJ, we . . . we're a thing."

"A thing? What the hell kind of a thing?"

"We're seeing each other, London. He's my boyfriend."

"What? What the fuck? When? How? Where was I when it happened?" I plopped down on my couch with my legs underneath me.

"London, you never see what's right in your face, girl. Me and DJ been fucking since I was sixteen. We got together as a couple on my eighteenth birthday. We've been doing this for a while."

My mouth was wide open. I was stunned to silence. "And he knows about Laylah."

"Yes, Lon, they know about each other."

I had so many questions. What the fuck? Was I really so blinded by my reality that I didn't see things right in front of me? First there had been DJ, who showed me another side of himself. Then there was Saint telling me Daddy owned a bank in Goodman And now, my brother, my cousin, and my best friend were in a three-way love triangle. I didn't know what to feel. I listened as Brash told me she and DJ didn't want anyone to know what was going on between them. Brash got DJ to let Laylah and Chance live, rent free, in one of the houses he owned in Goodman. DJ knew about Laylah because she told him. DJ had been fine with that until Laylah was going through Brash's phone and found out she and DJ were together. Since then Laylah has been at DJ's neck. This morning everything just boiled over. Now it made sense as to why Laylah always had something snide to say about DJ.

"Damn, Brash. Girl—"

I got cut off when I heard DJ yelling expletives in the background. "Motherfucker, what?" I heard him yelling. "When?"

"What's going on, Brash?" I asked.

"I don't know. Somebody just called DJ and now he's mad. He's getting dressed about to leave. I'ma call you back."

Before I could ask my next question, she hung up. I sighed. I tried to call Daddy, but he never answered. He was probably pissed at me. I called my mother but she said she was entertaining company and would call me back. I cooked. I cleaned. I waited anxiously for Saint to call or text me back. He never did. I didn't hear from him until four days later.

Chapter 11

Saint

All eyes were on me. I stood, arms crossed, in front of a black leather sectional couch, which had several of my homies chilling on it, including my brother and my uncle Red. We all hooked up to give the details I learned about Marvin. We sat in the basement of his meeting house, as he called it. The place always switched because, being in the type of business we were, once niggas learned your secrets and patterns then that left you ass out and open for anything.

Me and my select crew of runners—minus Jelly, Silk officially took that nigga's place—were in the basement of my uncle's meeting spot, sequestered on the edge of Roanoke. Yeah, I lied to London when I said I had never been to the Roanoke neighborhood. Part of it was true, though. This spot was directly near the train line that cut both areas on half. All I had to do was walk from the shop, disappear in the forest, then pop up on the edge where my uncle's old Victorian with a wraparound porch sat on a hill near a lake. No one could pick up on that pattern, which made it an ideal location.

Going to his place was the farthest I'd been in Roanoke.

Some of the crew would take back roads to get to this spot, making it appear as if they were going to the Roanoke neighborhood of Jonesboro just to do whatever.

That also helped with throwing off the pattern. But, anyway, above my head was a sunken ceiling with recessed lighting. New bamboo flooring was laid down and the once musky, moldy smell that was here was gone. My uncle's hobby of fixing came in handy here. On the wall next to several paintings and drawings Sin created were security monitors for our shop and for where we were.

My uncle sat tapping his silver lighter against his armrest in thought while glancing down at his cell. "So, what ya saying is this whole time Marvin, junkie-ass Marvin, has been making moves to fuck up our pipeline?" my uncle asked evenly. With a calm movement, my uncle measurably glanced around at every one of us. That let me know that he was thinking and internally trying to move all the pieces together like a puzzle. When my uncle was in that type of mode, he was not someone you wanted to press.

"So, this little nigga had the ingenious idea to move Guerilla's crew into our territory and essentially help them gain our zone? Just outta the blue he thought that up 'cause Guerilla made him?" Chuckling low to himself, my uncle gave an annoyed smile and began flipping his lighter off and on. "And they basically have our money and stash?"

O.G. was mad, but keeping his cool. I decided to speak up because I was getting exactly where he was coming from. Without a doubt, this unit of us in his home, my personal unit, was trustworthy. However, the others we worked with and trusted might need to be pruned and spoken with but, for now, I needed Blanket to continue trusting that we could handle this.

"Right now, that's what was told to us by Mellie," I explained.

Silky sat wide-legged brushing his beard line when he raised a finger to get my attention.

"Go for it, homie," I said, leaning back against the wall.

"A'ight, so, I sent a message through Rabbit about meeting up. Choppa and I had been doing like Saint and Sinner told us and that was to sniff out some shit." Putting his brush away, Silky glanced toward our homie Choppa who sat with his hat low, diamond studs sparkling against his dark skin, as he listened.

Quickly interrupting, I added, "Choppa learned that Guerilla has new product and support that will contrast what we got."

"So when I got word that Mellie was coming through to G-Town, I made sure Rabbit got word to Saint and Sin," Silky continued. "Broad was on some white tears shit, talking about Marvin beat her."

"Yeah, the fuck right!" every homie in the place said while some threw their hands up, laughing. Our small crew of seven wasn't just dudes; we had some bomb lethal women in the mix, including Hotep and Sassy.

"We all know Marvin lived in Mellie's vanilla pussy whenever he got the chance. He always was keeping her laced up and shit," Hotep said, laughing as if offended.

My hands slid in my pockets with a shrug. "Shawty was like, 'I can pull my pants down and show you.' Like? Where they do that at?" I shook my head in thought while watching the crew. "But I ain't knocking her. I just wasn't feeling her."

"Man, look, she walked up in Silky's pop's place like she just had the best payoff of all time. Cheesing 'n' shit in fresh clothes. If he was beating her ass like she said, no way she'd make it around in them tight-ass clothes she had on. Fuck that shit," Sin said as if reading my thoughts. We both locked eyes on each other and gave a nod of solidarity.

"Regardless. Her shit wasn't rosy and something was off about it," I said, moving this meeting on.

"No doubt about that," Sin added.

Silky also nodded his head and we all focused back on my uncle, who sat silently. The sound of him flipping his lighter off and on became the only thing we heard in the room while we sat in thought. Reaching out to his cell, he gave a low sigh and began typing.

"This is what is going to happen. Like y'all know, I'll be going over everything that was said here tonight with Blanket. He heard everything said, of course, and we both aren't happy about this shit," Uncle Red said, looking at us all.

My uncle's face was in a deep scowl, and he pushed his legs out then stood. "None of this shit should have gone down like it was. There's a breakdown going on and I'm not good with that. The fact that one of our own decided to cross over to another crew isn't what's fucking with me. We've had that happen before and since Guerilla is growing every day, that shit ain't surprising."

Uncle Red turned my way. He jutted his chin out, pointing, and in a carefully controlled tone said, "Like Saint said, Guerilla is growing and trying to take pieces of our zones. But, what's pissing me the hell off is that one of our own felt his nuts were big enough to steal from the hand that fed him all this time. The hand that took care of his woman, his kids, and helped wipe his fucking ass. In the end of the day, we're family. Am I wrong?"

Everyone, including myself and my twin, said in unison, "No."

"Then I want y'all to go in the street and help me understand why the fuck niggas like Marvin were able to play us and assist in another crew taking from us, and when you do, I'd like you all to indoctrinate them with a bullet. Understood?" Eyes narrowed, my uncle thumbed his nose and glanced at every one of us. "That includes yourself if you playing us. Because if any one of you, including our niggas in the street, are turncoating, best believe we'll smother your ass to sleep, feel me?"

"You know we are your truth council, Red!" one of the homies said. It sounded like Silky.

"Right, we'd never play you. We'd die before that," Hotep said behind that.

"No matter what, we all grew up together—" Choppa spoke up.

"So none of us here are running foul," Sassy ended for him with a wink his way.

"We'll shake down our houses, and weed out the niggas who call themselves fam," Sin said, standing to face our uncle.

"And as we feed them a rope, we'll watch them hang," I said in finality, fisting my hands together. "Because none of us here like a rat and a turncoat."

"True that," everyone said.

My uncle gave us a nod and a smile. "A'ight, go get our shit from our crib. You lay your head in what we own, and fix it up as if it's yours; then we have a right to reclaim whatever is in it. Fair exchange is no robbery. I'm out. The meeting is over, y'all," he said in finality.

On our way out of the basement, my uncle said one more thing: "Oh yeah, nephews, tell Maya that I'm about to go play some ball with Luther."

Luther was our goduncle/cousin. He had no part of the business with Blanket, yet I always felt like he should. Dude was built like a lumberjack and bodybuilder all in one. He had a cropped beard the color of milk tea and a dimpled smile. As kids, Sin and I called him Black Ninja because he had those type of skills and was usually silent. Uncle Luther was always at Mama's just posted. I never understood why we never saw him running the streets with Uncle Red, but it was what it was.

Once my uncle left, I glanced at Sin and my twin gave me a smirk. It was time to plan and that's what we did. The next day, our unique crew split up to watch the other zone houses while Sin and I sat in my mom's house, waiting for feedback on our zone house. According to Silky, the place had about five niggas just squatting in it. Nothing out of the ordinary was going on with regard to any product being moved in and out.

For now, the crew reported that they were waiting for an open window to smoothly get into our place and take it back from within. Via our cells, and the occasional people who would stop by my mom's place to send us messages, this was what we were waiting on while we chilled. One of the only reasons why we were at my mom's house was to keep our activities undercover. If Guerilla was really watching us, then I didn't want them thinking anything but what it appeared we were doing and that was spending a day at my mom's eating.

The house smelled damn good. Mom was in the kitchen cooking some greens with smoked turkey because she didn't like cooking with a lot of pork. Sin and I were already going in on some cornbread. Goduncle Luther was in the back grilling some jerked red snapper, with some rib tips, while Uncle Red was out getting Jamal.

While we chilled and shit talked like we did, Sin and I made our plans on what to do about Guerilla once Blanket gave us the okay. Halfway through our conversation, I abruptly walked away from the couch looking down at my cell reading the texts from the crew. In my thoughts, I walked into the kitchen and gave my mom a hug and kiss on the cheek.

She stood like she was in a meditative moment while she worked on some mac-n-cheese she planned on putting on the grill because it was too hot to turn on the oven in her opinion. Relaxing in yoga shorts that

I felt were too short for her, though they stopped in the middle of her thighs, she had on a simple tank that made me shake my head again.

"Sup, Mama. How you feeling?" I asked, opening up the fridge to grab a bottled water. I stood back, arms crossed, studying the side of my mother's face.

Her body wasn't tense, but her jaw was clenched. She and I got that bad in micromanaging our emotions. When she turned my way, she walked up to the refrigerator and pulled a white envelope down from where I had previously set it under her stack of bills. "Take your money back, baby. I don't need it," she sternly said, looking up at me.

"Ma, stop stressing and take it. Call it Sin's rent and his half of the bills. I know it's my half of what I pay for my place over the shop," I said then took a swig of icy water.

Clearly my mom was eager to fight me about the money. She tucked her hair behind her ear and gave me a glare. "Oh, trust me, sweetie, I took that part out of it. The extra that you tried to mix in there, keep it. I don't want it," she said with a gentle slap to my shoulder.

Fuck, here we go. "Mom, it's needed. I save up every month to pay you on regular. Don't do this."

Of course, Ms. Maya Black had to turn her back on me. She walked up to the stove, went to stirring, then turned to chop an onion. I watched her use that chef's knife with a calm expertise that had me keeping my distance from her.

As if on cue, she turned to point it at me. "You know I don't approve of how you are getting your money, Santana. As I told you, whatever you make you keep because I don't want any part of it."

"Ma, how am I getting my money, huh? I work for the towing company; you know how I get my money. The extra I make is favors for working on friends' rides or fixing some stuff in their house. I've told you this before," I said, mixing lies with truth.

Flexing her wrist with the knife, she turned and swung it around. "And like I told you, I'm not stupid. I've lived in this community longer than you and I know the streets very well, honey. You and your brother aren't just popping up with extra money from 'working' on friends' cars and random house maintenance. Isn't that right, William?"

Sin stood next to the kitchen table grabbing some cornbread. "Don't know what's going down, so I'm not in it, Mama. Love you."

He got ready to turn and leave, but our mom reached out and snagged him by his shirt. "No, we're talking about this right now, because once again I am not happy about my only sons out there in the street, trying to live some trap life!"

Both Sin and I glanced at each other and mentally prepared ourselves for our mom's preaching. A large part of me wanted to call her out on her foolishness because rumor had it that my mom used to be something in the streets too. Nah, she wasn't a trap queen or nothing, but she could hold her own and fight when she had to back in the day.

"Mama, dear," Sin said, putting his cornbread down, "I have a part-time job online. I work Web sites and design book covers and shi . . . I mean, stuff. That's where my money is coming from."

Sighing, my mom looked between us and pulled us into a loving hug. "You two are all I have. Regardless of how you two are effortlessly lying to me, Mama knows. I need you both to be wise in how you handle your business. I heard about that shooting, heard about your friend Marvin. That boy has been a handful since a child. His father was an addict and his mother tried to pray that boy's demons away until he lost his way in the street. You two know she stays in the Roanoke neighborhood now? Has a nice little house on Broadway. I think I saw him go up her way last week while I was shopping. I know I've seen that Mellie woman of his has been that way," she said, kissing us on our cheeks and letting us go. "Anyway, I need you two to keep safe and out of this crazy business. Your father would be on ya asses if he was still around."

Both Sin and I glanced at each other, as she went back to cooking. Like usual our mother had to preach to us, but what was weird about it this time was she threw us information.

"Hey, get your phone, William, it's going off. I hate that damn 'Flex' song. Grown-ass man sounding like a sick cat," she said, laughing at the same time.

"I got it, Mama," Sin quickly said, motioning for me to follow him.

Once we got into the living room, he glanced at his cell and frowned. "I swear Mama is hiding shit, but whatever. We need to ride out. Silky said come through."

At that same time, my cell went off and I looked down, reading my text. "Nah, it's more than that now. Red got the go from Blanket. We get to play, twin."

Sin gave a wide grin and headed out the door.

Taking a look at our mom in the kitchen, I studied her as she turned up some dancehall and started winding her hips at the same time Goduncle Luther walked in with a tin pan. Shaking my head, I chuckled then told her that Sin and I would be back and that we were going to go out to get some more drinks, since Uncle Red was taking a million years. Once out, we headed to our zone house, which was to the left and behind Dee Dee's.

Both Choppa and Silky were waiting in an empty house watching. Entering from the back, Sin and I walked in and grabbed a black bag. Inside were masks, gloves, and guns.

"What's the energy like over there?" I asked while pulling on some gloves.

"Quiet. About three niggas walked out the house. We had Hotep trail them with Sassy and some chicks. Looks like they are heading across Jonesboro to get some food," Silky explained.

I felt anxious and ready to handle business for Blanket, which had me rubbing my chin. The fact that these niggas were straight squatting in our place, with our shit, was still bothering me and had me eager to kill. "A'ight. Blanket gave us the okay. No need to be nice about the shit. Grab our stuff, reclaim the house, paint the walls, and leave the bodies on the block as a message. Let's go."

Pulling masks and gloves on, then checking our Glocks, we all rushed across the street.

All of us knew this area well; it was our zone and the house was one we purposely picked because it had a good view of everything. That didn't mean we didn't know how to sneak up on it. Using Dee Dee's backyard, we climbed a fence, and used the back way to make it to the house. Lighter in my hand, I glanced at my twin, who had his spray can ready to tag and let them know that this was our place.

Giving a quick nod, we all spread out. Sin started tagging the walls. Choppa and Silky headed upstairs. Music blasted and what was once a clean joint was full of trash, needles, and other crap. I stepped over bottles and felt myself getting pissed off. *Marvin let whoever the hell he wanted in this place? The fuck is that?* As I walked quietly down the hall, I heard boisterous laughing.

"Nah, nigga, you fooling. You literally let that snaggletooth bitch suck ya dick? Nigga, she stay in the Crack, dirty as fuck, too. You straight fooling."

Immediately after that, a lanky nigga walked into my vision. "I'm saying, though. She was easy pussy. She didn't struggle or nothing after I pumped her vein."

Laughter continued but it quickly silenced when that nigga dropped to the floor. Ruby liquid pooled on the floor. I stood there, head tilted, watching with my silencer in my hand.

"Oh shit!" I heard.

Reaching in my pocket, I pulled out a glass bottle, threw it, watched it crash on that nigga; and then I dropped a lighter. Flames started to blaze, and I saw the form of another dude rush to see who I was. Of course, it was just easier for me to introduce myself.

Stepping over the body, I pointed my silencer. "Sup, nigga."

Two pops to the head, and that nigga dropped his gun then fell over table full of money, white powder, and beer. The paper they had I wasn't interested in, so I left it there and exited through the back door, jogging to the garage. I could hear people inside talking about possibly hitting up another zone house. It was at that point that loud shouting could be heard from the house.

Immediately, I picked up a brick and jammed the lock to the garage. Lighting another bottle I had in my jacket, I crashed the window and tossed it inside. Sometimes I liked to play with fire and since niggas wanted to squat in a house that wasn't theirs, I figured it was only fair that I let them burn with it.

A loud whistle called to me. It was a signal from Sin that they had our stuff. Running around the front, I went back into the house and dropped to the floor. Bullets rained from upstairs. Sin used his blade, slicing niggas across the throat, while Choppa was running down the stairs. His boot-covered feet were banging on each step as he attempted to make his way out of the house with several big body bags.

"Where's Silky?" I shouted, letting rounds go off, gazing through the smoke.

"He was behind me," Choppa yelled, his eyes full of worry at the door.

Gritting my teeth, I pushed up to look at Choppa. "Kill anyone who comes out that garage. I got Sin and I got Silky. Ride out."

Choppa gave me an uncertain look then took the bags with him.

Back inside, I looked around; the basement door was open. Flames lit up the kitchen, but it hadn't made it to the front yet, so I knew I had to be quick. "Sin, where's Silky?" I yelled, watching my brother go toe to toe with another nigga.

"I'ono, bro!" was all I got as he threw a nigga down a stairway.

Cursing, I caught that dude, crushed his trachea with my foot, and then took to the basement quickly. Lo and behold Silky was there surrounded by two dead bodies, shaking his head as he stared down the barrel of a gun. Behind him was a map detailing our zone houses and territory lines. A huge X was on the white board and I noticed a circle.

Without even a thought, I jumped over the banister, watched Silky duck as a gun went off, and I ran up on the back of a beefy motherfucker with a glassy eye. "Fuck a Guerilla," I shouted out, wrapping my arm around that motherfucker's neck.

Smoke clouded the basement and made it hard to see. I felt myself flung across the room, landing hard on my back. "Get out, my nigga, I got this. Get what we said," I shouted, painfully getting up.

"They've been watching us. I'm getting their intel, man," Silky said, rushing around the room grabbing shit. "Don't get killed. I'll fuck you up if you do, homie."

"I got this," was all I said.

Big meaty tried to snatch up Silky, but nigga was nimble and used running back moves to pivot and snake out of his hands. Noticing that he wasn't going to catch my homie, he looked around for a gun.

By that time, I had gotten back up and pulled out my switchblade. Flipping it open in my palm, I rushed that nigga again only to be punched by him. "Shit! Nigga, the fuck is up with your fat-ass bear-looking self?" I said, wiping my masked mouth.

Sumo beefy laughed, and thumbed his sweaty nose. "Fuck a Blanket," was all he said in a husky grunt.

Cracking my neck and shoulders, I gave a big up to the upstairs, and rushed him. Taking that nigga down was difficult. I slammed my blade into him several times while trying to climb up his body. Because that nigga was getting winded from the smoke, his movements became sluggish and allowed me an opening for me to take the blade to the back of his sausage neck and drive it home. Forcefully pulling it out, I switched hands and slammed my knife right into his milky eye as he stumbled backward.

I then jumped down, reached into the back of my pants, pulled out my gun, ran up on him again, and forced a bullet up under his cheek. When his eyes widened and all I saw was red painting the walls, I smirked and stepped back.

"Like I said, fuck a Guerilla." Looking around, I found another bag, grabbed it, and took to the stairs.

Flames were blazing and we had no time for stalling. Sin appeared at my side covered in blood. He took the bag and we ran outside away from the burning building.

"Anyone we can take with us?" I heard asked by Choppa.

I rushed to the garage. When I got there, I opened it up and saw a few niggas still breathing, passed out and partially burned. Adrenaline kept me hyped, because when I saw that shit, I knew to act quickly. Dragging them out, we shot the rest, closed the garage so they could burn, and took two Guerillas as prizes.

"Yeah, these two roasting niggas, let's go," was all I said.

Making it to Choppa's ride, we all headed to Guerilla's zone, leaving our old place burning with the Guerilla tags on it. Everyone knew Guerilla stayed close to our train district near Broadway, where old abandoned trains sat next to Cracker Jack–looking houses mixed with beautiful Victorians. Parked across the street of that place, still in our masks, we stepped to the streets, dragging the bodies. I knew that all eyes were on us as I spoke.

"War accepted," was all I said, shouting in the street. I kneeled down, sliced open the necks of their two goons, then used their blood as paint while my boys stood behind me in their masks.

"From Blanket: fair exchange."

Chapter 12

London

"Daddy, I have some questions," I said on Friday night.

Three days not hearing from Saint had turned into four. I chalked that shit up to him not wanting to talk to me like he claimed. Maybe he saw me as easy pussy and when he saw I wasn't going to give it to him or that he had to work for it, he lost interest. Inwardly I shrugged. I was nineteen and had had sex with four guys: the boy I lost my virginity to, my boyfriend in high school, and two guys since I had been in college. I had no qualms about sex, but I normally made the dude who wanted it prove it. Maybe Saint was used to the girls in Goodman being easy. Or maybe I was just being snide because I was mad he hadn't called or texted like he said he would.

"Okay," Daddy said as we all sat around the dinner table.

Things had been pretty touch-and-go as far as conversation was concerned. Daddy was talking to DJ about how he was planning to extend the realty business. Mama talked about what she planned to do with the women's shelter she owned and ran. I just sat and listened like usual. Mama was dressed to impress as usual. Cream silk dress slacks that adhered to the roundness of her hips, with some kind of red dressy blouse. Her hair was tapered down and brought out her exotic features more. DJ sat on the left of Daddy while I sat next to Mama. DJ was in navy slacks with a black polo-style shirt. Daddy was dressed similar, as Mama required we all come to dinner on Fridays dressed accordingly. Most family had these kinds of dinners on Sunday; not in my home. Duck à l'orange was on the menu, one of Mama's favorites. The grand dining room was decorated as if it was going to be in one of those home style magazines. Cream and gold made up the colors with specks of silver accentuating throughout.

"Why do so many people dislike you in Goodman?" I asked without trepidation.

Daddy chuckled. "People who have less than you will always find a reason to dislike you," he answered.

"London, baby, those people over there have very few hopes and dreams. They're the kind of black people who like to wallow in the 'woe is me' self-pity kick," Mama chimed in.

"But there are more than black people over there," I said.

"Well, I'm talking about the black people because everybody else is just as racist as the rich white folk. Your father does so much for those damn people and I don't understand why, to be honest. He goes over and fixes up those damn shacks they call homes. Built that damn community center that they tore down and destroyed, but God freaking forbid we decide to send our children to the best schools, and teach them to speak proper English and to want something more out of life. It's like those people never want anything more than what they have and if anybody speaks against it he's an Uncle Tom," she said, righteously indignant.

I looked at DJ and wondered if Mama knew he code switched. Code switching was when a black person switched dialect from one way of speech to another depending on who they were around. DJ had turned into this person I didn't even know. And he had a gun!

Daddy grunted and nodded as he put a forkful of duck in his mouth. "You have people like Maya Black who convinces her kind—"

"Her kind?" I interjected.

"Yes, her kind. Her kind, those people over there, listen to every word she says. Her kind. The kind who have babies out of wedlock and then teach their sons to continue to perpetrate that cycle. Women like her are what's wrong with the black community. I tried to have a meeting with city council to open another community center. She blocked it, got people to vote against it claiming it was self-serving to me and not the community. How is it serving me? Doesn't she get tired of kids roaming the streets with nothing to do? Humph. Doesn't she get tired of the drugs and homeless running the street?" Daddy asked. "Then she had the nerve to pull a gun on me. If I weren't the man my father raised me to be . . ."

Daddy let his words trail off once he saw that I was all ears. I swore he called Maya a "fucking cunt" under his breath.

"What's the deal with her?" I wanted to know. "Anybody want to fill me in on why this woman hates Daddy so much she and her sons pulled a gun on him?" I asked.

"I know Maya," DJ spoke up, surprising me. "She's been robbed at the shop a hell of a lot. So maybe she pulled the gun for safety and not because of Daddy," he said.

Mama cut her eyes at DJ as she started to aggressively poke her duck with her fork. "I don't know why the fuck you do business with that woman. Of all the people you could get rentals from, you get them from her. Don't get it. Don't understand it and I never will. Devon, will you talk to your son?"

"It's his business, Tamika. He made the best call for his business."

"Does she know it's you?" Mama turned back to DJ when Daddy didn't give her the response she wanted.

"I don't know," DJ answered. "More than likely not. If she knew it was me, we wouldn't be doing business. I never show my face. I always send a representative."

"Keep it that way," Daddy said. "She doesn't need to know, but you need to watch her boys. Don't underestimate them. They're dangerous. Blanket uses them to do his dirty work."

I kept turning my head as if I was in a tennis match. "What kind of business?" I chimed in. "And who is Blanket? I keep hearing the names Blanket and Guerilla. Who are these men?"

Everybody's head whipped around to look at me like they had forgotten I was there. Quiet as kept, that was how it had always been in my family. They always kept me busy: Girl Scouts, dance recitals, science fairs, chemistry camp. There was always something I was doing to keep me away from home. I was always kept out of the loop. For the first time, it angered me. I was older now, nineteen, so whatever was going on in this family, I should be in the know.

Daddy looked at DJ. Mama looked as if she wanted to bolt from the room. DJ kept his eyes on me. He had always been the one to tell me things when Mom and Dad wouldn't.

"I have to go pick up Brashanay," DJ said out of the blue. He wiped his mouth with the cloth napkin, stood, and then tossed it onto the plate.

"DJ," I yelled.

He paid me no mind. I looked at my parents. I knew not to ask my father anything. The look on his face said so. My mama was no better.

"This is such bullshit," I snapped.

"Watch your mouth, London," Daddy warned.

"I'm grown, Daddy. I can speak my piece."

"Can you pay your own rent? Buy your own car? Pay your own tuition? If so then you can speak whatever the hell is on your mind. And do know that it comes with a price," he countered.

I shook my head. "All because I want to know what's going on around here you're threatening me with this?"

"Some shit just ain't your business, London. Now leave it be."

"So is it true that you're taking people's houses over in Goodman? Are you really snatching houses after you give them loans from the bank you own? One I didn't know you owned?"

Daddy's eyes narrowed. "In case your sheltered ass didn't know, that's what happens when people don't pay their rent or mortgages. They get evicted."

"How is that legal? How is it legal for you to own the bank that gave the people the loan and be the owner of the company that buys the houses when they default?" I asked.

"That's enough, London. Leave it alone," Mama said.

"So what those people over there are saying has merit? Daddy is the Big Bad Wolf? He is taking homes? Is that why Maya Black doesn't like him?" I wanted to know.

"Don't mention that woman's name at this table again," Mama snapped. "Not even in this house again, understand me?"

"What did you take from her, Daddy?"

"London, that is enough!" Mama said.

I pushed back from the table and tossed my napkin in my plate. "Fine. I'll go ask her."

Mama jumped up so fast, she knocked her glass of wine over. "You will do no such thing. I forbid you to cross those tracks or speak to that woman!"

I made a face that said I was confused. "So you don't want me to ask you questions, but you forbid me from seeking answers myself? Yup, sounds about right. That's how you've treated me my whole life."

"I don't know what has gotten into you, London Royal, but you have only one more time to disrespect me or your mother in our home and that will be the last," Daddy threatened as he slowly stood from the table. There was fire in his eyes. "Now, we turned a blind eye to the stunt you pulled by going to that party when you weren't supposed to. Don't push it."

I wanted to ask what exactly I'd done wrong by going to a party but I knew better. Daddy wasn't to be messed with when he had that look in his eyes. I had so many questions, but I knew I wasn't going to get the answers, at least not ones that would make sense. I stormed from the dining room, then grabbed my purse and keys. I was out the door when Daddy called me.

"London?" he said.

I turned, hoping the look on my face told him I didn't want to be bothered. He has a cigar in between his fingers, and his left hand was in the pocket of his slacks. Daddy looked important and stood like he ruled a kingdom. His eyes held a glare that said he wasn't in the mood to mince words.

"Yes, Daddy?"

"Take heed of what your mother said. Don't associate yourself with Maya Black or any Black, for that matter; that includes her sons. Stay away from those people and stay away from Goodman."

He gazed at me for mere moments as if he knew something I didn't. Before I could protest, he turned and strolled back in the house, closing the door behind him.

"Bodies were left on the tracks between Goodman and Roanoke as masked men seemed to stand taunting the residents of Roanoke. It was a tragic sight to see the bodies that had been laid out like the men in the masks were sending a message. Cell phone footage showed one of the men shouting. There is speculation that he was saying, 'fair exchange is no robbery,' as if someone from Roanoke had done something to him. There is bad history and bad blood between the residents of Goodman and Roanoke. . . ."

I'd been gone from my parents' house for hours. I didn't feel like being bothered with anyone after that whole fiasco but I did plan on calling Laylah. I hadn't heard from her since the incident with her, DJ, and Brash. I watched on in horror as a reporter from Fox 5 Atlanta spoke. I shook my head as the reporter talked. I still hadn't heard from Saint at all and as much as I hated to admit it, he'd left an impression on me. Which was probably why I was hoping one of those bodies shown wasn't him.

After the news depressed me more than I cared for, I called Laylah hoping she would answer. "Damn, girl. Where have you been? You okay?" I asked as soon as she picked up.

With all the noise in the background, I knew she was at Auntie Nikki's place. "I'm straight. Just got off work," she answered. Her reply was curt, like she had a problem with me.

"Are you mad at me or something?" I asked.

"Nah."

"Then why does it sound like you have an attitude every time I ask you something?"

"I don't. You straight."

"Laylah, we're family and yeah, we fight, but we've always been good and straight up with one another. What's up?"

"You knew DJ was coming over here?"

I shook my head. "No, I didn't even know the three of you had anything going on!"

"I'm sick of that nigga. Sick of him. Fuck him. Blood or no blood, fuck him," she spat venomously.

"Why do you hate him so much, Laylah? What did he do besides get with Brash?"

"He always got some smart shit to say. I ain't want Brash fucking with that nigga, but you know her. She do what the fuck she want. So it's like, whatever, you know. I love her so I have to deal with them two being together or whatever. But me and Brash will be hanging out and this nigga will just show up and like take her and shit. It be my time, but he don't respect me, Lon. He don't respect my time with her. I been real quiet about that shit, but I just snapped the last time. Sick of him."

Laylah was huffing, sniffing, and puffing. I knew she was crying. I was about to say something, but she started talking again.

"Then I walked in on him telling Brash that they should adopt my son, like take him away from me because I don't have time for him. Fuck that! I may be a lot of fucking shit, cousin, but a bad mother I ain't. And DJ think 'cause he got a dick and money he can just run over me and Brash don't say shit, cousin. She don't say shit. She let him say whatever the fuck he wanna say to me and I am fucking sick of it!"

I knew Laylah to be a lot of things, like she said. But I'd never seen a young mother work harder to provide for her child. At one time, she was working three jobs, but I started giving her money just so she wouldn't have to. Yes, Laylah did party a lot, but she worked hard, too. She wasn't in school, but she worked and she provided for her kid.

I didn't know how I felt about all of this. I didn't know what to say. I never knew my brother to be unfair to anybody and I hadn't heard his side of the story yet. I did know that Laylah was only seventeen and shouldn't have been even going through this kind of thing so young.

I didn't really know what to say so I asked, "You want me to come take you somewhere? Need to get out the house?"

"It's kind of late for you, ain't it? But whatever. Come through if you want to. If not, I'm cool either way."

"I can come take you out the house for a bit. You can bring Chance, too."

"Okay."

About an hour later, I'd picked up Laylah but Auntie Nikki decided she wanted to keep her grandbaby with her since it was after hours, so Laylah and I rode out. I wasn't as scared to come over the tracks as I had been only days before. Quiet as kept, my heart always kicked up a notch when I crossed over. It was like walking out of the land of everything perfect into the spice of life for me. While Roanoke had the best of everything financially, it was like Goodman was always full of life. Most people called it a jungle, but to me it was like the Brazilian rainforest.

Everything and everyone in Goodman had adapted and evolved. What they had evolved into was still up in the air.

I was dressed casually in a sundress and sandals while Laylah had on shorts that looked to be painted on her ass. She had on a long tee that hung to her ankles and was split on the side, with the latest pair of Jordans. Her hair was pulled back into a sleek ponytail. And her purse hung over one shoulder and across her chest.

"So you want to go chill in Ro or here?" I asked.

Laylah looked at me then smiled. "Look at you trying to hang with us po' folk," she joked.

"Oh, whatever," I said as I pulled off, glad she was in a better mood than before.

"If you're hungry we can hit up Silky's pop's spot or we can go to the arcade and chill or something. I ain't trying to be in Ro because if I run into your brother, I'm pepper spraying his fuck ass on the real."

"Stop it, Laylah. We're blood."

"He don't be thinking 'bout that shit when he being a dick."

I was just about to respond when I saw Saint and his twin, Sin. They were sitting outside of Dee Dee's house. Dee Dee had her pussy damn near in Saint's face and her friends were all over Sin. I sat at that stop sign and mean mugged Saint so hard you would have thought he was my man I'd caught cheating.

"Girl, you gon' go or nah?" Laylah asked me after realizing I had been sitting at the sign for a while. She followed my gaze and then a slow smirk eased onto her face. "I knew it. I knew that nigga was gon' get your ass," she said with a laugh. "St. Good Dick gets all the hoes," she continued, jokingly so.

"Shut up. Nobody checking for him."

"Could have fooled me."

"Anyway. I was looking at those girls. They were the ones in the bathroom talking smack about us at the party." It was at least half the truth. I was checking for Saint but I wasn't about to play myself by wanting a boy who didn't want me.

"Who was talking about us? That funky cunt, Dee Dee?" Laylah asked like she was about to get out of the car. That was the thing about her and Brash, they were always ready to fight.

"They all were." I repeated some of the things I'd heard being said.

"Bet not one of those hoes will step to our faces and say nothing," she said so loud I knew they heard something because they all turned and glared at us. "Jealous and petty. But why you staring Saint down, though? Don't think you fooled me by telling me that shit about Dee Dee 'n' 'em. I appreciate it, but nah."

I sucked my teeth as I finally pulled off at a slow speed. "Nothing. He was supposed to call me after we hung out the other day, but he didn't."

"Ayyyy, Saint," Laylah yelled out the window.

My eyes widened, nerves started twitching. "What are you doing?" I asked.

She ignored me. "My cousin said why you ain't hit back the other day, nigga? You cute, nigga, but you ain't cute enough to be ignoring my people. She bad as fuck so don't be trying to play her like you do these stank pussy bitches in Goodman," she yelled as I rode by the house.

If I hadn't been driving, I would have slid down in my seat and tried to disappear. Sin threw his head back and laughed. Dee Dee cocked her head to the side and looked at Saint like he had said something offensive when in fact, he hadn't said anything at all. He did look back at her like she had lost her mind, however; then he shot the same look at Laylah.

I sped off, wishing my cousin knew how to keep her mouth shut. We ended up at the arcade. The place was bigger than I thought it would be and the parking lot was crowded. Laylah told me to park across the street so I wouldn't get blocked in so I did. The music was loud. The latest song with the latest dance craze was blasting on the speakers. "Watch me, watch me. Watch me, watch me," greeted us as we made our way across the street. I'd never been grabbed and hollered at so many times in my life. I felt violated in a way. Laylah was used to it, though, because she just laughed it off.

The arcade was alive with noises and murmurs of people. Dance games, racing games, and everything in between blended in so you couldn't tell one game from the other. The carpet had the shapes of planets, moons, and stars, and it glowed in the dark. The walls were blue in some places and red and green in others. I paid for Laylah and me to get wrist bands and then we set off to play around.

Brash called to see where we were because Marsha and Brandy wanted to hang out. Really Marsha wanted to get to Goodman so she could meet up with Lank, the guy she met at the party. We all met up and played games and then I sat down to eat. Things were going good for a while and then went left. By left, I mean Saint and Sin showed up.

Saint walked through the place like he owned it. People parted and gave him wide berth like he was king of the hill. I was at the table picking over my pizza, trying to pretend I didn't see him walking my way. I smelled him when he sat next to me. Saint had a distinct smell, one that told of his uniqueness. From the red hair and brown skin to the brown eyes, he was in a league of his own.

"So we just gon' sit here and pretend we don't see each other?" he asked after a few minutes.

I couldn't front like his voice wasn't melting my insides. I cast a curt glance at him over my shoulder. "Like we'll pretend you called or texted like you said you would."

He chuckled a bit then picked up my pizza to take a bite. "So," he said, chewing, "you mad, huh?"

"Not mad. Just wish people kept their word like they said they would."

"I got no excuse other than the fact duty called and I had to answer. Been busy and shit, you know?"

"No, I don't know."

"Well, I'm telling you. You can believe me or not. Won't change a thing," he replied, taking another bite of my pizza.

"You can't buy your own food?"

"I can, but I'd rather eat yours. It tastes better."

I turned to fully look at him to see a smirk written across his face. I rolled my eyes and turned back around then almost jumped out of my skin to find Sin sitting on the other side of me. He was grinning like the Joker.

"What up, beautiful?" Sin spoke.

"H . . . hello, Sin."

His grin turned into a smirk to match his brother's. "So check this out. Your friend Brandy, she here?" he asked.

"Yeah, why?"

"No reason. Just asking. She single?" he asked then took a slice of my pizza.

If I didn't eat a slice soon, they would be sure to eat it for me. I shrugged. "Last I checked."

"I mean I don't give a shit either way, feel me? But I'd like to know if I'ma have to cut a nigga after I blow her back out."

I frowned. Didn't know if I liked him speaking about my friend that way; although, I was more than certain Brandy would go for it. Still, he didn't know her like that to assume he would be getting anything from her.

"You don't know her like that to speak about her in such a manner," I said.

Sin nodded and chuckled a bit. "My bad, my bad. But I figure since Saint said you were too green for him to fuck with I'd see if I could say something to get your gears grinding."

"Excuse me?"

Sin cackled again.

"Nigga, shut the fuck up," Saint quipped behind me.

"Ay, bro, mama got some fire in her. She may not be too green after all, feel me?" Sin said. He then took the slice of pizza he was eating and disappeared into the crowd.

I turned to Saint. "So I'm too green?"

"You are, but I didn't say what Sin said I did," he answered.

"How am I green?"

"We had this conversation before, mama, but look, I'm sorry I didn't call, okay? I said I would and I didn't, but let me make that up to you right now. Why don't you and your homegirls come to my crib and chill with me and my brother?"

"Chill? Is that another code for fucking?" I asked, knowing how the game went.

Saint shrugged. "Do you want it to be? Because if you want it to be code for fucking, we can make that happen."

"You're so used to getting what you want, huh?"

"Maybe, maybe not. So we chilling or not?"

"Let me see what my girls want to do," I said.

He nodded then tore into another slice of my pizza. I walked away hearing my daddy's voice in my head. *"Stay away from Maya Black, and her sons."* I glanced back over my shoulder at Saint. It was going to be hard to stay away from a man who moved me the way Saint did.

Chapter 13

Saint

Having people in my spot wasn't something I was chill with, but seeing London and reading her body language had me doing things differently. After taking care of business with Guerilla's crew, Goodman had become tense with worry about what was going to happen between us. Marvin being the catalyst of it pissed me off. Blanket had made it his main rule to keep all gang war minimal as a means to keep the people of Goodman safe from being collateral damage. Now, that shit was crossed out.

It was all or nothing and we had our zones to protect in the community, along with the people who lived in them. With that in my mind, it led me to Dee Dee's, where I was really checking up on the neighborhood and shit talking on her porch. I was still working, trying to do Blanket's business while making sure our crew at our various zone houses knew to stay on guard, when I saw London mean mugging me.

Honestly, the shit was comical. I really did mean to call her, but shit, the old saying goes you want what don't want you. London wasn't reciprocating the type of vibe I was giving her at first, so I decided to be slightly chill on her. When she saw me on the porch, the look in her doe eyes gave me nothing but money and now, watching her walk away, I pretty much felt like I could get her.

I low-key admired how nice her hips rocked as she stopped to speak with her girls. I then slid my hands in my pockets and noticed my twin by my side. He was geeked up about this mini-party in my crib and all I could do was shake my head.

"Note, I'm only doing this for one thing," I said to him while still watching London.

Sin knew that my place was my sanctuary. I never invited anyone but family to my crib.

"Pussy," Sin said with no type of respect our mother drummed in his skull as a kid.

"Basically," I said back with an off-handed chuckle. Shit, I had none of that respect in me right now either.

"Permanent or one time?" Sin asked.

"Not even sure, twin. But I am curious to turn the Roanoke in her out, feel me? Since she's showing she's bad enough to be in our social mix here," I said, chuckling with my twin.

I never ever was interested in the type of female who came from the Ro side, I repeat, but London felt different. I guessed it was because a small part of me wanted to run into her father again, look him in the eyes and let him know I had his prize; another part was something else I wasn't sure of and pretty much wasn't trying to discover. I was young, and I wanted to celebrate the success of getting our product, money, and fresh information on Guerilla to Blanket with the crew and my people. Trailing London here was the extra icing on that. She looked like the right one to fuck with on that celebration level.

On some real shit.

"Yeah, her girl Brandy looking bad as fuck too," Sin said, rubbing his chin. Head tilted, my twin was sizing Brandy up like a meal. He gave a slight chuckle then slapped his hand on my chest, pushing me back to get in my face.

"I'll grab Silky. We'll keep this thing small," he started.

"You know it ain't going to be that way. You know that shit, right?" I said, scowling. In my mind, I knew this thing was going to explode.

"So, what you wanna do?" Sin asked in response.

"Grab Choppa, and take him to our house," I advised.

Everyone on the block knew Sin and I had an old house inherited from our dad that we were fixing up. It was really our secret zone house for him and our immediate crew. It was right up the street from our tow yard and right next to G-Town Grill, Silky's pop's restaurant.

"Damn, good idea. That area is deeply protected so we shouldn't get any flying bullets, especially since it's away from Guerilla's scope and they don't know it's ours," he said as if taking my thoughts right out of my head.

I stopped my brother from walking away, then rubbed my chin in thought. "Wait, man, this is just us and London's chicks, no one else. Silky and I will meet you there with the girls."

"I'll do what I can do, but you know how I am," Sin said, quickly walking off.

After a bit, London came back my way with a smile. "They said they are open to it."

"Y'all sure? Don't want any y'all talking shit about being scared," I sad, just joking. Clearly London didn't get my joke, because she was staring at me with a hostile look that disappeared when I smiled.

"Remember when I took you to G-Town Grill?"

Following me, London gave me quick nod as she linked arms with her girl Brash. "Yeah?"

"My place is on the corner of it," I explained.

London's soft, "Oh," was all she said because as soon as I opened the door for them, Dee Dee walked right up to me.

Dee Dee dramatically threw back her teal hair, stepped to me with a haughty smile, and slid her hand against my chest. "Where you going, Saint?"

"About to handle some business," was all I said.

"Ooo, can I handle some business with you?" Of course as she said that, she gave a flirty laugh that had her hand sliding down over my dick, while she licked her lips and gave London a slick side look.

Some females kill with the extra shit; that's why I walked out the door, holding it, and said, "Naw, this business isn't about you. We'll talk some other time."

I heard Brash suck her teeth and look Dee Dee up and down as Laylah said, "Tasteless ass."

London said nothing. Her attention stayed on me and I respected that. It had me taking her hand and closing the door in Dee Dee's face. Yeah, I was rude, but how my dick was made up, London had its attention.

After not even fifteen minutes, we rode up to my and Sin's place and parked in the garage next to Sin's ride. The empty lot next to us was ours. We had put a fence around it to keep it protected and help drown out sound from our main house.

Walking to the front, I glanced at the three-story brick and oak Craftsman house. Rusted metal Spanish tile lined the room. One bay window rested in the front of the house and the black wooden door with three-panel glass tinted windows marked the entrance. The front of the home was still tattered but part of it was fixed by my and Sin's hands. Our father had bought the home for my mom. He was going to give it to her as a wedding gift the day he was turning in the marriage license, my brother and I learned from my uncle.

But, all things fell apart and he died and the house was left here half fixed up. Because my dad had been rehabbing it himself, it stayed in shambles. My mom couldn't bring herself to move in and fix it or sell it, so she gave it to us on our twenty-first birthday as a gift. Now it was up to me and Sin to handle business and work on it as best we could with our uncle Red and goduncle Luther.

Lights were on and I used my key to let everyone inside.

"Wow, this is a nice house," London said by my side.

"Yeah, there's a lot of nice property here in Goodman. It's just hard keeping them up. If you work on one house then other houses feel the heat with taxes, ya know?" I explained.

The scent of wood and paint tickled my nose. Outside, across the street, I saw a light turn on in a house. I knew that was a signal that we were protected and watched by old heads in our crew. Closing the door, I heard loud thumping of feet on the wooden floor in the entryway to the living room that made me cringe. I really wasn't a people person when it came to places I tried to protect.

Security turned on, I headed to where everyone was. Sin had hooked up a flat-screen TV to a laptop and had us streaming movies. Silky was working out the music, and Choppa was laying out the food with Hotep and Sassy. That left me with moving paint buckets and other things out of the way so the crew could dance. As I did that, I grabbed a red cup of Hennessy White, took a deep drink, let the burn relax me then went to work, dragging stuff from the living room to the hallway so that I could take it to the kitchen.

"Do you need help?" I heard behind me while in the hallway.

Music started blasting and we heard Brash say, "Let me see your list, Silky."

"Nah, I control the set, mama," we heard him say after that.

Several tracks shifted until we heard, "Baby, is you drunk 'cause you had enough?"

All the ladies in the house shouted, "Ey!"

I stood up with an amused chuckle while brushing my hands off, feeling the track playing.

"Nah, this is stuff that should have been out the way," I explained. "But you can follow me if you want."

London gave me a look, then grabbed a gallon bucket. "So what's up with you and that Dee Dee chick?"

We heard next, "Are you here lookin' for love? Ohh!"

Smoothly, I took the heavy bucket from her, grabbed a bag of tools then walked to the kitchen. "Nothing. We used to chill from time to time, but that's it. She's not my girl if that's what you're asking."

"Got the club goin' crazy."

Because the old-school swing door to the kitchen creaked and I heard the slapping of sandals, I knew London was behind me. As soon as I set the bucket down in a pantry closet that we were using as storage, I turned and almost ran into London, who had more things in her hand.

"She's saying or feeling otherwise," she said, walking past me to drop everything.

I gave an amused chuckle while studying her and wondering what was going on in her mind. "That's not my fault. I'm upfront and honest with her about everything. I'm not trying to be caught up by her."

"Ah, but why mess with her then? It's stupid how some of you so-called men play women," she said, looking down at her hands at the dust there.

"Yeah?" I said with a tilt of my head. "What about when the woman says she just want some dick and nothing else? Dee Dee likes being messed with. But, she likes to be territorial with it, too. Now why do some of you females do that, huh? I think that's stupid." Stepping to

London, I took her hands and brushed them off. "Does that bother you, mama? You mad?" I said in a low voice.

London slowly looked up at me while I stared down at her.

There was a quiet pause between us as we both heard, "All these bitches, but my eyes on you."

"Nah, why would I be?" London finally said.

I reached up, curled my finger under her chin, then shrugged as I leaned into her personal space. "I don't know either, because my attention is between me and you."

Our lips touched and it was crazy but her lips seemed to feel like butter. It had me taking the light kiss deeper by running my tongue against her lower lip to coax her mouth open. In that kiss, I tasted something like sweet candy; no, mint, but something like cherry. It was intriguing and made a nigga's dick thicken on hundred. Honestly, I didn't plan on me kissing her. I did it because I wanted to. The vibe in the house was running through me and the fact that I saw something like jealousy behind her eyes made me want to kiss her.

Feeling how heated our kiss became when she kissed me back, I knew I made the right decision. Tongues dancing, I dropped my hand down her back then down to grip her ass. When she didn't push me back or play coy, I lifted her and turned to sit her on the wooden kitchen island my uncle Red had just installed. A sharp but soft, mousy squeak came from her when I picked her up. She weighed no more than a feather and a stone; it was wild to me but I liked it. Little mama wore a simple thin sundress, so that awarded me easy access to not only feeling her softness against me but in pushing her dress up.

Hands on her thighs, I slipped them to the side and hooked the folds of the fabric against my thumb and pointer finger. It was interesting to me how soft like silk were her legs. I enjoyed the smoothness. Not that the chicks I messed with didn't handle their business when it came to shaving or nothing, but this was different. I couldn't explain it and didn't want to.

Inhaling, she smelled good, too, a light honey scent this time. "Damn, London," I said because of how she curled her tongue over mine.

When I claimed her mouth again and dropped her back on that island, my fingers read her body like braille. Brushing against the middle of her covered slit, I strummed and felt her gasp and jerk her hips up to feel my knuckle more. Rhythmically stroking, playing her keys, she moaned, turned her head as if bashful; and I dropped down like a vampire and bit her neck, licking the flat of my tongue there.

"Ahhh, London! These niggas are clowning," we both heard over the music in laughter.

While we were kissing and touching, I liked how she jerked, how she held me when I did that, but when she pulled back, I frowned. "What's wrong? Want me to stop?" I asked, breathing hard.

"I didn't come here for this," she said almost stammering.

"Yeah, but we're here, so, I mean . . . I have protection if you're worried about that, and I've never had an STD eva', mama. I got my test papers, new, if you want," I said, going in my pocket.

"Damn, really? I'm proud of you, Saint. Look, I'm not about to give it up just because you kiss good, and thank you for telling me that," she started as her pretty eyes narrowed at me in annoyance.

It was then that I looked up at the ceiling in frustration. *Here we go.* "What you wanna do then, huh? Because I'm standing here, dick ready to give it to you, but you're backing up. What changed? Your girls' loud laughs?"

I tried to think about how I was handling her as I took some steps back. Maybe we should have kicked it off upstairs. I didn't know, but I wasn't willing to stop kissing her in that moment to go upstairs.

London sat biting her lower lip, looking at me. When she reached out and kissed me, I sighed in relief and returned to where we stopped. Holding the small of her back, I spread her legs wide and lifted her so she wouldn't fall while on that kitchen island. Working the top of her dress off, I dropped my head to graze my teeth over her nipples. Her moan let me know she was heating up again and that made my night.

Music continued its thing. I reached between us and dropped my head to introduce her my gift of mouth. Speaking in tongues was my thing. I slipped her underwear to the side with my tongue hooking around that moist fabric there; then I dipped in and out. It was interesting to me how she seemed to tense a second as if surprised, then seemed to relax and open up more for me. I guessed she never had a nigga go down on her? I didn't know. But how I was doing things, I knew she liked it.

Figure-eighting with my tongue, I stiffened it then drank her like Henny. I was high off of her moans. High off of how her fingers gripped my kinky fade, and high off the fact that I had her wilding out for me. All my focus was on working her. My gift of mouth came from dealing with an older Goodman college girl when I was about eighteen. She showed me the ropes and I was keen on learning the lessons and I learned them well. Seeing how when I held London's pelvis and butterflied my tongue against her pearl, I knew she was ready to explode.

When she almost slipped from the island, I smiled against her kitty, chuckling then leaning up over her.

"You're about to fall, mama, and you're getting a little loud. Think you can handle me taking you upstairs?"

I hooked my finger under her chin again, to glance in her dilated eyes waiting for her response.

"Hmm . . . ah, yeah. We can go," she said as if in a daze, watching me as if I were something new to her.

I licked my lips. I adjusted my dick. Then I helped her down, and fixed her top. "A'ight, follow me upstairs. Ignore everyone else."

We held hands as I took her down the hall. Bass had the walls vibrating. I literally touched the wall and felt the rhythm flow throw me. It made me nod and look behind me at London, who watched me then smiled when I smiled at her. We were still locked in that moment, ready to go over the edge. Too bad that before we could make it upstairs shit popped off.

Brash rushed our way with something like panic across her face. She then stopped in front of London and grabbed her wrist. "Lon, we have to go. DJ called. He said your daddy is looking for you and something is going on."

Disappointment shined in London's eyes as she stepped forward. "He's just mad because he probably knows I'm in Goodman."

"Yeah? Then you know he'll come up in here fooling like he did at the shop. We need to go because I don't feel like arguing with DJ tonight, please." Brash seemed to be deeply worried. She dropped her hold on London only to hold out a hand to her. I watched as London took it then looked over her shoulder at me with a nonverbal sorry in her pretty eyes.

"We'll be back when the dust clears, Saint. I'm sorry about this," Brash said, taking London with her.

Frustrated, I followed. "Hold on. I'll open the garage so y'all can get ya ride."

After watching them all pile up in their car, Sin ran up on the car and I followed. He was putting his digits in Brandy's cell and I was keeping my cool as London watched me and mouthed that she'd call me.

I was rolling my shoulders as they pulled off into the night. It was around two in the morning. Streetlamps flickered off and on and the heat of the summer had somewhat dulled.

"Well, damn, that was abrupt, wasn't it?" Sin said with a scowl. "Brandy is feeling me, though."

I kept my thoughts to myself about what was about to go down with me and London while I laughed. "Yeah, I'm proud for you, man."

As we walked up the steps to our house, the sound of an engine revving drew our attention. Turning, bullets flew our way. Guerillas were on our block. They had taken the war to the next level by crossing into our boundary yet again, when we only left bodies at the border of theirs. Steel sliced into and out of my side. Another against my arm. The force was strong and had me falling back, as did my twin. I saw he was hit too. We both pulled out our Glocks and returned fire as our squad rushed out the house and sprinted after the Guerillas. Sin and I were pumped with adrenaline because we both were neck and neck, running as if in track, shooting back, hitting the car and watching it run into several parked rides.

"You fucked up yet again!" I shouted, feeling dazed.

Several niggas spilled out the car trying to get away, but again, they were in Blanket's zone. That meant our crew, those from other zones, were coming out of their houses letting out rounds. Catching one nigga, Sin slammed his Glock across that nigga's head, and I ran up to jam my gun under his chin, blasting brain matter everywhere. Heat was blazing through me, had me glassy eyed as I held my side.

I saw Sin holding his shoulder as he dropped back to keep near my side. In the middle of the street, I ran out of rounds, and stumbled to my knees. I was losing too much blood and all I could think about was my family, the fact that these niggas were looking for anyone associated with Blanket, and oddly enough London crossed my mind too.

Succumbing to black, all I heard was my brother saying my name.

Chapter 14

Guerilla

"They've been hit," was said to me.

I held my cell to my ear waiting for confirmation that we had moved in on Blanket's turf again. How that nigga felt he could leave bodies as a message to me was baffling. But that was the thing with that nigga Blanket. He thought he was untouchable since nobody knew his face. I guess you could say the same shit about me. I'd been in the game a long time. Had seen a lot of shit. Being a kingpin didn't come easy, but I was willing to respect Blanket as long as he kept shit copasetic; however, it was a dog-eat-dog world and times had changed. I was ready to run metro Atlanta with a grid-iron fist and Blanket could either get down or get laid down. I had no intention of letting this nigga get out of this alive, but I couldn't kill what or who I couldn't see. I wanted to flush him out, make him show his hand and his face.

Taking that house in his territory was easy. In fact, it was too damn easy. Marvin was a basehead who was looking for a come up. I had money to blow so it was nothing to pay him off. I figured that Blanket would find out sooner or later and he did. Leaving those bodies by those tracks was comical to me. But it was also a wakeup call. Blanket was too big for his breeches it seemed. The nigga seemed to forget I was eating in the hood long before he was. A nigga was being generous by even letting the nigga come to the table.

Most people in the A or around the A knew of cities like College Park, Decatur, East Atlanta, or Zone 6, and the like. They knew of places like Cascade, Godby Road, and East Lake Meadows, better known to us old heads as Li'l Vietnam. Those places were the worst kind of ghetto. The shits used to be made up of tenement houses or drug- and rat-infested apartment buildings. We wouldn't mention how the roaches used to park on a nigga's shoulders and chill wit'cha while we smoked. The memories made me chuckle.

Those places had the worst drug problems. The crime rate there had made the crime rate in other crime-ridden cities look like child's play. Most of the niggas who grew up there had few options. You could luck out on a scholarship and get out, but that was only if you lived long enough to see high school or if you were lucky enough to stay out the system or sell drugs. Most niggas only left those places on a stretcher or on an extended state-sponsored vacation. I got lucky, most people would think.

I happened to come across an O.G. who showed me the ropes early. Made me go to school and to college. He taught me how to be the drug dealer who the drug dealers wouldn't see coming. Taught me how to blend in with the elite while running a criminal enterprise so smoothly I'd never have to show my face if I didn't want to. I took that shit to heart and made it so only very few people knew what my shadow even looked like.

I said all that to say, as a businessman, there was no need to do business where there was already heat. Don't get me wrong, Goodman was hot, but it wasn't East Atlanta hot. See, I dealt in the cities and areas that the feds wouldn't pay attention to. The local cops could be paid off easily. Import and export were a breeze 'round these parts. I had no issue finding workers anxious to get put on, as people were starving and dying to eat. Therefore, Goodman made a great spot to have my home base and conduct business.

"How many died?" I asked.

"Not sure. Haven't gotten the head count yet," my worker said over the phone.

My voice was distorted so he wouldn't be able to pick me out anywhere if he heard my real voice. I grunted for my response.

"Got word that one of those twins went down though."

That got my attention and made me sit up. "Say what now?"

"One of the twins. Saint, I believe. Word is he went down in the middle of the street."

"That nigga dead?"

"Got no confirmation on that yet. They just said he went down."

I was quiet for a minute before speaking. I had to think. Blanket's response to my takeover of one of his houses was to have his enforcers leave bodies for me to see. Kind of reckless if you thought about it. Yeah, they had on masks, but I could use what he had done to my advantage.

"Set up a meeting for me with all the suppliers. I think it's time we talk about the heat Blanket pushed our way by leaving those bodies out in the open like that. Guess that nigga think he El Chapo or somebody. All that heat ain't good for business. Let the suppliers know that we want to double our orders, too. We're paying for everything up front. If we double up, that pushes Blanket out as far as product. It'll take him a minute to re-up."

"Got it, boss. What about that other thing?" he asked.

"What other thing?"

"The chick at the shop."

"I'll handle her."

Maya Black had secrets and I intended to find out just what the fuck they were. She was a problem for me. I always kept my eye on her. There was a time she and I, along with her sons' father, were friends. I knew most people wouldn't believe it but the Royals used to be a part of that clique as well. I knew the Royals never wanted that shit made public knowledge. They'd never want to be exposed as having ties with people like the Blacks. They were trash, lowest of the low.

They were also things that people would never believe. They were killers, sadistic killers, and it seemed Maya had passed the genes to her sons. I wondered if Maya Black still thought her husband's and his father's deaths were an accident. I rolled my shoulders then looked out over Roanoke from my office building. I had my secrets too, ones that I would take to my grave with me.

Chapter 15

London

As soon as we pulled up to my place after dropping Brandy and Marsha home, DJ came rushing over to the car. I thought he was coming to fuss at me about being in Goodman again. I didn't have time for his shit on top of what I knew I was going to hear from Daddy. But to my surprise, he jumped in Brash's face.

"London, Daddy's in your crib waiting on you. Brace yourself," he said all the while staring Brash down. "So you're just going to go fuck with Laylah and lie about it?" he asked her.

The tone of his voice was so eerily calm that it alarmed me. I wanted to tell Brash to tread lightly because him being this calm meant he was at his deadliest. But she had been fooling with him a long time. She should have been abreast of that knowledge.

Furthermore, I was upset because DJ called Brash to have me leave the party like there was some dire emergency. I had a feeling I was about to get the fuck of my life. The way Saint had rewired my pussy with his tongue still had my body humming. I seriously had the feeling he was about to have me seeing past lives and I was ready for it. The fact that he had condoms and papers with proof of his status that he was willing to show lit a fire in me. I didn't think dudes from the hood cared too much about shit like that.

Obviously, Brash still didn't know my brother that well because she lied when she said, "I was nowhere near Laylah. I was with London. We was chilling—"

DJ visibly bristled. "We was chilling?" he repeated as if he was offended by her misuse of the English language.

Brash rolled her eyes. "We were chilling at the arcade."

"So Laylah wasn't there? You weren't locked in the bathroom, finger up her pussy?"

"No," Brash said defensively. "What are you talking about?"

I knew Brash was lying by the way she kept switching her weight from one foot to the other and by the way she kept looking everywhere other than at DJ.

"So you're just going to stand here and lie to my face? Like that ghetto bitch didn't send me pictures of you and her to my phone? I guess when she was face first in your pussy you didn't pay attention to what she was doing with her phone, huh?"

I was about to interject and say something about him calling Laylah a bitch, but the bass in my daddy's voice when he called my name stopped me.

"What?" I responded without really thinking about the tone of my voice. I was annoyed at that point.

Daddy stepped down the front stairs of my place then walked up to me. "I think you have a problem with your tone of voice, first off. Secondly, you were over there gallivanting with trash while your mother is having a medical crisis," he snapped.

"Mommy? What's wrong with Mama?" I asked, all other emotion giving way to fear.

"She was over in Goodman looking for you."

I frowned as her looking for me didn't explain her medical emergency. "Looking for me? Why was she looking for me and how did she know where I was?"

"We pay your phone bill, London. It's easy to use GPS to locate the area your phone is in. Your mother felt bad about the way we made you feel at dinner so she came over to apologize. You weren't here. She went to Goodman and got robbed at gunpoint."

My hand flew to my mouth. "Oh, my God! Where is she?"

"She's in the fucking hospital where I would like to be, but we had to run around here looking for your disrespectful ass."

I dropped my hand and clamped my mouth closed. For as bad as I wanted to tell my father to go fuck himself, I knew now wasn't the time. I could tell by the look in his eyes he was itching for me to speak up and say the wrong thing. And God knew that I wanted to. Daddy had never raised me to be silent on anything, but I guessed that only counted when I wasn't disputing him.

We stared one another down so much that the left corner of my upper lip twitched, which made Daddy cock a brow.

DJ broke the tension. "Dad, Mom is asking for you and London," he said with the phone to his ear.

I'd been so put off by Daddy, I hadn't heard whatever was going on with DJ and Brash behind me. We all piled into DJ's truck and made our way to Southern Regional. As soon as we walked into the hospital, I frowned. The place smelled damp. The waiting room was overflowing with people and I felt as if I was going to get sick just looking at them.

Daddy bypassed the reception area, and pressed a button by two brown double doors that flew open, granting us access. No one stopped us or greeted us as we went into the triage area. I could hear Mama before I saw her.

She was pissed off. "Did you just really try to touch me without gloves on?" she yelled. "What kind of place is this? Where did you get your degree? Online? This freaking place is filthy and it's disgusting."

Daddy opened the door. As soon as he did, the male nurse who had been in the room shook his head. Clearly he was angry by the way his mouth was balled and the mumbling under his breath as he made a hasty retreat from the room.

Daddy and Mama had always been in love. I'd never seen them at a time they weren't. Even when they were mad at one another the love they had for one another still shone in their eyes.

Once Mama came into full view, I gasped at her face. When Daddy had said she was robbed at gunpoint, he forgot to mention that they had assaulted her as well. Her light face was red with bruises and cuts. Her lips and jaw were so swollen that they looked to be stuffed with cotton balls. As soon as she saw my father, she rushed into his arms.

Daddy held her tightly, his big hands fisted as he bit down on his bottom lip. He was seething with anger. Malice leaked through his pores. For seconds he stood there holding her as she cried.

"Get me out of this place," she wailed. "I told those stupid-ass cops to not let the ambulance bring me here. They didn't listen."

Daddy leaned back enough so he could caress her face. "Did you see who did it?" he asked her.

"It . . . it was dark and I was trying to call London. Stopped at a traffic light. It was late and I was scared with her being in Goodman by herself. I . . . I don't know what I was thinking. I don't know why I went over there, Devon. I don't. I should have known better."

Daddy cut his eyes at me when I stepped forward.

"I'm sorry, Mama. I am," I apologized while reaching out to hug her. She returned my embrace. "I didn't hear my phone or I would have answered for you, you know that. I'm so sorry," I told her.

"Where were you?" she asked as she pulled away from the hug.

"I was with Brash and Laylah."

"You were with more than Brash and Laylah. When DJ called Brash all I heard was loud music and talking. What in God's name—"

I cut my father off. "Mama, did they do anything else to you? They take your purse?"

She nodded. "They have everything. I was able to call 911 from the car. I'm shocked they didn't take that from me."

The doctor walked in, stopping anything else we were about to say. All Mama wanted him to do was release her so she could go to "real doctors and nurses who knew what they were doing." I was sure the doctor was insulted but he was more than happy to oblige. DJ and Brash had stayed outside since DJ had already been with Mom until they had to leave to find me. Once we walked back up, Brash rushed up to me with urgency in her eyes.

"They shot Saint," she said low enough for me to hear.

My eyes widened and I felt the bottom of my stomach fall out. Yeah, Saint and I hadn't really known one another for long, but I was still feeling him on a level I couldn't really explain at the moment. All I knew was I liked him a hell of a lot and to hear he had been shot alarmed me.

"What? When? What happened?" I asked.

"Laylah said not long after we left somebody rode through shooting. Saint and Sin got hit, but she said when she looked outside Saint was lying in the middle of street."

"Oh, God," I whispered. "Is he dead?"

Brash shrugged while she slowly shook her head. "Nobody knows."

I didn't know why I felt like crying. First my mama was assaulted and robbed at gunpoint; then to hear Saint had been shot and was quite possibly dead weighed heavily on me. I had to get back over there to find out for myself if he was alive. I didn't give a damn what my daddy had to say about it, either.

Once we got to my parents' home, I stayed with Mama until the next morning. Since Daddy wanted to be a dick, I asked Mama if I could sleep with her just to piss him off. Since DJ and I had been kids, Daddy hated for us to sleep in their bed. He always wanted Mama to himself at the end of the night. Surprisingly, he didn't put up much of a fuss. He and DJ left and didn't come back for the rest of the night. God only knew what they were doing.

Mama tossed and turned most of the night. She kept saying something about a rooster or something. I didn't know, but I could have sworn I heard her say something about Maya Black. I gave Mama Valium and brandy. She slept like a baby.

I didn't know what I was doing or why I was doing it, but I called Laylah early the next morning and asked for Maya Black's address. I'd been calling Saint all night, but his phone went straight to voicemail each time. I didn't know Sin's number's so I was taking a gamble. I pulled up to a yellow two-story Craftsman-style home. I didn't know what to expect, but it wasn't for the house to be surrounded by men and women. I was under scrutiny as I did so. All eyes were on me as I stepped out of the car. I was nervous, wasn't sure I would be allowed in to ask questions or anything. I got a sinking feeling in the pit of my stomach.

Did all those people mean Saint's family had gathered to wish him farewell? If so, I didn't know how I would feel about that.

"Can I help you?" I heard a female ask me.

She had an attitude off top so I knew I had an uphill battle. "Yeah, ah, I'm looking for Saint," I answered.

She narrowed her eyes, looked at my car and then back over at me. "What for?"

"She's cool," I heard Sin say before I could answer.

I looked up and saw he was shirtless but had a big white patch of gauze covering his left shoulder. I took note of the fact that the silky hair on Sin's chest was just as red as the hair on his head. His abs constricted each time he took a breath. His eyes were red and puffy. He looked tired.

The men and women guarding the front of the house parted to let me through. I rushed up to Sin on the steps of the house, trying to see if his eyes would tell me what I wanted to know. "Is he dead?" I asked.

Sin shook his head then held the door open for me. I stepped in to find just as many people inside as out. They were all visibly armed and it made me uncomfortable, but it attested to how well-loved the Blacks were. I could smell food cooking, but it seemed as if all eyes were on me. Clearly I was an outsider. Just as I was about to ask Sin where Saint was, Maya Black came rushing from the kitchen.

I stepped back defensively just in case the woman was crazy and was going to try to hit me or something. She and I hadn't really seen eye to eye the first time we met. Her eyes were just as red as Sin's and, quite frankly, the woman didn't look to be all there. Her eyes held a crazed look in them that gave me pause. I guessed if my sons had been gunned down I would feel and look the same way.

"Can I help you?" she asked blandly.

"I wanted to see Saint. I heard what happened and wanted to see for myself that he was okay," I answered.

Maya's face frowned and she looked as if I repulsed her for a second.

"Mama, chill," Sin said. "She's cool."

She turned her anger from me to Sin. "I told you I didn't want anything to do with the Royals. Why is she in my house?"

"Ma, I think Saint would want . . . I don't think he'd have a problem with her coming to see him," Sin answered.

"I do. My house, my son, and I don't want a Royal anywhere near my house or my son."

"Okay, fine," I said, albeit with a smattering of anger laced in it. "I'll leave. Just wanted to know he was alive. Now I know, I can leave. Thanks anyway, Sin," I said then turned to leave.

I couldn't front like I wasn't ready to cuss that woman to hell, but she was right. It was her house and her son. Since it was her house he was in, she had the right to tell me to leave.

"Good," Maya said.

I turned to look at her when I made it to the door. "I want you to know I'll be back, every day, same time, until he gets better or you change your mind about letting me see him." I looked at her in her eyes for a few seconds more so she would know I was being 100 percent truthful and 200 percent serious.

"Like hell you will," she snapped and rushed for me, but Sin stopped her.

"Then I suggest you get one of these people to shoot me or have the police here to help escort me away every day."

Sin hid a smile.

I shrugged and walked to my car.

For the next week, I did exactly what I said I would. Every morning, same time, I was back at Maya Black's house trying to see Saint. I'd knock on the door and ask to see Saint and Maya would slam the door in my face. The one thing my father had passed on honestly was my stubbornness. When I set my mind to something, I stuck with it.

Although, the news of the wave of violence that hit Goodman couldn't be denied. I was afraid of my own shadow every time I stepped foot in the place. There had been fires set to houses, bodies were turning up in ditches. Even headless bodies left on spikes at the railroad tracks. I think what got me most was the news of the police who had turned up dead. Whoever Blanket and Guerilla were, they gave no fucks and held no prisoners.

That Friday morning Maya Black stormed out to my car and snatched my door open. Her hair was pulled back into a ponytail. She had on denim overalls, and a tank top that showcased her big breasts. The woman looked almost as young as I was. Her eyes had turned to slits. And I couldn't help but notice the cuts and bruises along her arms, neck, and chest.

"Don't you have a job or something? Why do you keep coming back to my house?" she questioned, using her hands to do so.

I was eating breakfast in my car, a chicken biscuit I'd gotten from Silky's place. I wiped my mouth and shook my head. "No. My parents are rich. All I have to do is bother you since school is out and I'm not taking classes this summer. Can I see Saint today?"

"No! It will be the same answer each and every day," she yelled.

"Then I'll be sitting here until I get tired and then I'll be back tomorrow."

I heard some of the people who had been around the house laughing. For the last six days people rotated in and out as I sat there sometimes from early morning until late night. Sin left home every day and came back late at night. There were two doctors who came in and out of the house daily as well. I'd seen Dee Dee and her friends come in and out too. Dee Dee even stopped to stare me down then smirk. I couldn't front like that hadn't pissed me off, but I still wouldn't be moved. Unless Maya Black shot me or sent the police to stop me from coming, I had no intention of stopping until I was allowed to see Saint.

Maya reached inside of the car and snatched me out by my hair. My food, car keys, and cell phone fell on the ground. Before I could react, the woman's hand was around my throat. Gotdamn it she was stronger than she looked. My eyes watered when she intensified the pressure to my throat as she pushed my head back.

"Little girl, I don't know who you assume I am, but I'm not the woman you want to go toe to toe with. You get in this fucking car and you leave. Don't come back or I won't be this nice about it."

The people guarding the outside of the house were on alert. I could feel my anger I always worked hard to suppress rising to the surface. My eyes were watering and my claws were digging into her wrist.

"Let me go, Maya," I snarled.

Her pupils were dilated and she was sneering at me as if she was seeing someone else. Looking into that woman's eyes, I knew she wasn't all there. There was something under the surface that told me Maya Black was more than what the naked eye could see.

"London," I heard.

Both my and Maya's heads whipped around. Maya dropped her hold on me and I coughed hard, trying to regain my breath. There stood Saint on the stairs. His abdomen was wrapped and his arm was in a sling. She started up the walkway to her house.

My heart was beating a mile a minute. I hadn't seen him in days. He didn't look any worse for the wear. I found myself smiling. The clothes he wore did his body little justice. His arms, chest, and what I could see of his abs were sculpted to perfection.

"Come here, London," he demanded.

"She's not coming in my house and I mean it," Maya said to her son. "You need to be back in bed."

"Mama, I love you, but you're tripping and I mean that with as little disrespect as possible," he said. "Let me talk to her real quick. She's not like her pops."

"They're Royals. That means they're all the same to me."

"I can take her to my place at the shop—"

"No, that won't be necessary," an older man with the same color red hair as Saint stepped in to say. "Let her see him, sis. I know you're pissed, but we got bigger fish to fry, feel me?" he said to Maya.

I'd seen a lot of people roll their eyes, but Maya was in a league of her own. That woman cast a look at me that damn near froze my heart. I was genuinely afraid of what that look meant.

I swallowed slowly then looked up at Saint, wondering if the relationship—yes, relationship—I was trying to establish with him would cause damage to the relationship with him and his mother. But, I didn't want to be Saint's friend. I wanted to be his everything.

Chapter 16

Saint

Hurricane Maya was on the loose. No doubt, I had to be stern with my mama to keep her chill, but I could see London being in her presence wasn't going to help anything. I stood there in pain as my mother brushed past me, disappearing into the house only to come back with a large vase of soft white and pink tiger lilies. My jaw clenched as I saw them. I tried to grab my mom's arm but she moved like she had the spirit in her.

In her dramatic rage, she threw the glass vase with flowers at London's feet, pointed her finger at London, and scowled. "Since my damned house ain't my own, you do this for me. Tell your gotdamned father to stop sending me this shit. You do that since you're bold enough to park your ass in front of my home and ignore my wishes."

Water and broken glass was everywhere. The lilies lay on London's kicks with a signed card that I knew had her father's name on it. Not catching it, but shocked by what my mom did, London looked my way with confusion.

For years, my mother had been getting those same flowers around this time, the anniversary of my father's death, and each time my mother would become unhinged. I figured that was only a small part of why she had gone off on London like she did. The other reason was that Hurricane Maya could get as ratchet as she wanted to be when in a foul mood.

All I heard was cussing, shouting, and slamming doors. A nigga was in bed trying to sleep and heal when I had heard London's voice from upstairs. Dizzier than a motherfucker, it was Sin who let me know that our mom was about to paint the street. As quickly as I could, I knew that I had to get to London before my mom did harm. That's how I ended up outside watching my mom go Super Saiyan on London.

Stepping forward, I held a white beam that was part of our porch and I tried to keep my balance. "Ma, clearly she doesn't know shit about that," I said in London's defense.

"I don't give a fuck. Now she knows," was all my mother said as she marched to the screen door, pausing to lay a hand on my forearm. "Royals think that they are entitled to you. They play people against each other, friends even, and exploit their weakness. Once you get locked into what they want it's too late. Later when you wake up from the bullshit and back off, they take the only thing you love. Watch yourself, since your nuts seemed to be swollen and you don't think that I have your best interest at heart. Be careful of Devon Royal and his seed."

She cut her eyes at me, angrily walked through the door, and left me confused.

"Mama, why do you have to be like that?" I heard Sin say for me as he followed her. "What happened between you and them, for real?"

"Will, leave it alone!" she shouted.

I stood there slowly closing my eyes. The summer heat wasn't helping with the pain and medicine rushing through me but my thoughts were on London and that kept me standing where I was. "Come inside with me, shawty. She won't touch you now," I said, holding my hand out to her.

London stayed in place. She seemed to be cautious and in thought. From the way her hands were fisted at her side, I could also tell that she wanted to fight my mom. A small part of me was amused by that, but a larger part wasn't about to let her put hands on my mom. That's just how I was wired. I'd keep them apart before I let that happen, in this case, again. I was too late to stop my mom and I wished I had.

Anyway, once London came out of her zone, she gave a defiant look around at the spectators, who were my cousins and my mother's church friends, then she walked up to me and took my hand. Once inside, I took her upstairs to my old bedroom, closed the door, locked it, and had her sit on the edge of my bed where I lay down. Because I had lost so much blood, I knew moving around like I did was going to be a problem. But I didn't want to look weak in front of London so I lay back, elevated in bed.

I studied her body language and checked how London inspected my old room. There wasn't anything special in it. When I moved out, I took the majority of my things, but there were old posters of sports, athletes, and luscious vixens. My old high school basketball jersey hung on a wall, boxing gloves hanging on the doorknob of my closet. There were also some pill bottles and some random things including medical shit just added in there by me.

"Ah, you literally have an IV machine in here, Saint. Why aren't you at a hospital?" London questioned like I knew she would.

"People coming in with gunshot wounds, like how Sin and me got hit, draws attention. Brings eyes to Goodman that we don't need any more of, and we all are just looking for a little peace in the mix," I explained while sliding my uninjured arm under my head.

"How bad is it? What happened, Saint?" London started, looking at me with deep concern.

"You like me, huh? The camping out at my place these past . . . How long was it?"

London gave me a hard eye roll. She then shifted to hook her leg on the bed while rubbing her hair. "A week and a day."

I chuckled deeply, wincing at the pain. "Give me a kiss."

She blushed then smoothed and tucked her thick hair behind her ear, pinning it with bobby pins she had removed from her disheveled hair.

"No," she said in a singsong voice. "How bad is your wound, Saint?"

"Kiss me." There was no joking in my voice, just seriousness as I locked eyes on her. When she saw that I wasn't budging, she carefully dropped over me, partially caging me where her one hand was resting by my side and the other was over my chest. From that angle I could see how her brown eyes seemed to dilate. It had me feeling good and forgetting that I was in pain, especially when our lips touched.

Carefully, I held her in place, even though she was over me. Slicking my tongue over her lips, she immediately parted them so that I could take our kiss deeper. Locked in the moment, our kiss was long as fuck and deep. It had me thinking about how sweet her pussy tasted on my tongue and that only caused my dick to harden in response.

When she pulled back, I felt myself feeling a little annoyed it as I sighed. She wanted an answer so I gave it to her.

"There was some complications because I was losing so much blood. But it was taken care of and I'm lying here healing up and good. The bullet that shot me, the bullet just passed through the muscles surrounding my abdomen, and never entered abdominal cavity at all, I was told. Went through clean leaving nothing dirty behind. Same for my shoulder." Having removed my hand from under my head, I rubbed her arm and continued. "If I keep taking these antibiotics and limit my movements, I'll be good and shit in a couple of weeks possibly."

Relief spread across her face, and London quickly hugged me. Grunting, I hissed out, slightly laughing, "Damn, mama! If you keep holding me like that you might open the wound back up."

"I'm sorry! I was worried, Saint," London said while scrambling backward looking at my bandage.

I pulled her back with a lopsided smirk and had her lie by me. "Hey, come back. I didn't say you had to get off me completely now; and you can call me Santana now." Though I couldn't lay on my side, pulling London on me was good enough. I slid her leg over my waist and stroked her bare thigh while watching her watch me.

"What happened? And what pull do you have that you can get doctors to come fix you in your home . . . Santana?"

Lazily watching the ceiling now, I quickly thought of a way to explain it without her knowing my true business. As I scratched my now growing beard, I turned my head to look down at London's pretty face. I felt the need to trace her face with my fingertips. Running the pad of my fingers over the wide bridge of her nose, over the large spans of her lush lips then the tip of her chin, I didn't want to tell her about how I saw her face in my dreams as

I blacked out. I wasn't sure why I was so hooked on this female but I was.

"You have a lot of questions, damn," I said, half-joking voice low in thought. "I don't really know what went down. Word on the street was that with Blanket and Guerilla going at each other, a lot of us were being dealt the aftershocks."

"And you being shot had to do with that? Are you a part of them?" she asked, closing her eyes.

When she did that, I traced those too. I swore whatever it was about her, it had me feeling like she had shot me with a truth serum. The truth was on the tip of my tongue, but I was too quick for that, so I flipped it with half-truths.

"I've done easy work for Blanket, like watched if anything crazy was going down in their zone, that's it. It never was nothing deep for them to blow bullets my way."

"Oh. It was just the wrong place and time?" she asked, opening her eyes.

By this time, my fingers were running over the curve of her check. I felt how her pulse quickened and it caused the heat between us to rise.

"Yeah, something like that. They probably were gunning after someone else in the street and I just got caught up," I explained again, partially telling the truth.

Gently, I outlined the curve of her breasts, slowly pulling her shirt up to get a palm full of her honeydew-size melons. Nipples rising to greet my thumbs, I continued my light touching of her as we spoke.

"So, you're not part of Blanket's crew?" she asked again as if needing reassurance.

The heat of her mound was my friend at that point. Gliding down into her black leggings, I massaged her slowly, then gave a shrug, enjoying the silky folds of her kitty's opening lips and the hardening pearl of her kitty's tongue seeking the heat of my rubbing fingers. Hips rising and her moan making things harder for me, in and out I went as I got her off on my finger strokes.

"Maybe a little, but it's not something you have to worry about, mama. I just watch, that's it," I explained.

"Saint, I don't want you hurt like this. You scared me." Shifting against me, London moved to straddle me, giving me a view of the plump curve of her ass. It was tiny, but it still had mad curve and it made it difficult to deal with her sitting on my dick like she was.

"I had to find out about you while in the hospital. My mom was robbed and got hurt all because she was looking for me at the same time. If I hadn't left, she'd be shot at too," she said with emotion in her voice.

"I'm sorry to hear that, mama. That's the last thing that I'd want too. I didn't know any of that was going to go down, for if I had, I wouldn't have taken you there." Grunting, I looked down where she and I connected and my teeth scraped against my lower lip.

"That spot was supposed to be safe. It was safe. That wasn't . . . Shit, London. You need to get off my dick." I grunted, keeping my eyes on the way her pussy was calling for me.

"Saint . . ."

I looked up at her then she gave me a smile, quickly crawling off me. I watched her pull off her shirt for me, then kick off her hi-tops not saying a thing. No lie, the act of her undressing was poetic. It had me gripping my dick while I lay back, hoping she wasn't playing with me right now. When she turned and bent some to pull off her bikini briefs, I watched that thin piece of fabric remove itself from her ass and I gave a painful grunt again.

Mama had a body like Rihanna and it was killing me, because she also had a tattoo in script that ran against the side of her hip that said, MY LIFE IS MY OWN.

Coming back to the bed, she stopped and my eyes drank her in as they zoned in on her trimmed pussy. Mama only had a strip there, gotdamn.

"Santana, condoms, where are they?" she asked, grinning as if my facial expression of pain was funny or some shit.

For a second I didn't hear her, but when I looked up at her and saw how the sun created a red halo though her dyed hair, I pointed. "Top drawer."

She walked with confidence and I watched her go through my drawer and pull out what she needed. By that time, I was up and standing behind her using the dresser as brace. There was no damn way that I was going to let her kill me like this. If a nigga was going to die, he wanted to die showing her what he could do, and that's what I did.

I stood pressing her against the dresser. Dropping my head, I kissed her shoulder as my hand reached around to play with her strip. Feeling her petite ass press back against my nine, I immediately began slipping over her silky lips enjoying how her legs parted for me.

"Hold the dresser," I muttered against her in urgency.

When she complied, I let my fingers dip in and out of her again, until she was using her toes to bounce up and down. Several "damns" and "shits" aggressively slipped from my mouth as I touched her all over her. For a moment, my hands couldn't stop their outlining of her body, but eventually they did, especially when it came time for me to bend her over, put my condom on, and trace that juicy pussy from behind with the tip of my manhood.

Both of us gasped at the first break of skin as I entered her. All games were out the window while I made that dresser rock and she threw that shit back as best as she could. See, my girth was no joke. I could tell for a second that she had to get used it because she kept flexing and gripping the sides of the dresser.

It made me laugh, which only traveled through her body. Goosebumps lining her spine was proof of that. "Relax and let me teach you," was all I said while I spread her wide from the front, used my digits against her then introduced her to my slow grind.

Sweat dripped down my face. I wanted to beast her, but I couldn't because of my wound. I didn't want to open that shit and leak blood on her, so I damn sure had to be careful. However, I was grateful at the same time. I couldn't thank her more for giving me the gift of her pussy because this sex was needed and was making me forget about the pain of my wounds.

As I held the front of her hips, teaching her to find an angle that made this work to her benefit, I busted that shit open once I felt her body quiver and relax for me, giving me my invitation to ride her.

Thump, thump, "Shit," was our music. It blended with the laughter, loud voices, and the gospel music that was playing downstairs. Yeah, a nigga was zoned in on London, but I couldn't help but chuckle myself as I got a handful of London's squishy breast and the song "I Luh God" flowed with our groove. Shit was wrong, but shit was good, too. Guessed that's why I was considered a Saint.

After some time, both London and I got our kicks off. In the midst of trading places, I guessed my dick game hyped her so much that I ended up back in bed playing with her kitty as she rode me cowgirl style. Mama made me feel like a damn king and I appreciated her last name because of it. Sticky and sweaty, I smirked looking at how sexy London was against me.

Her natural hair felt like cotton as it covered my good side. The heat of her body continued to act as a healing balm, and I lay there chill. There was a reward in this moment between us and I was good with it. Eyes closing, the loud bang of someone knocking woke both of us up.

"Yo, Saint! Mama is on one; she's heading to that town hall meeting. I'm just letting you know. Unk is downstairs still as well," I heard Sin tell me.

"A'ight, follow her. We don't need anything happening to her because she's riling up the neighborhood," I said in return.

Silence then shuffling started before Sin responded, "Y'all good? I mean, y'all were loud as fu—"

"Nigga! Ride out," I barked out, swallowing my laugh.

When Sin hit my door twice, I knew that was his way of saying bye. Dropping back against the pillows that kept me elevated, I looked down to see London watching me. Her walnut flesh had a slight red tinge and I knew it was all because of me.

"How you feeling, mama?" I asked in a husky voice.

Lips kissing where my chest was bare, London rose up to kiss me with a smile. "So good. I really pissed off your mama now, huh?"

Studying her, I laughed then sighed. She was right. I knew my mom had to have heard us. There was no way she wouldn't since she always checked on me every five minutes. I kind of felt some type of way about how she came at London, but another part of me didn't. London held her own and I couldn't be

Mama's boy forever. However, I wanted them to have some peace between each other if this was going to go deeper, because I wasn't about no female fuck shit.

Which was why I came up with a brilliant idea. Gently sitting up, I kissed London again. "Yeah, but she'll get over it. Today was my pop's death and anyone could sneeze wrong and she'd get lit. I guess . . . Look, that's why I want you to help me out of here and go with me someplace. It won't be long and we'll be hidden in the back. I want you to understand my mom some so you can be able to handle her if y'all face to face again."

"You can make it out?" she asked in concern.

"Yeah, trust me," was all I said.

After cleaning up, we both took to Goodman with the help of my uncle Red. Down the street from my father's house was Goodman Baptist A&E Church. Hella cars lined both sides of the streets and the parking lot. Music could be heard along with loud voices, and I held London's hand. While we sat in the truck, I felt my cell vibrate in my pocket.

Pulling it out, I checked the messages and shook my head. Looked like Blanket had a new job for me and my brother and that was babysitting and scoping out DJ Royal. I didn't know why Blanket would be looking his way, but I figured it had to do with the realty game.

London gave me a light smile. I didn't want to break up our chill vibes, so I quickly erased the message and stuffed the phone in my jeans then kissed her lips.

"Welcome to another side of Goodman. I think you'll be surprised, mama," I said, giving her a smile. She dropped her head against my shoulder for a second then we headed inside.

Rows of pews were filled up with people. Because it was so packed, London and I chilled in a corner near the front of the church by the doors. Young and old stood up talking about their losses and how every time Goodman seemed to be getting better, more drama always hit. In the middle of it all was my mother, who stood in leggings, with a white high-neck sleeveless dress that cut at the sides of her hips. She wore white hi-tops as well, always prepared if she had to fight.

"I grew up in Goodman," my mother said empathically. "I was here with Mr. Black, who dedicated his life to continue building up this town. Trust me, I know the blood that has been spilt because we've been losing economic outlets and finances to keep us surviving here," she said, looking around with passion in her eyes. "I've fought to keep regulated daycares in our area, to help our family here from signing those damned predatory house and car loans. Yet, even I am struggling to keep my head up. My sons were shot at and it's broken my spirit. I'm pissed about that and I am not just going to let that go down without a fight!"

I wasn't sure if my mom and London would ever get along but at least they could get to look at each other differently behind their dislike of each other. Either way, as long as they didn't kill each other, a nigga was good with working it out how I was now. London's fingers laced with mine, and gripped me hard as she watched my mother in frustration. As the meeting went on, that frustration slowly melted away as her features softened into something like that of new understanding. Next time I'd work on my mom's skewed view.

Listening to how our town was losing only made things hard. But, it also put a perspective on how important it was to handle Guerilla and how deep Royal Realty was working its hooks in our community. As the meeting went on, we eventually left in the middle of it to head back to my mom's. We eventually found our way in my room where we chilled, and I taught London some more things before she left in the morning.

Chapter 17

Blanket

"But that damn Devon Royal is taking our houses and taking over our businesses. All while these foul thugs are at a war keeping us all scared in our houses!"

I detected no lies in what was being said around me in this town hall meeting. Ms. Philips was right. My unit, my rooks were at war and it was all by my order. See, my underground railroad ran thick. The bulk of my business was handled in Roanoke as a means to take out the upper elite who looked down on us from Goodman. I see it like this: I was Robin Hood. Taking from the rich and giving to the poor. In the middle of it all, there were casualties as there usually are in any battle of war, but my aim was to keep it to a minimum. See, as a kingpin in the A, I had to keep up a certain je ne sais quoi. Especially when it came to my enemy Guerilla.

Before I became the invisible Don that I was, I was just another kid in the street bent on helping my community. As I got older, I realized the only way that I could do that was protect it from niggas like Guerilla, though I didn't know then that he would be who I was protecting Goodman from. I spent time being involved in knowing everyone in Goodman. I had a gift for remembering faces and names and, because of that, I knew everyone's story here. I knew who to fuck with and who not to. I learned who to strategically place around me to work them to my benefit and who to move out of the way with a swift manipulation.

In the beginning like any hoodlum, I had my stumbles in my lessons, but had it not been for my mentor, I never would have made it as far as I did without being ousted and killed. My mentor gave me the world. Made sure I learned the art of deception. He made sure I appreciated getting an education. Had me work my ass off to pay my way through college. He insisted everything I did be work. I went from Atlanta Metro to Georgia State. Soaked up all I could before it was time for me to come back to Goodman as a new person and that's what I did. No one would think that in it all I was being groomed to be a killer and a street entrepreneur. See, people like Guerilla believed that I wasn't around as long as him, but I was. I was the shadow in the streets watching, waiting, and learning, building up my brand little by little in Roanoke and on the low in Goodman. See, the method that nigga was using against me now was how I got myself stable in this game.

Having my rooks dump the bodies how they did served a purpose. It was about being sloppy and it was about watching how Guerilla would handle the next move. Like everyone in the streets, I didn't know who that nigga was, but I was aiming to find out. He needed to be dealt with, just like that nigga Devon Royal.

The name Royal left a bad taste in my mouth. That nigga and his business was like an infestation that was causing problems for me in how I protected my property. With him swooping in and taking everyone's houses, it was becoming harder for me to protect everyone who came my way. Every abandoned house in the hood was important to me. Shit, it was easy to get away with unlawful activity if you had houses that were empty, or houses that you could use as a form of distraction.

But back to Mr. Sunshine with his million-dollar smile on every sign around Goodman. Since I was a kid, Devon Royal was an issue to me. Nigga walked Goodman like he owned the world, as if his shit didn't stink. But, I knew better. Devon was a foul motherfucker with dark, deep, and deadly skeletons in his closet. Him and his trick Tamika, though she wasn't bad back then, she was just the common wannabe. Being the type of kid I was, it was easy to be overlooked when people like him and her walked around on their high and mighty pedestals. Mixing with the Blacks didn't clean the shit off of Devon Royal by a long shot; it only made it worse, especially for the city of Goodman.

"Listen, everyone, you know me and you know my family. We Blacks have willingly sacrificed our all to help our community and I promise you we will continue to do so. We all know this community works together to help each other even in this war and we will continue to do so. Let me talk to Blanket through my sons. I allowed my sons to mix with him because I knew that we'd need his help, his protection, which was why we turned a blind eye to some of his unsavory dealings. Let me talk to him. If I have to, I'll even speak with the Royals."

I listened to Maya Black speak passionately to a house packed with Goodman residents in the local Goodman Baptist A&E Church. Of course it was hot, and sticky. Everyone had a fan and everyone's hair was springing to life and walking off some people's heads. In the middle of it all was Maya Black standing behind a pulpit as if she were the next female Martin Luther King with all eyes on her. She was a slave and a leader to this enclave.

"I know that he will work to save our homes. He just bought Ms. Lovejoy her home, no strings attached for her; and he built that new urgent care clinic for us. I fought for that. It was my family who took the hit and accepted the attached strings in negotiating with him willingly. Trust in me and I can work my ass off and do my damned best to keep us as safe as I can."

Ms. Maya Black? She was right in that. Those strings I wrapped all around her family. How could I not? Like the Royals, the Blacks were movers and shakers, well respected in the community. Their power I needed as an in and, in return, I kept them protected. Which was why when my rook Saint was shot, I sent nothing but the best his way. I always protected what's mine, and retaliation was going to come swiftly toward Guerilla.

People made their disgruntled complaints and I noted it all. When a church organ started to play, Ms. Maya slid into her seat. It was then that I took that time to excuse myself. Stopping in a narrow hallway where the bathrooms were, I dropped a yellow envelope with a fat wad of money in the collection, and exited the premises. It was quite simple to do so, since no one would even associate me with the Big Bad Wolf around town or anyone off-putting. No one knew who I was but my right, and I aimed to keep it that way. My secrets were mine to keep and no one else's.

"What's the 411?" I offhandedly asked while climbing in the passenger's side of my blacked-out ride. Smelling the scent of a sweet mix of a cigar and weed, I reclined in my seat and watched the lights of Goodman pass us by.

"I received word from the underground that there will be a meeting with the suppliers," my right hand relayed in between the draw of his cigarillo.

A smile played across my lips in thought. *Guerilla.* Nigga was trying to cut off my pipeline by buying my suppliers and snuff me out of my territory. Lines had been clearly drawn and he got bored with it, so he wanted to fuck with my money and my reputation to flex his power. Interesting. I figured that he'd gun at me hard, but I wasn't sure exactly how he would come for me in his next move. Now I did, and I was very amused by the situation.

"Good, keep your ear to the streets and your eyes all around. I want to know everything, and if they are stupid enough to double-cross me, make sure you take what is mine and cut off their airway," I coolly ordered.

My right gave me an intense nod. "You know I will. Nothing like a smothering to get a nigga's dick hard."

In the game of warfare, sometimes you have to sacrifice to gain a better footing in the battle. If Guerilla succeeded in this, the kickback would hurt me, but that wasn't nothing to me. Stretching out my units and making them run the streets harder would be my cover in appearing to be weak. In reality, the money I made by selling in Roanoke was so good that losing a small piece of the Goodman pie wasn't going to hurt . . . that bad. Especially after dropping my new shit, aimed to hit the Guerilla squad while taking out those in Goodman who would entertain the thought of working for Guerilla over me. Never bite the hand that feeds ya.

Driving through Roanoke we pulled up to my high-rise parking area and my second glanced my way while gripping the steering wheel with gloved hands. "Check it, as for the new-new. I got eyes on him as well."

Being deceived by a crackhead named Marvin truly fucked up the rotation of my squad, but at the end of the day, that nigga did more good than harm. He let me know that Guerilla was spreading out without even realizing it and he also let me know of a newcomer in the streets: a little entitled brat sporting Royal nuts.

I tapped my fingers against the side of my door. Of my own accord I then opened it and climbed out. “Good. Keep him on our radar. Goodman isn’t fond of nobles moving through the streets at all hours of the night, especially going to a house just repossessed from a sweet elder. I want to know exactly what DJ Royal is really doing. Tell Mrs. Lovejoy thank you by dropping her off something special for her keen eyes.”

Nothing good comes to a Guerilla or a Royal in the Goodman mist. With that, the sound of light jazz relaxed me as I walked into an elevator with my right and headed up to my apartment. It was a long night and I had some niggas to chop up in the morning. “The best part of waking up . . .” was the hoarse screams of a Guerilla hanging from a meat hook in my walk-in freezer.

Chapter 18

Devon Royal Jr.

The wind was whipping through the air while mists of rain fell on me. The scene before me was a beautiful one. I stood in the mountains of Georgia overlooking the business that had become very profitable to me. While my father thought I was working hard and keeping long hours to eventually step up to run his business, he had no idea I was creating a legacy of my own. I had degrees in business and economics, which worked out well for me in the end. There was only one other person who was in on my scheme: my cousin, Mudbuster.

"Cuz, this shit between Blanket and Guerilla getting crazy," he said as he smoked a joint then offered it to me.

I declined it. For as much as I loved my cousin, that nigga loved eating ass. So I wasn't keen on sharing joints with him. I was a nasty motherfucker myself, but eating ass wasn't one of the sexual playtimes I took part in. There was no grocery shopping in my world.

"Nah, I'm good," I told him. "I see. Good idea you had to do that shooting at the party and make it seem like the Guerillas had done it. I couldn't have had a better idea myself."

He nodded then blew out smoke. "But most of them young niggas with Guerilla stupid, you feel me? They took credit for that shit like some dumbasses just to seem hard. I guess they thought saying they went after

Blanket's people would make them look good in Guerilla's eyes. I'm surprised that nigga ain't said nothing about it yet. That's the one thing Blanket has over Guerilla; for the most part, Blanket's folks are loyal and smarter. Marvin surprised me."

"How so?"

"I was at that house when Saint and Sin came looking for that nigga. Was over there looking for Niecy, but fell back when I saw her talking to Saint. That nigga crazy, fam. Nigga pulled out his gat and blasted that fucking pimp right in front of everybody. He got pull, cuz. Nobody said shit. They just dragged that nigga's body outside. If you about to stage this takeover, folk, you need a nigga like Saint and his brother on your team. Real shit, fam."

I nodded as I had been eyeing those twins for a hell of a long time. There was only one problem: our families didn't jig to one another like that. I had no problem with the Blacks as my pops and moms did. Saint nor Sin had ever disrespected me and we passed one another often in the streets. But their mother was a problem.

"I know we could use them. With what I got planned, I'd need thorough niggas like them on the team. I mean like right-hand men in on day-to-day business, but I don't fucking know how that shit is going to come into play," I said.

"Shit, them niggas loyal as fuck. Only way to get them on the team is to take down Blanket. They won't deter from that nigga any other way," Mudbuster confirmed. "Was at that town hall meeting. Maya Black said she had been communicating with Blanket through her sons. Supposedly, that nigga built that urgent care center and other shit in town."

I frowned as I watched the immigrant workers in the 500-acre marijuana field. Best business move I'd ever made. The shit was even more profitable because I had pharmaceutical companies, government officials, and weed dispensaries all over the US in my pocket. This shit had been well thought-out on my end. From the fleets of vans and trucks I rented from Maya to the fact that my father thought I was only using Maya's vans and trucks to transport illegal immigrants to work on houses in other areas, no move I made was without thought.

In order for me to get the serious backing from government officials I needed, I had to get rid of Blanket and Guerilla. Both those niggas were making shit too hot for me. See, most niggas thought the weed business was a dying drug trade. And when you looked at it from their standpoint, they were right. Any drug lord worth his weight knew that coke and heroin moved more money than weed on the small scale of things. However, for a business and economic major like myself, I never thought on the small scale of things.

I watched the news, shit like Bloomberg and Business Insider. I watched the stock market. Kept my ear to the ground when my father went to these meetings with top officials from the state capital and Washington. Since I was sixteen, I'd been putting this plan together. Purchased the empty plot of land when I was eighteen and all the surrounding land. Had workers brought in to till the land and start planting. So while I was in place to take over Daddy's realty business, I was also my own businessman.

"We need this shit to take off," I told Mudbuster. "But like that nigga from Washington told us, the shit going on in Goodman doesn't go unnoticed; the town is just too small for them to give a fuck really. However, with this shit I got going on here, they can fuck with what I got going on, but not with Blanket and Guerilla running around like King Kong and Tony Montana."

My cousin chuckled. "What you need me to do next, fam? Say the word."

I looked at my cousin and appreciated him. As soon as I brought my thoughts to him on what I was doing, that nigga was on board. I was sixteen talking to him when he was twenty. He never disrespected me or made me feel like my idea was too much to take on at sixteen. So once I got shit going for real, I brought him on. He was smart enough not to be flashy or run his mouth. That's why we worked so well.

"Burn down the urgent care center," I ordered.

"Any particular way you want it done?"

"What day is the busiest?"

"Wednesdays and Fridays mostly. You know a lot of us over there got no insurance. Maya Black got it set up to where the docs see folk for like a few dollars and shit. So people go there more than to the hospital."

"Pick a day, but not for a few weeks. Wait until the busiest hour. Block the front doors. Lace the outside with gasoline. We need the town to turn against Blanket. They're too loyal to that nigga. We need to flush those niggas out. I need Blanket and Guerilla gone so we can do real business around town. I need that separation between Goodman and Roanoke to end. Burn down a couple houses tonight. I'll come in and offer to move the displaced residents to Roanoke for free. I got a few houses I can let go for nothing. Then a few weeks later, take out the urgent care center."

Mudbuster tossed the end of his joint, blew out smoke, and nodded. "Done."

We slapped hands and pulled each other in for the shoulder bump. "Don't get caught," I reminded him.

"Never that and if I do, I go out in a blaze of glory, fam," he said.

I nodded. "You find Niecy yet?"

"I did. She at some older woman's house."

"If she doesn't get clean and come off that shit, you can't fuck with her no more. She's a liability. So she better make sure she get shit together."

Mudbuster's face fell a bit. He had been in love with that damn addict all his life. But she couldn't be around if she didn't get clean and stay clean. I couldn't risk it.

"I love her, cuz," he responded.

"I get it. I respect it, but what we're doing here is bigger than love."

He rolled his shoulders and looked like he wanted to say something, but thought better of it. "I understand," was all he said as he walked off.

Once he was gone, I pulled my ringing cell from my hip. "Speak," I answered to one of my watchers.

"Covers rustling. Also, ambulance called to your Auntie Nikki's house. Laylah's son got burned. She was sleeping. Left the stove on. Her son got in a chair, touched the burners. Burned his hands really badly," the voice on the other end said.

"Good deal. Go to the bank to see Ms. Brown. She'll give you your pay," I said.

"'Preciate that."

I hung up then placed a call to Southern Regional. Once the doctor I wanted picked up, I said, "There's a kid coming through with burns on his hands. Call child protective services on the mother. Have them call the police. Lock her ass up. Put the son in my personal foster mother's home. I'll take it from there."

"Done deal," the doctor said.

I hung up the phone, thinking about how I was going to get Saint and Sin on my team and how to get rid of Blanket and Guerilla. I knew one thing for sure: I had to make a move and do it swiftly. My time was running out.

Chapter 19

London

The smile that had been plastered on my face for the past few weeks showed that my love was under new management. Saint and I had been going heavy for a least a month or two now. So much so that Sin and Brandy were going on double dates with us. School was going to start in a few weeks for me so I was trying to get in as much time as possible. I was no longer allowed in Maya's house, but that was because I made that decision.

While I was still pissed at the woman for putting her hands on me, I understood her better. I knew the laws of nature versus nurture and Maya was a product of her environment. I loved her son so she would have to deal with that. However, I wouldn't make it worse by antagonizing the woman. I got what I wanted, which was Saint. In a sense, I'd won.

Saint had lied to me about his relationship with Blanket. He had no idea I'd seen and heard what had gone on in that kitchen when that white girl had walked into Silky's place. I wasn't mad at him, though. No. Any man worth his weight in the streets wouldn't reveal who he was to a chick he just started messing with so soon. I may not have known a lot about the hood, but I'd read enough books and seen enough movies to figure it out.

I'd wait on him. If he wanted to tell me, fine. If not, I didn't care. He and I had been up under one another a lot. The sex we had tended to leave my head spinning. His dick had to be laced with oxytocin. That sex with him made me fall more in love each time we did it. I'd even gotten him and Sin to come to my place to chill with me and Brandy. Brash had been MIA a lot and Marsha was prepping to head back out to Cali for school. So Brandy and I were hanging together a lot.

Not to mention, Laylah started to stay home more after Chance burned his hands. DFCS had taken him away from her and she had been a mess since then. Every time I saw her, she was crying and depressed. She didn't want to hang out, didn't want to talk on the phone. She didn't even want to be bothered. I supposed if I got locked up and accused of child endangerment, I'd be the same way.

Around the way, houses had been burned to the ground in Goodman, but what surprised me most was DJ offering the single mothers who had been displaced free homes in Roanoke. I'd never seen children so happy when DJ walked them into their new homes. I was proud of my brother.

"My thing is this," DJ had spoken in a live news conference, "people are sick of being in the middle of drug and turf wars. I believe, just as my mother and father, that if some of the single mothers have better options than what the Goodman section of Jonesboro has to offer, their children can grow up to be productive citizens of society. The way these criminals, Blanket and Guerilla, use the people of Goodman as pawns is sickening. So I spoke with my mother and my father and we agreed that Royal Realty has the power to change people's lives. So instead of just rebuilding the homes in Goodman, we'll offer those displaced a new start," he had said passionately as he pulled three sets of keys out his pocket. "We want to offer the three mothers and their children three free brand new homes right here in Roanoke."

Before the mothers had been angry and crying pissed-off tears. Now, they looked on in wide-eyed excitement as DJ presented them with keys to their new homes. The crowd cheered wildly. There were even people saying they wished their houses had been burned down, because they, too, wanted out of Goodman.

"Not only that," my mother cut in, "but I have job openings in my women's shelter. I'm willing to guarantee these three mothers jobs if they want them."

That part even had me clapping. I knew Mama took that shelter seriously. So the fact that she would give them jobs made me happy.

"Also," my father jumped in, making the crowd laugh, "my new car dealership would like to offer these women transportation. So," Daddy said, waving over his workers who drove up in three barely used cars, "we're offering them the cars needed to get back and forth to work as well, along with $5,000 shopping cards to Toys 'R' Us, and vouchers good at any furniture store in Roanoke."

"London! London Royal, do you have something to offer?" a reporter in the crowd joked.

I smiled and put on a show like Daddy had taught me to. "Yes, although mine isn't just materialistic. I'm willing to offer afterschool tutoring for two hours to help with homework while the mothers are at work once school resumes in a few weeks, along with free laptops and the tablets they will need for classes as well."

By the time my family finished, the kids and their mothers were jumping up and down, screaming with glee. But, there was something about the way my daddy turned to the camera and smiled that rattled me. It was as if he was sending a message to someone who we couldn't see.

That had been a few weeks ago. Since then things had been quiet. I was on my way to see Saint as I hadn't seen him in about a week. We kept missing one another. He was busy with work at the shop, he said, but I knew it was a lie. I didn't trip, though. It was what it was; as long as he wasn't moving with some other chick, I was cool. That brought me back around to Dee Dee, who had been trying her hardest to pull me into some ghetto street brawl over Saint. Every time we ran into one another in Goodman, she had something to say. I was better than that, though. Wasn't any need for me to fight over Saint. A man was going to do what a man was going to do. She did everything in her power to provoke me, but I kept it moving. Just as I kept his nuts empty and stomach full. My mama had taught me that lesson well.

"When you get a man you trying to hold on to," she had lectured me one day, "you fuck him so much that the thought of his dick getting hard when you're not around annoys him. Keep his nuts empty and stomach full. Never let another woman feed your man and never give him a chance to be energized enough to be fucking another one."

I guessed that was one of the secrets to her and Daddy's marriage.

I got to the shop, parked, and walked up to the front door, hoping Maya Black was nowhere around.

"Saint ain't here," Sin said as he opened the front door for me to walk in.

"He told me to meet him here. Where is he?" I asked.

"Uncle Red's son got sick and shit. Saint took him to urgent care. Come on, I'm about to walk over there now."

I nodded and waited for him to lock up. Sin and I had become close as well. We were always laughing and cutting up about something. He was the brother I wish I had. Don't get me wrong, DJ was a good brother, but Sin was a clown. Always laughing, joking, or talking about someone. So he was always fun to be around. Not to mention, he was good to my girl Brandy. He was a bit slick at the mouth, but good to her nonetheless.

Anytime Brandy and I walked around Goodman with Saint and Sin, the chicks looked on like they wanted to kill us. The same could be said the one time Saint and Sin crossed into Roanoke. People looked on at the red-haired, tatted-up black boys like they were foreigners.

"I hope your uncle's son is okay," I said.

"That li'l dude is a fighter," Sin said. "He'll be cool. Just need the fever to come down. You and your fam done being the good Samaritans and shit, though?" he asked in the funny way he did.

I chuckled as he threw two fingers up, speaking to someone who had called out to him. "What's wrong with my family helping out people who lost their homes?" I asked.

He tsked. "Shit, I wouldn't be surprised if them niggas burned it down just to do some shit to show how 'good' they are, feel me?"

I cast a sidelong glance at him. "First y'all say my daddy is taking homes and now he's burning them down, too?"

He smirked. "Sorry, mama. I don't trust your pops like that. But yeah, I'll cut him some slack on the burning down the houses part. Your mom looks like her injuries healed well."

I nodded, not surprised he knew since I'd told Saint. "Saint told you what happened?"

Sin shook his head. "Nah. I know what happened, though."

I stopped just as a pest control van passed us. I looked up and saw we were almost to the urgent care center, where the van was going.

"You robbed my mama, Sin?" I asked incredulously.

"Robbed her? Shorty, you forget a nigga got shot up that same night? How the fuck was I gon' rob her?" he asked with a frown. “Yo’ mama ain’t get robbed. Shorty got her ass handed to her fucking with my mama.”

I was confused as fuck now. “What?” I asked.

The smell of gasoline drew my attention. I glanced around and saw the pest control people spraying around the urgent care building. Didn’t know why the smell of gasoline was so strong, though.

“From what I heard, your mama walked up to my mama’s shop talking shit and mom dukes got wit’ her ass, feel me? Now I don’t know what they were arguing about, but my mama ain’t too bright in the head or too crazy about the Royals as you can see. A fight ensured and your mama got her ass whooped . . . And why the fuck do I smell gas?” He yelled that last part.

We both looked over toward the urgent care center just as one of the pest control people backed the van into the front door. When the man stepped out in a ski mask, I knew something was off.

“What the fuck?” Sin whispered as he started jogging across the street.

I followed. One of the pest control people was on the side of the people. The driver of the truck jumped out, flicked a match, then tossed it. The van went up in flames. Sin started sprinting full speed ahead. I was right behind him. We both almost got hit by cars as we made our way across the street. Saint was in that building along with countless other people. Just as we made it across the street, someone football tackled me to the ground just as I saw Sin knock the other dude to the ground.

“Get off of me,” I yelled.

I started swinging as soon as he turned me over. The man behind the ski mask wrestled me until he had me pinned down.

There was a wild look in his eyes when he said, “Get the fuck out of here!”

It confused me as I stopped struggling. The man's voice and eyes were familiar to me. He was about to say something else until Sin ran up behind him, and grabbed him up by wrapping a forearm around his neck.

"Today's your lucky day, nigga," Sin snarled while shoving a knife into the man's back near his kidneys over and over in rapid succession.

The man yelled out, trying to reach behind him. He backed up until he slammed Sin's back into one of the steel poles connected to the building. That made Sin drop the hold on him. His knife fell and slid across the concrete. The man's mask was halfway off his face, which made my eyes widen. He looked at me before pulling the mask back down, turning, and sending a flurry of punches to Sin's face.

Sin dropped to one knee while the man took off running full speed like he hadn't just been stabbed. The screams and cries coming from inside the building clawed at my insides.

"Sin," I yelled, "people are trapped inside. The building is surrounded by fire."

"I know," was all he said.

I got up from the ground as Sin pulled me away. "No," I screamed. "Saint's in there!"

I kept screaming over and over the same thing, wishing, hoping, and praying for a miracle. Truth was the building was engulfed by angry flames. Sin ran around the building to find the back door had been blocked as well. I saw people beating on windows and the front doors. By now the whole neighborhood was out. I could hear sirens in the distance, and screams and yells of friends and families who knew their loved ones were in the building.

I looked around for Sin and saw him running for the building next door. He pushed people out of the way as he rushed inside.

"Move. Move. Move!" he shouted on the way in.

I didn't know what he was doing, but I followed him. He rushed through the pharmacy, then through double doors in the back. By the time I caught up with him, he was heading through a door that read BASEMENT. I was hot on his heels. When he made it down the stairs, there was a loud banging on the wall. Sin pushed file cabinets to the side.

"Help me move this shit, shorty," he demanded.

I did as he said. Once we got all the shit from the wall, I noticed a small latch.

"Help me. My shoulder still fucked up from getting shot. When I pull, you pull," he said.

I did. He pulled, I pulled harder. The wall went sliding over and Saint came stumbling out. Smoke was behind them, but he yelled for people to head up the stairs and go out through the front of the pharmacy.

"I gotta go back," Saint shouted.

I didn't even think he had noticed me until he said, "London, take them out of here."

"Why you going back?" I yelled.

"My uncle. He won't leave without his son. I gotta go back. You get out of here and I don't care what happens, London, don't bring your ass back in here after me," he ordered.

I had so many questions and emotions floating around in my head. But I nodded. I watched on in horror as he and Sin rushed back through the tunnel. Nervousness had me shaking as I led people out the front of the pharmacy like Saint had said. It took us about ten minutes to make sure everyone was out. But once outside, I could still hear the screams and yells of adults and children in the urgent care center being burned alive.

The shit was heartbreaking so much so that there wasn't a dry eye in the crowd. My flesh crawled at the thought of the torture those people were enduring.

"Oh, God. Oh, God. Oh, God," someone screamed.

"Why? Why would they do this?" another screamed.

"Take 'em home, Lord," came someone else.

I paced back and forward like a caged animal in front of the building as firemen tried without success to move the van blocking the front door.

"Gas leaking from the van," one of them screamed.

"Get back! Get back," they bellowed as they came running toward the crowd.

The explosion was so hard and loud that even as we ran for safety across the street, the force knocked us a few feet in the air. I was disoriented as I came to. Felt blood trickling down my head. I looked toward the pharmacy to see the windows had been blown out. Still, through all the smoke, three bodies emerged. One cradled something to his chest while the other two were running toward the crowd, covering their faces with shirts.

"Saint," I tried to call out, but got choked on my own blood and spit.

I gingerly made my way to my feet then over to him. He looked fine but there was a wild look in his eyes. For a second, I feared his uncle's son had died, until I heard the baby crying. I was relieved to say the least, but still saddened by the fact that people were still burning alive in the urgent care center.

"We got out all we could through the tunnels," Saint said two hours later as we sat in the shop.

Maya Black paced the floor with a frown on her face. She'd shown up as soon as we all got to the shop. She was deep in thought. The woman was hurting and she didn't try to hide it. The firemen had gotten the fire under control, but the damage was so severe that death had settled over the community like an eerie haze. News vans and cameras were crawling over the area.

"How bad was it, Saint? The body count, I mean?" she asked him.

He shook his head, but his uncle spoke up as a doctor walked around the room checking them out. "Only reason we were able to get out so many was because the tunnel is at the back end of the center. Anybody at the front or in the middle we couldn't get to," Uncle Red said.

The man had been holding his son close to him since the doctor had assured him the baby had no smoke damage. After he finished checking Saint, Sin, and even me, Maya paid the doctor and he left. Saint had one arm around my waist as he sat in a folding chair and I stood beside him.

"Body count," she demanded to know again.

"Last I heard, fifty," Uncle Red answered.

"Oh, dear God," Maya groaned.

There was a knock at the door. Sin stood, grabbed a shotgun, then looked out the window. "Mama, you better come look at this," he said.

We all leaned forward and saw so many people that it alarmed me.

Uncle Red handed his son to me. "I'm going to trust you with my seed's life. You understand? If some shit pops off, no matter what you do, you get him out of here. His mother is in Roanoke. She lives on Lake Spivey. The address is in the glove compartment in the truck. Take him to her. Drive the black van out back; it's bulletproof. If anything jumps off, you take my son and you run. Understand me good, London?"

I took the kid into my arms and nodded then looked at Saint.

"Do what he said and don't come back looking for me if you don't hear from me. If I'm alive, I'll come for you," he said to me.

Maya walked to the front door and yanked it open. The crowd was loud and anxious.

"You said Blanket would help us. You said you'd get him to protect us, but look at what just happened," an older man said as he moved to the front of the crowd. "My wife was in that building, Maya, and she didn't come out. Forty years we stayed married only to have this happen?"

The man was crushed and, sad to say, I felt his pain. Tears stained his sepia-colored cheeks. There was a woman in the crowd who kept moving back and forth like she had something on her mind. She had a black cap low on her head and a bag clutched underneath her arm. The denim jeans and windbreaker jacket she had on were too big for her. She was kind of behaving weird. Something was off about her, but I guessed if I had been a part of this community after what had just happened, I'd be acting a little weird too.

"DJ Royal was right," a woman yelled. "Blanket and Guerilla are using us in their war and we're losing daughters, sons, husbands, wives, and grandchildren. Goodman can't take another hit like this, Maya. We just can't. This is enough!"

Cheers and yells of agreement fiddled throughout the crowd.

Maya nodded and spoke calmly, all while Saint and Sin stood behind the door armed. Uncle Red stood next to Maya with a shotgun strapped to his back. I stood near the back window rocking the baby in my arms while watching. I couldn't help but think about the person who had tackled me to the ground. Why would they warn me to leave? When that mask almost came off the man's face, I could have sworn it was . . . I shook my head. *No, it couldn't have been. Could it?*

My thoughts were put on hold as I listened to Maya while texting DJ. Have you seen Leon? I texted.

Maya said, "I'm just as angry as you all are about this tragedy. I can assure you, Blanket had nothing to do with this."

"How?" someone yelled.

"Fires aren't his MO. Never have been."

"Yeah, but I know his boys set that house on fire the Guerillas had taken over, so fire may not be Blanket's MO, but his hitters got no problems with setting fires," a young boy said from the back of the crowd. "And I know some of Guerilla's boys were in the urgent care this morning. That's why I ain't go in. Seen them boys in there. I don't like to be nowhere 'round them kind of niggas. So I chose to go back home."

"Glad you did, baby," an older female voice cut in.

"Now we know Guerilla ain't gon' set his own peoples on fire. Not heavy hitters like Marco and Don who was inside," the boy continued. "How Blanket gon' explain this shit, Maya? He ain't no better than that nigga Guerilla. They both the same kinds of people. I don't care that Blanket built this and that. At what cost, sis? We gotta look the other way while he peddle in drugs for an urgent care center and a few good deeds? We gotta keep losing lives because his evil ain't as big as Guerilla's evil? It's still evil. Shit, you sold your sons to him, for what though?"

"Most of all you around here either working for Blanket or Guerilla. We killing each other up while these niggas sit behind closed doors giving orders. Who the fuck are these niggas?" another young kid yelled. "We ain't ever seen either one of 'em."

The people in the crowd looked around agreeing with one another. Maya looked at Uncle Red. She knew she was losing control of the crowd. They needed answers and looked to her as their leader.

"We need to take back our neighborhood," someone yelled.

Yeah, he's with me. We're on our way up from Florida. Why? DJ finally texted back.

I'd forgotten DJ had told me he was going out of town. I didn't know he had taken Leon with him, though, but I was glad to hear it. I could have sworn he was the man in the ski mask. Thank God he wasn't.

My mama was calling me. Shit, with the fire and all that had happened, what Sin had told me about Maya and my mama fighting had slipped my mind. Why would she lie about what happened to her? For what reason?

If I didn't know anything else, I knew one thing was for sure: it was time my parents came clean about why the Royals and the Blacks hated one another so much.

Chapter 20

Saint

My mother was looking around as if her heart was breaking. Every time she opened her mouth to interject, someone would interrupt her until she got loud. "Just like every-damn-body here, I want Goodman to be safe as well. I had no idea the fire would happen and that we would lose so much! This is breaking my heart," she pleaded.

"You sit in your home never losing a damn thing, while some of us are homeless. You lied," someone spat out.

Tired of the bullshit, I whispered to my goduncle Luther to take my shotgun and to stay near London and my baby cousin. I stepped by my mom's side as the crowd became disrespectful.

"Hold up!" Thumbing my nose, I dropped my hand then fisted it. I then turned to check on my mom by resting a hand against her back. I was a dutiful son, and I wasn't about to have any harm come to my mother. I carefully had her move behind me and I shielded her in protection. I then leaned down toward her to mutter against her ear, "Let me take care of this, Mama."

She didn't need this shit. It was time for me to take up the reins. The little piece of tranquility that was going on before everything fell down was clearly officially over.

"Thank you, sweetheart. This is too much," she painfully said.

There was a look of deep sadness in her dark tawny eyes and something else when she looked up at me. Something like hard-edge anger and it reminded me of how my uncle Red would look in our meetings about Blanket. Shit, something was ticking off in my mom's mind and I wasn't sure what it was.

Whatever it was, I knew it was time to speak up for my part in running the streets and doing ill in our community.

"My family appreciates you all coming here to voice how y'all feel. I understand the fear that everyone is feeling, but let me be clear here. My mama has lost as much as you all," I said in respect to everyone there.

"We as a family have been in these streets with every one of y'all. We lost just as much as y'all, so I got you. My mama can only do so much when it comes to Blanket, because she asks me and my brother to speak him, a'ight? Every day she cusses me and my twin out for our choice in linking up with the streets on that level. She almost lost me and my brother for our decision to work for Blanket." Licking my lips, I looked down at everyone around me who stared up at us.

Frustration, along with a slight pain irritating my side, had me rocking back and forth fisting my hands while I spoke. "Every day she worked herself to the bone with our business to serve Goodman, only to now have that shit being threatened by a new car business coming through. Ain't none of y'all come up to hold her down with that shit!"

Grumbles started in the crowd and I cut that shit down with a slash of my hand in the air. "Naw, check it. Every day Maya Black worked with the churches and schools to counter the shit all of us young dudes and females were doing in the name of Blanket and even Guerilla. She swallowed her pride about all of that by asking us to talk to Blanket to clear that zone so we could work with our community legislators to get that urgent care dropped in. But y'all stand here and try to blame her for some shit she had nothing to do with?"

Silence was the only answer until a lone voice spoke up, "It is her fault! We never should have accepted Blanket's deals."

My eyebrow rose and I shook my head looking at my mom. When she shook her head, I shrugged and went with it.

"Y'all want some truth? Here it goes. Had my mama not negotiated the deal like that, guess what? *All* of Goodman would have been nothing but empty lots and bodies. Because of the deal it kept Blanket from settling with some other kingpin who wanted to turn this whole block into nothing but hoes and drugs. Blanket stopped that with my mama's quick mind."

Gasps sounded and I gave a nod.

"We're supposed to be a community, right? Blame us young people for trying to go out and find avenues to line our pockets for y'all and for those who have fucked-up habits. It ain't right but it's just real. Some of y'all been in the streets longer so you know what's up. Blanket ain't have shit to do with that fire. That I can tell y'all factual. All Blanket has been doing is trying to curb the bullets. All Blanket has been doing was trying to keep the addicts outta Goodman and manage the ones who are here without feeding them drugs. I mean, that's what I've been told and so far seen." I knew what I was saying was truth but the fear was still thick in everyone and it was pissing me off.

"Yeah, this shit is crazy as fuck but it is what it is. The little good he's done has been a lot. We got a new art center, focused school programs, better afterschool programs, and got some of y'all to have ya open some business without dealing with predatory loans and shit. But, check it, who was the face in fighting for all of that?" I looked around at every motherfucker who kept challenging my mother's authority with heated passion blazing in my eyes.

"Maya Black! And it was me and my brother who managed to make safe zones in the area for this shit, because we promised ourselves to work for Blanket against our mom's wishes. We sacrificed and lost too, fam! Almost died being shot and almost died in that fire just now, but I'm here. Something ain't right here, but y'all can't put that shit on Maya Black! My family upholds my grandfather's, uncle's, and father's promise to y'all. We don't intentionally break that shit." Swinging my arm out, I glanced at my mother, who was fighting tears, and I glanced at my uncle Red, who watched on with a stoic expression.

"Man, fuck that. All the Blacks have done is bring us trouble!" was shouted somewhere near the crowd.

I turned my head to look, glimpsing a black truck that watched in the distance. Suddenly bullets rang out with the harsh shout: "Fuck a Black!"

"Ma!" sounded from Sin.

It was so harsh and raw that it made me take my attention off the crowd and on to my mother, who lay on the asphalt of our shop in her own blood. Utter shock had her eyes wide. They darted back and forth before settling on me in sadness. I wanted to go to her. Drop down and will her to stay with us, but I didn't. Brittle anger slammed into my body, my soul, like I was hit by a hammer square in my chest. The blow of it literally had me stumbling backward to turn and home in on the scattered crowd.

Several people ran. The people who were really about my family stayed and rushed to the shop.

"Get down!" I growled as I jumped through the crowd.

One look backward, I saw London with my baby cousin as she and Luther rushed back into the entryway of the shop. By that time, I was sprinting like it was the Olympics. I looked left and right for any sign of who shot my mom. Rushing up to people, I grabbed them by the shoulder, seeing fear in their eyes. Each person had tears and shook their head immediately, asking who got shot. When they did that, I let them go and ran on.

Fire lit my lungs up and anger pushed me on ignoring the sharp pain in my side. Some motherfucker had the nerve to shoot at my mother. All my mama did was sacrifice her all for this neighborhood and this was how they treated her?

Bitches had to die.

Huffing, I ran for blocks only to stop at the sound of my name. "Saint!" Behind me was my twin, Sin.

Exasperation had me looking up at the sky then back at my brother as I harshly breathed in and out. "You find them?" I asked, voice cracking, sweat pouring down my face.

Looking down at the cracked street, he shook his head. "Nah. Found an envelope, though."

I let out a brittle yell then punched the air in fury. I then walked past my brother, briefly glancing at him. "Where's Mama, man?"

"They got her in the house. Everyone's there. What you about to do, man?" Sin asked, following me. There was a heated tone to his voice as we fell into sync while we walked.

What was I going to do? I wasn't even fucking sure, except as I walked back home, I saw an unfamiliar face in a hood. Anger had me seeing red. The image of my mom being shot had me taking my gun and blasting the nigga who watched the house without any regard.

"Yo, Saint man!" Sin shouted, walking up on me and taking my gun.

"What am I going to do?" I finally answered, turning to see Sin walking up on the rolling nigga. "Nigga ain't dead? Shit, I need to get better on my aim," I said in hatred.

"Saint, fam, chill a minute," my twin said, kneeling on the dude. "Fuck you want, nigga?"

I took several strides toward my brother and the dude. I stared that brotha down and saw that that guy appeared to be around our age. He had nothing but tattoos on his contorted face. Looking back and forth at us, he shook his head, gritting his teeth and shrugging his shoulders.

"Nothing! Fuck. I mean, I got a message," he said, hissing in pain.

Blade against the nigga's neck, Sin added pressure and tilted his head. "Speak."

"I was told to tell y'all to watch the cameras and check the vans. It wasn't Guerilla."

Not giving two fucks, I glared at my twin and he sighed then shrugged. "A'ight. Thanks, nigga." My twin then sliced that guy's throat with no remorse.

Slowly rising back up, he wiped the knife off then looked my way with a raised eyebrow in question. "Think it's a trap?"

"I don't know," I said, looking around.

When members of our family came out to remove the body for us, Sin and I headed back to the shop and to our workman lounge area.

"If it is, I'm done on this shit. Niggas gotta die and I'm done protecting a neighborhood that's ungrateful." Storming into the room, I noticed London sitting at a long table we used to chill or have lunch. Before her was an envelope, with pictures and paper spread over its white surface.

I wanted to ask why she looked upset, but when I heard Mom's scream my attention stayed on that. Rushing down the hall to her office, I felt my arm being pulled back. Turning, it was London, pushing a picture in my face.

"Please, wait a minute. Look at this, Saint. Look at this, Sin," she said, her voice trembling.

I was straight-up confused, because I almost pushed her back in anger, not realizing who it was. My uncle Red appeared in the narrow hallway. He looked past me then eventually my way.

"Go ahead and handle that. She's . . . she's critical but she's not dead. It's too much going on in the room right now so just go with London, nephew," Uncle Red said with pain in his eyes. "I'll come out when it's clear and I'll talk to y'all . . . about that."

Glancing back at the pictures, I stared at him in confusion before he walked away.

"What is it?" I said, looking down at what London showed me.

She held it up and I saw a yearbook. It was of our local high school. Each page was marked, but the one she showed me had a single picture on it. A group one; and when my gaze focused on it, it had me turning around and taking the book, leaning to show Sin. Locked frozen in several poses of happiness were my mom, my pops, London's dad, Uncle Red, and another female.

"That's my mom," London muttered.

"Hell, naw," I said in disbelief.

"There's more, you guys. Come here real quick. I'm sorry, but . . . just look," she said, pulling me by my arm.

Reluctantly my brother and I followed her to the table where more pictures were.

"I can't fucking believe it," London muttered then pointed. "That's my mom and your mom getting into it."

When I looked, I shook my head. Had my mom not been in her office possibly dying, I would have laughed about that shit but, right now, I was all laughed out.

"I don't understand. So they know each other?" I asked as if she could answer me.

"Bruh, I think so. I just told London I heard about when that went down and it wasn't pretty," Sin explained. "I don't know what was being said except some bitch this and that but, yeah, that shit was crazy, fam."

"A'ight," I solemnly said while dropping into a chair. "So, someone dropped this here to pull up some bullshit. Had another nigga outside talking about check the cameras and vans. Send Silky and Choppa over there to handle that, Sin."

I glanced at London; then she reached out to wrap her arms around my waist and lay her head on my shoulder. "I'm sorry about your mom and all of this. And it's cool about the rest. I'm not tripping, though I was scared for you."

"Already on it, Saint," Sin said, taking a seat next to us then turning a picture his way while texting.

I exhaled slowly while coming down from my emotions. Everything was on some fucked-up shit and it was hard to process. So all I could do was kiss London's lips before focusing back on the papers in front of us.

"Now, we're looking at our mom going at it with yours, and this yearbook . . ." Flipping through it, I shook my head. "They all grew up together. Like ya parents and mine were close. Why am I not shocked about that shit?"

A news clipping of my father's death was in the mix, along with medical files showing the autopsy and other notes. With that were various receipts that I didn't feel like looking through and real estate papers.

Then London reached out to grab a card like the ones that always came with the flowers my mother would get. Curiously, she glanced at us both then scowled. "Wow. Listen to this: 'Once mine, always mine, even if you move on to someone else. You can't just love me one day then decide you don't. Don't say my love is all you need then choose another over me. Who does that?'"

Head tilted I stared at my twin, who looked at me with the same confused expression upon his face.

London flipped the card in her hand and shifted on my lap. "There's more: 'Then you tell me I can't tell you what to do, but give me hell for taking Tamika out? Why him? Why that fucking redhead cock-looking nigger? I mean we're cool, he and I, but not cool enough for the shit y'all pulling.'"

"Damn, shit's dated 1989," Sin said, sitting back. "Are there any return letters?"

"I . . . I don't know. Let me look," London said, shaken.

Me, I kept flipping through the yearbook, looking at little scribbles here and there.

Sin said, "Hol' up, check this one out: 'Fuck you, Maya. Fuck you and I should kill you and you know why. You called me an opportunist, but you gotdamn know you're the whore here. You took Rooster from me and had to marry him? Fuck you! I hope you all burn in hell for taking what's mine, but I won't complain all the way about that. Ha! I got the money and the power. I hope you and he suffer. You deserve each other.'"

"This one is signed from Tamika." Exhaling, I flipped through cards. "But these," I said, holding up the other cards, "are like the same ones Mom got with the flowers. They all say, 'Once mine, always mine,' signed with the initials DR."

"A'ight, I need some answers," I said, standing.

"And I got 'em, nephew. Your mom is resting. We almost lost her but she's 'sleep now resting in your apartment," Uncle Red said, walking our way with a large box.

He set the box down, then reached inside, pulling out a black card, which he handed to me. "Read that, then breathe and let me talk to you all about what's really going on," he solemnly stated.

My temple began to throb as my eyes glanced at the card in black and I read it out loud. "'I would say sorry for her loss, but you know how I felt about you, nigga. Never thought red was your color until seeing it splattered all around you. I told you I loved her to death, nigga. Never said it had to be my death to prove it. Rot in peace, Will. DR.'"

Once I read that, silence filled the room. My fingers dug into the table and I saw Sin matching me in manner. London slid off me slowly, taking the card and reading it over. A news clipping was attached to it and dated.

The sound of my chair backing up was all that I was aware of until I felt my uncle holding me down.

"Let me talk, nephew," he said, struggling to hold me in place. "This is going to take awhile. That note was left on your father's grave."

I saw Sin also being held in place by my uncle. He looked between us both and then at a dumbfounded London.

"Back in the day, the Royals and Blacks were cool, mad close, but teenage shit always gets in the mix of friendship and fucks it up," he started.

Licking his lips, he continued, "Maya and Tamika were inseparable. Best friends and like sisters until Maya fell in love with my brother. Tamika felt like Maya had changed the day that happened and started working at my pop's shop. So that started the strain. Tamika crushed my brother and me at one time; everyone knew it, including us. We thought it, okay, but we weren't into her like that. Your pops only had eyes for Maya. That shit only got complicated when Devon got in the mix. Tamika tried to get at him hard, but he only had eyes for Maya.

"We were cool with him, too, but nigga was mad unstable at times because of his temper. We all were popular so everyone wanted to chill with Rooster, Devon, and me. Anyway, Devon always found a way to be near ya mom and Tamika. Tamika and Maya were always having small fights about Maya getting all the attention or when Maya felt Tamika was getting too much attention from Rooster. Devon would send her flowers and gifts and Maya would give them to Tamika. He would try to walk her home, but because Tamika was getting annoyed about it, she'd have Devon walk Tamika home."

Pausing to light up, he took a deep drag. After taking a moment, his eyes red with pain, he continued. "He'd show up at y'all's grandmother's making breakfast and she'd give it away. At one point, she thought it was just him being nice and because she was there to help him about losing his mother. But shit, we told her he crushed her hard; she just was always about Will and not hearing it. I told her then that Tamika was feeling neglected over it but that stopped when Devon decided to date her."

I walked up to where my mom kept bottles of drinks. I poured some Hennessy for my uncle. Grabbed a couple of beers from the clear fridge for the rest of us, and a coffee for London.

"Anyway, how ya mom explained it, we were all at Luther's house kicking it when Tamika gave her something to drink. Trusting her friend she took it and chilled through the night. Toward the end, ya mom was going to leave with ya pops but Tamika said she saw him leave. So she told her that she'd take her home. Ya mom waited for Tamika but felt sick and ended up running into Devon."

With a deep sigh, he sat down and ran a hand through his hair. "Ya mom ended up somehow in a room with Devon, they ended up fucking, and when she came to and realized what was up, she went off on him and left, only to find Tamika and ya pops fucking in his car. Maya was so upset she ended up dragging Tamika out the car and they started fighting until I pulled them apart.

"I was chilling with another female when I heard what was popping off. As I pulled them apart, we found out that Tamika and Devon had planned the shit, but I found out later that Will was high on some shit as well given to him by Devon. Anyway, ya dad ended up going at it with Devon. Both of them crashing into each other like monsters. Will would have killed that nigga hadn't the cops shown up and hadn't he been drowsy. Maya and Rooster ended up in jail until Luther bailed them out and Tamika and Devon ended up free," he explained, watching us all.

"Everyone in school knew Tamika to be about popularity, wearing the latest, and money, so her and Devon hooking up didn't come to a surprise to anyone in the school. What ended up being more fucked up was that they claimed Maya was a lying trick and ya dad was caught up on his own dope and tried to rape Tamika. Ya dad lost hella grants and scholarships after that. Devon endorsed that shit, too. Eventually we all graduated, and Tamika and Devon left Goodman."

Uncle Red took a deep swig of his drink then sullenly set the glass down. "Years later, Will and our dad died turning in the marriage license. A month after Will and our pop's funeral, ya mom got pissed and wanted revenge after Tamika showed up at the funeral and started a fight with Maya. She spat out shit about how Maya betrayed their friendship and took Will."

My uncle gave a dejected, anguished chuckle. "So, after that, ya mom wanted revenge. She went to Devon. They did what they did, had an affair and all, but ya mom quickly cut it off. Since Will's death she kept saying something wasn't right. She told me that it was one night with Devon when he said some strange shit about Will's death when she ended it. Grief and anger is fucked up. Ya mom realized that she was being stupid and left everyone alone in her grief. She started rebuilding the towing company with me and that was that until the letters. Devon sent her a card talking about sorry for your loss. In it, he was on one saying how he felt ya mom had lied about caring for him."

Reaching out, he flipped the black card over that he said had been found on my pop's grave and pointed at it. "When she got this final one, about Will's death, ya mom knew her suspicions about his death were true. That my pops and brother were killed and Devon had something to do with it. Our past is what started the battle between the Blacks and Royals."

Silence was our friend. It was London who finally broke it. "So, the hate between them and her was about some bullshit? My daddy is not crazy like that!"

Uncle Red sat back and shook his head. "Naw, you see the proof around you, baby girl. Whoever left this is showing the links to my brother's and father's deaths and your dad, London. I'm sorry but ya mom's hatred is valid in this part of it. She set my brother up to be killed, baby girl, and this, along with what I got in that box from our own investigations, proves that shit one hundred."

"Fuck this," London said, leaving.

When the door slammed, Sin and I sat there in quiet saying nothing until I got up and flipped the table over. In unison, Sin and I walked out, saying nothing after that.

Chapter 21

DJ

"Ay, yo, Santana and Will?" I called out to them as I exited my truck.

The brothers had stormed out of their mother's shop. Maya Black had been shot. That was a crying shame. The people loved you one minute then hated you the next. I bet that was how Maya felt standing in front of that crowd.

The twins turned to eyeball me, weapons drawn. Sin was a motherfucker with a knife so I wouldn't let him get that close to me. Saint was a shooter. At least I could run, duck, and dodge if that nigga started to feel froggy. As soon as they laid eyes on me Saint charged in my direction.

"Saint, chill for a minute," Sin yelled, trying to hold his brother back.

"A Royal ain't safe around this parts, nigga," Saint snarled at me. "Yo' pops ain't teach you better than to walk in a lion's den, motherfucker?"

"You're mad at me and I have no idea why," I stated calmly. "Okay, that's a lie, but I come in peace."

"Fuck your peace, nigga," Saint spat.

I held my hands up and backed away a bit. "I just saw my sister storm out of there as well. I take it she saw what was in the envelope? And judging by the way you're trying to get at me, I know y'all seen it too."

Sin stopped holding his brother back then turned to me. "You left that shit, nigga? You were here when they shot my mama?"

I saw my truck move then held a hand up. "Stay," I said to the person in the truck.

"You saw who shot my mama?" Sin kept asking as he advanced on me.

"I saw them, yes. But," I yelled as I tried to back away from that crazy nigga, "I come in peace."

I already knew I was walking into a hostile environment. I wasn't quick enough to stop the jab Sin threw at me. When his meaty fist connected to my nose, blood spewed out like a leaking faucet.

"Shit!" I yelled.

Most of the time I forgot Sin was the oldest because Saint's quick temper and quick thinking made him stand out. However, in this moment, I would have preferred to deal with Saint. *Gotdamn!* Sin's fist felt like hard steel against my skull. I could have fought back and I did, but not enough to cause any damage. My intent wasn't to cause damage, not to me at least.

I tried to shield myself from as many blows as possible, but when a gut-wrenching punch to my back where my kidneys were located from Saint took me to the ground, I almost pulled out my .48 and shot that nigga. He was a lucky motherfucker. My sister loved him and she was always talking about how much he meant to her. So I wouldn't shoot his red-headed black ass, nor his brother. That hit took the wind out of me, though. I found myself on the ground being stomped and kicked mercilessly. I'd take it. I had an agenda.

"Guerilla sent somebody to do it," I yelled through punches and kicks.

Those niggas weren't hearing me, though. I knew when I was on the verge of passing out that if I didn't get them to listen to me, my whole plan would come undone. The passenger side door to my truck opened. Six-inch heels clacked against the pavement. I heard the Taser before I saw it. Sin dropped to the ground first. The prongs had so much electricity in them that boy's hand clawed up like rigor mortis was setting in. His eyes rolled to the back of his head while his back arched and his legs jerked wildly.

I slowly stood and saw that Brash had her gun aimed at Saint.

"That's enough," I told her.

She stopped the electric shock treatment of Sin, who lay on the ground groaning.

"I'm sorry," she said looking at Saint then Sin. There was a conflicted expression on her face.

I took the gun from her hand and kept it aimed on Saint. The boy had a scowl on his face that would set the devil himself straight.

"Now, listen," I stammered. "I stole some of that shit from my mom's trunk in the attic at their home. St . . . stole it a few months back and been trying to piece shit together. I ain't ever had beef with either of you niggas. I said I come in peace, motherfucker. Now you listen to me before I shoot the shit out of you. Guerilla had your mom shot. I can say that with certainty because I know who the fuck Guerilla is."

Saint's eyes held a bit of madness that made me want to just shoot that nigga. I was afraid he'd gone off the deep end. He said, "There is only one reason this bitch ain't bit a bullet. The roundness of her stomach. But you on the other hand," he said, raising his gun to match my aim at me, "I'll kill you, nigga, and not think twice about it. Make your kid another statistic, nigga, just like me," he said, menacingly so.

I knew there was no rationalizing with this nigga. I had to speak up and I had to do so quick. “Santana, I’m going to give you two options, understand? I can give you Blanket or I can give you Guerilla. Which one do you want?”

Chapter 22

London

"Mom!" I yelled as I walked in the front door.

My kicks softly thudded against the Italian marble flooring as the bright lights from the golden chandelier lit up the foyer. I looked up the grand staircase trying to determine if she was upstairs. I was halfway up the stairs when I heard her call me from the front room. Since finding out the history between the two families, my mind was all over the place. I had every intention of talking to my parents, but my first stop had been home so I could make sense of everything. I stayed there for over an hour trying to rationalize the whole mess.

Afterward, I went downtown to her shelter and to Daddy's office looking for her.

Normally, she'd be working late or sometimes with Daddy while he worked late. Not to mention I'd called to the house and she didn't answer. I called her cell and got no answer. Once I got to the women's shelter, they told me she had left with my father and was headed to one of his offices. Since I'd gone to the realty office and they weren't there, Darryl and Tap told me Daddy had gone to Royal Enterprises and Mama had gone home.

I rushed into the front room. The scream that erupted from my lips upon seeing my mother could have shattered glass. Six or so bullet holes riddled her chest. The white blouse she had on was soaked in blood.

"Come here, baby. Co . . . come here," she wheezed as she held bloody hands out to me.

I ran over to the spot where she lay. Her back was against the couch and her legs were splayed out around her. I slipped then sloshed and turned in her blood. Tears clouded my vision as I got my balance and crawled over to her.

"Mommy, Mama, what happened? Oh, God, what happened?" I wailed.

She held her bloody fingers out to me and once I got over to her, she caressed my face. Tears mixed with blood and mucus dripped down her face. She was in obvious pain, but was trying to hold on to life with all she had.

"Always, always remember you reap what you sow," she said.

I'd come with the intention of confronting her about the lies she told about being robbed and all the stuff that had been in that envelope only to find someone had shot her!

"Who, Mama? Who did this?"

She shook her head then moaned out in agony. "No matter what they say about me after this, I didn't kill nobody. I never killed anyone, okay?"

"What are you talking about?" I yelled while trying to cradle her in my arms.

"Long, long, long time ago, I had a best friend named Maya Black. Sh . . . she and I were thick as thieves. We loved one another very much. There were two men we both loved very much as well, Rooster and Devon. It was all one big mess. One big mess."

I knew the story. I'd heard Saint's uncle tell me. I told Mama as much. Just so she could quit talking. It seemed she couldn't talk and breathe at the same time. I told Mama all that their uncle Red had told us. Mama surprised me. She laughed, well, tried to anyway. She coughed up blood and almost strangled herself.

"I . . . I never felt a fucking thing for Red. That ugly nigga wished," she croaked out. "But for Rooster, yes. Yes, I was in love with him. Dated him, but he loved Maya. Maya dated Devon, but loved Rooster. Quiet as kept, I think she loved Devon, too, but not as she did Rooster. I know Devon loved Maya. He loved . . . loves me too, but not like he did Maya. Sad, tragic fucking shit, London. Oh, baby. Love can make people do some fucked-up shit. I did some fucked-up shit. But I ain't never drugged my fucking friend. Would have never done that shit to Maya. And Will wasn't on no fucking drugs. Will was as lucid as ever when we fucked in the back of his car. Red is a fucking liar! Don't trust that nigga for shit. He's a liar."

I was seeing and hearing a side of my mother I'd never witnessed before. She was quiet for a moment. She closed her eyes and I thought she'd left me. I frantically searched for my phone that had fallen once I slipped in her blood, to find it had slid underneath the settee. I couldn't reach it while holding her.

"Mommy, please wake up. Please, Mama," I begged her.

I'd been so angry at her moments earlier. The thought that she would be barely alive when I got to her didn't even register with me. The last two months of our lives had been shaken, from senseless fights to me trying to rebel in my own way. None of it mattered. None. I thought about Maya Black. The woman was still a mystery to me, but I knew she would survive her injuries. My mama wouldn't.

Tamika Royal's eyes fluttered open. "I can't and won't make no excuses for what I've done, London," she said softly. It was as if that brief moment of her closing her eyes gave her more strength. "I've . . . Your father and I, we've been horrible fucking people. Our bad outweighed our good. Devon killed a man many years ago. He killed two men because his pride and jealousy wouldn't take a back seat to Maya being happy with Rooster. I helped him cover it up because I knew it would hurt Maya. I knew losing Will would hurt her more than anything. She came back, fucked my husband for a few months until . . . She had an affair with Devon after he killed Rooster."

Mama stopped and coughed violently. Blood from her mouth splattered on my face. I gently laid her head on a pillow from the couch then rushed for my phone. I wiped her blood off my hands on my jeans to I could slide my finger to unlock my phone. Once 911 was on the line, I told them to come quickly to the Royals' residence. I made my way back to my mother.

"Don't matter if they get here or not. I'm dead anyway," she said. "It was like seeing a ghost. His father's spirit had to be inside of him."

Her eyes were wide as if she was still seeing whatever ghost she spoke of. I had no idea what she was talking about. She was incoherent.

"Is Maya dead?" Mama asked.

I shook my head. "No, she's still alive."

My mother's face turned into a disfigured mask of anger. "If I had another chance, I wouldn't miss next time. She didn't give a fuck about me as her friend. Completely fucking ignored me for both of them. I loved her."

I frowned down at her, trying to see if she was saying what I thought she was. Had she shot Maya?

She looked me in my eyes and, before she took her last breath, she said, "Fuck Maya Black." However, for as much hate as she tried to say it with, I could hear something different in her voice.

The next hour was like a blur to me. Paramedics were in and out of the house. DJ had come in just as they were carting Mama out. His yells and demands that somebody tell him what happened only mirrored my pain. I didn't even notice the bruises, scrapes, and cuts to his face. I was so detached from the moment that all I could do was sit there in a daze. I realized I didn't know either of my parents as well as I thought I did. What kind of hate must my mother have harbored for her last words to be, "Fuck Maya Black"? Who carries around that much hate for so long?

What had Maya really done to my mother? The story Uncle Red had told made it seem as if Maya was only guilty of choosing one man over another. Not to mention she'd had an affair with my father, which my mother knew about? Who were these people?

Where was Daddy? Why wasn't he answering his phone? Who had killed my mother?

I thought about Saint. Hadn't heard from him since I'd stormed out of the shop. Where was he? Was he okay? What had my mother meant about seeing a ghost? I had so many questions, but my mind was too fuzzy to give me logical answers. I'd lost my mother. I had no idea that I would be parentless come morning.

Chapter 23

Saint

Two hours before.

The steel of my nine stayed even on DJ as he kept his distance from me with Brash behind him. “Which one will you pick, Saint? See, once you pick it, you gotta open it once I bounce.”

Under any other normal circumstances, I would have categorized DJ as shifty. Yet, how he came to me and Sin, spitting information out like a rat, my current assessment of him now had me feeling like he couldn’t be trusted; and I didn’t like niggas who couldn’t be trusted. The very aura around DJ felt like he was a manipulator and it was crazy to me, because the little bit I did know about this dude, I didn’t take him to be on this level of rat. Rich, and entitled, fuck yeah, but manipulative, shady, and shitty? Naw. This was something new and this was something that would get a lesser man killed.

Just ask Marvin.

As I thought about my choices here, I felt Sin get closer after picking himself up. We were communicating without words.

Brah, you trust that nigga? reverberated in my psyche from him.

I gripped my Glock while I shifted on my feet. I then pointed at DJ, never dropping my position. *You know I don’t,* I said back without talking.

Thumbing his nose, my twin cracked each of his fingers while moving in a way to keep a lock on Brash, snarling. *What you gawn do then?*

I let out a low laugh then chuckled to myself. Of all days, this drama shit wanted to pop off. Dealing with my mom being shot. The fire at the urgent care being some type of ploy and the truth behind my mom and the Royals was really fucking with me. All that time, it was about some teenage bullshit. Then, on top of that, it was about the possibility of London's pops having killed my dad; and now his son was in front of me?

An agitated smile flashed across my face, and I watched Brash pull DJ back, who also was moving back on his own in unison.

Blanket ain't my concern right now.

Thumbing his nose again, my brother stopped his movements and that ended our conversation.

My twin held out his hand in an upright motion while leaning against me, as I said, "Guerilla. Once you put it in my twin's hand, for London's sake you got five seconds to get out my face, since you're eager to bounce—"

DJ reached in his jacket, pulling out a thick folder. As he handed it to Sin, who then handed it to me, my twin stepped up to DJ and said, "Hol' up. One more thing. What you know about this shit, Brash? I mean, since you ride and die now. Because I ain't got no qualms about cutting a baby out that belly."

I tilted my head in a measuring manner, jaw clenched in a menacing way while I locked my eyes on her to let her know all respect would be gone if she was in deep with this shit. I was my brother's keeper and dropping to the level of killing her even though she was pregnant wasn't going to be shit to me. I'd do what I had to do.

When DJ's hand fisted, I stepped forward. I slapped the envelope in Sin's hands in a way that let DJ know that I was about to fuck that nigga up.

DJ peeped game then quickly backed up. *Smart nigga.*

"It's just me," DJ quickly stated. "She's clear of this, on my word. You got what you need. We're out."

Gun still pointed, we watched them climb back in their vehicle and quickly speed off. The sound of Sin opening the envelope combined with approaching feet had me turning to see who was stepping to us. Coming from the shop it was Uncle Red. His eyes were still bloodshot and he had his cell in his hand.

"What did fuck boy want?" he asked, stopping in front of us.

Sin, being Sin, waved the package in front of my uncle then went back to digging into it.

"Damn, more bullshit. So it was him who dropped the first one. A'ight." Looking where DJ left, my uncle exhaled and shook his head. "Silky and Choppa combed through the surveillance and checked the vans. Shit came from some dealer on the Ro-side. Blanket didn't have anything to do with this, I need y'all to understand."

"And who the fuck is Blanket, huh?" I said with a snarl. "You?"

Confusion flashed across my uncle's face.

Before he could respond, Sin roared, "Fuck this shit!" He slammed the envelope against my uncle's chest then got in his face. "You knew about this, huh?"

"Speak calm and clear like I taught you, nephew. I knew what?" he firmly asked. His arms stretched out to show he wasn't a threat before holding the package.

"Mama, you, Devon Royal, his wife, all of this shit is some bullshit. That nigga is Guerilla! Both of them!" Sin spat out as if he were breaking with reality.

I knew when my twin got like this that no good was coming. It usually made me step back and chill in my emotions but today wasn't that day.

Uncle Red stared on in confusion. His cell suddenly vibrated, and he quickly reached for it. Looking it over, a dark expression slid across his face. He then slammed his phone in his pocket then went through the package.

When Sin backed up, pacing, holding his skull, I reached out for what my uncle almost let slip through his fingers. Skimming over it, tension made me roll my shoulders.

"There's transcripts of Devon Sr. speaking with our fucking transporters? The Dominicans, the Italians, the fucking Arabs. All our product distributors," Uncle Red said in disbelief.

What had me in the end was the signatures. "That letter from London's mom. Same fucking handwriting."

Holding out a tablet, I pushed play and we watched a video of Devon and his wife talking about business they were doing with Royal Realty. Everything would have sounded nonthreatening to novices, but being who we were, everything said, from movement of construction material, to client names, and then some, all coincided to how Guerilla moved in Goodman.

At the end, we listened as Tamika said, "We need to continue to stay as invisible as possible, honey. When that house went up in flames, I had to work twice over to get those niggas to clean up and move out. Covering everything you do, Devon, is going to be harder with taking out Blanket's marks. You do understand that, right? This isn't like when I had to invent Guerilla to hide you killing that bitch Maya's husband."

Devon strolled into view and caressed his wife's jaw. "I love when we talk business like this, beloved. I understand what has to be done. We're now dealing with a game changer. More money will come our way as we sell Goodman property and move those animals out of their homes. The bigger goal is to move into government. If

I can show that I can clean a slum like Goodman, then we're in there, remember?"

My mind was fucking blown as we watched on. "Yes, I do. I continue to stand by you like I always did. I never regret my choices."

"Good. Guerilla needs to continue to spread out. Send some of the crew over and start leveling the playing field against Blanket," Devon said with a smirk.

It was then that the video flipped to the event today. Watching it, the video displayed the front of the business. Shouting started and we heard the gunfire. I watched my mother fall to the ground. At that same moment the camera turned and followed the shape of a person who looked like a female. Watching it zoom in, the person threw a gun then headed behind an empty house with a Royal Realty sign. After the commotion cleared out, from that same area a woman appeared. Tamika Royal. She calmly looked around then climbed into a car and drove off.

My head tilted to the side in disbelief. At that same moment, all the pictures my brother also saw fell from my hands. Everything played in rewind in my mind. The turf wars, the suffering we all went through in Goodman, it all played back. All of it was done for the profit of Devon Royal and his family. Shit was fucked up on so many levels all I could do was process it slowly and make sure the pieces all added up.

I heard my uncle on his cell putting out a call to everyone in Blanket's crew as if he were the man himself. It made me turn and stare him square in the eyes.

"Who the fuck is Blanket?" I said as calmly as possible. "My mother is laid up in bed almost dead because she got shot by Devon Royal's wife, a bitch who's one of the people behind Guerilla. Who the *fuck* is Blanket? You?"

My uncle glanced between us, stepped back, and then exhaled, ready to talk before I interrupted.

"No bullshit. I'm loyal all damn day, but it's time for some truth. That bitch shot my mom!" I shouted.

It was then when my uncle yelled back. "Then buck up, nigga, and handle business. Stay loyal and step into your role, the both of you!"

Sin and I stared back and forth at each other in mirrored disbelief before what Uncle Red said slowly dawned on us.

With a curt nod of his head, Uncle Red thumbed his nose. "We are . . ." He dropped his voice. "Mainly, she is," he said, pointing back at the shop. "I am who I am: the nigga who will always protect the woman who my brother loved. Me and ya goduncle Luther. So, yeah. She is, and it's time you kept that loyalty."

Tears of white hot anger slid down my face. This shit went to a level I had no idea it was. None of it made sense to me. "Why would she come at us all these years like she did only to be the boss?" I asked in pain, knowing I knew the answer. It was because she was our mother, and a mother's care was a motherfucker.

My uncle shook his head and looked at us both. "What mother would want to watch her children in the streets? After my brother was killed, she created the boss. Our family is this world. The stories about my pop's are all true. He was the first."

He stepped up to reach out to protectively squeeze the back of my brother's and my necks as he spoke. "Our sources are old and come from his dealings in 'Nam. That's why we hold it down like we do and can. Your mom didn't want this for you both, but she saw y'all were going to do what ya wanted, so she brought y'all in. I brought y'all in. The best way to watch your kids and protect them is to do what she did. She felt like she had no other choice!" He shouted in the end, stepping back.

"Now what y'all going to do, huh? Because I know what I have to do."

Walking off, my uncle took the paperwork then headed back to the shop. "The pest control vans came from a commercial spot owned by Royal Enterprises," I heard my uncle shout to us as he gave us a final look.

Both Sin and I stood there in the red. Where I'd go was where he'd go, and once my uncle left, loyalty drummed in our blood, riding out.

We ended up in Roanoke parked in front of the Royals' home. Though our conversation was long, not that much time had passed between DJ leaving and us learning the truth.

We sat in silence before I climbed out of the ride. "Stay in the car. I need answers."

"I got you covered," Sin said, watching me walk off.

Fist banging on the door, I waited until it opened. Like some stank on shit, standing before me was the first half of Guerilla: Tamika Royal. She stumbled back into her house in shock. The look on her face gave me a quiet satisfaction because, like any Southern belle, she clutched her chest and pointed toward me as if seeing a ghost.

I really didn't care about what was going on with her on her end. But somewhere in the back of my mind where logic lived, the broad was annoying me. Stepping forward, I thumbed my nose then followed her around the house. Bitch moved around like she was on some next shit as she threw items at me, which I dodged.

"You're . . . you're . . . you're dead," she stammered in confusion.

When I stepped up on her, it was then that she changed. Mrs. Tamika went from damsel in distress to hood rat in a second. Swinging out a punch, she hit me in my ribs hard. In that same motion, she grabbed my shirt, using it to bring me down to slam her knee into me. Air rushed from me and she pushed me against a table. Bitch could move, but I was fine with it. I wasn't just good with a gun.

Flashes of everything my town had gone through, my boys in the streets, and my mother being shot splashed across my eyes. At first I was going to ask the important questions, I really was, but instead I found myself reaching out and dragging Tamika by the neck. Backhanding her, I sent a hard punch into her gut, snatched her by the hair to slam her face against a white pillar, then I took her by the neck.

Her screams were like music to me and the way she struggled only fueled me as I dropped her to the floor. No help came, no staff, or nothing. I figured Sin had ignored me and went to clear the house. I appreciated it kindly.

"First things first: why?" was all I said as I held her down with my gloved hand.

Tamika swung out. She missed and I slammed her head down against the floor. Images of the Royals' smiling faces in large canvas circled us. Everything they had was because of the death of my people, mainly my family. The hatred I was taught to have for the Royals immediately became dominant. I now understood my mother in that sense.

"Why?" I shouted, starting at her glazed eyes.

Wincing and coughing, Tamika's mouth opened and closed. When she found the strength to speak, she spoke as if she was still locked in fear. "I . . . I didn't want you to die, William." Her words faltered. "I . . . I loved you once and you used to love me too, but . . ."

She paused then her face contorted in malice. "Fuck you, nigga!"

A low snarl came from me. The disrespect left a sour taste in my mouth as I squeezed harder.

It was then that Tamika pleaded. "I didn't do it. Please! Devon could never let that bitch Maya alone! She was never loyal to me, never loyal to our friendship, you know that. She fucked Devon then acted like it was all about you. Why'd you have to be a nigga-bitch, huh? I never should have let you meet Maya. I knew . . . knew she'd go behind my back. That's why that bitch is dead! Please, you're dead."

Slamming her head down, I got tired of the rambling then stood up. "Yeah, and I'm here to do his business." Rounds escaped my gun. "You take from Maya then you take from Blanket."

As soon as I said that, her eyes widened and she tried to fling at me. Punching her dead in the face, I sent more rounds in her and watched her fall down. Standing over her, I studied how peaceful she was. She stared back at me with an aware stare as if she had more to say; and then I popped off more rounds. "Naw, bitch, you don't get to die in peace."

Her cries started then stopped. The sound of the horn of my ride had me exiting and going back in the streets of Roanoke. Devon Sr. wasn't there. Had he been, I would have nicely fed him my Glock.

"Uncle sent me an address. Nigga might be at his other office," Sin let me know.

I wiped my face, tugged on a cap, and stared blankly ahead of me. "A'ight. Take us there then."

"There's something else," I heard my twin say as I tried to focus. "Cops are around the shop. They want Blanket."

"Fuck!" I slammed my fist against the roof of the car and looked at my twin. "DJ played us?"

"Yeah, I think so, brah," Sin said in disappointment.

"I should have killed him."

Sin gave a quick nod with a slight chuckle. "Yeah, but nigga was intent on running. We'll handle him later; but, in the meantime, I'm keeping up with what's going down. It looks like they don't know who Blanket is in the physical."

"Yeah, Uncle will handle it," was all I could say.

In front of us was Royal Enterprises. Getting out, I kept my head low and face covered. Getting inside wasn't our issue. Once we took out his staff, and moved any phones around away, we made it to the security station. Sin wiped that out, turned off all cameras, then we made it to that nigga's office.

Devon Sr. sat back with a glass of amber liquid to his lips, taking leisurely sips. Sin stayed behind me, watching the door as I stepped forward and took off my mask.

"How may I help you young men?" Devon Sr. asked in smooth calm. "You look just like your red-headed bitch of a father."

Once again, my gun spoke for me. Several bullets slammed into Devon, hitting his right shoulder and arm, which made him drop his glass. He hissed out in pain and looked at us in cold amusement. "Damn, I meant that in nothing but love, nigga. You two should have been mine, not his," Devon Sr. said with a sick chuckle.

I really had no patience for his type of bullshit. I now realized why he was so easy to hate, and why when he was in my mom's shop he stared at her how he did and then at us. Nigga had no fear, none at all. And I wasn't upset about it at all. It only made things cleaner for me.

"You tried to kill my mom," I said, stopping in front of his desk.

Devon slumped to the side and coldly shook his head. "Kill your mom? No, I want your mother. Kill her? What good is dead pussy? All it leaves is a rotting smell, son."

Since he didn't give a damn about life, I decided to not give a damn either. Swiftly climbing up on his desk, I kicked that nigga square in the face. I then squatted down and pulled out a razor chain from my shoe. "I'm sorry, I wasn't clear there. Your wife tried to kill my mom and you knew it."

"Again, why would I be so sloppy to do something like that son? I'm just a realtor. I buy houses and property. Why would I have—"

I hated liars. Without blinking an eye, I hooked the chain around his neck. Just as fast, I then jumped off the desk and tugged down hard, pulling him from the desk. It allowed me to see that he had a large shotgun on his lap and a hunter's knife in his hands.

"Nah, see I'm woke, nigga. I know everything about you, Guerrilla. So explain to me why you'd not only turn a neighborhood that birthed you into a slum, but you also went after my mother. Wasn't killing my pops enough?" I snarled low between clenched teeth.

Struggling, a strength in Devon took over and this nigga's neck tightened like the Hulk. He strained then sent me flying backward. Thrown off by that, I looked up to Devon standing over me with one slumped shoulder. His hunter's knife was in his left hand and he threw it at Sin, but Sin ducked then rushed to tackle Devon.

Both fell to the floor of that office. Both laid blows against each other like maniacs, and both fell apart in exhaustion as glass and other things in the office lay broken around them.

"Killing your pops was only the start! Everything that Maya loved needed to die. Being Guerilla only helped that shit!" Devon snarled, hunkering low. "So tell me, how'd you know?"

A sharp laugh came from me and I narrowed my eyes. "Looks like your son has it out for you. That nigga told me and showed me it all. Now it's your turn to die, just like ya wife died, by my hands."

I ran forward, took that chain, and then slashed it across that nigga's face. Because that left me open, it allowed him to punch my side. Sin followed through and rammed a blade into his ribs. Me, I wrapped that chain around his neck, cutting and pulling.

Devon's strength was insane. He managed to knock us back while spittle and blood ran down his face. This allowed him to put distance between us by backing up some.

"Little pups of Rooster need to learn a history lesson," he said, holding the gash at his neck. "Your father was in my way by keeping me from Maya; but, on the real, a nigga needed to build his empire, and taking down Rooster and your grandfather helped me take their territories and drug connects, so I thought."

Devon spit a glob of blood. He shook his head and watched us as if in thought. "So my son told you. Hmm. Y'all know taking down urgent care wasn't my shit. I appreciated it, admired it, but it wasn't my MO. Y'all let that nigga Luther know since he's Blanket."

He turned on a flat screen that showed my goduncle being led out of the shop with my Uncle Red.

Anger had me tense and it didn't make things any better when Devon laughed then casually took a swig of amber liquid from a crystal decanter that had been on the floor.

"In all my years, I never would have guessed this battle between me and your family would transcend even us battling as Blanket and Guerilla. That shit is classic. Humph. After handling my son, I guess I'll collect your mother now . . . after I kill you both."

Gunshots rang in our ears. Bullets hit us, and we fell to the floor. I crawled on the floor trying to get to Devon. This nigga's madness was fucked up. He thought he was king, but I had some shit for him.

Blindsiding him, I slammed Devon down. My fist hit his face. My forearm smashed against his nose. Then my elbow slammed into that bastard's body until I managed to stand up and smash my foot down on his neck. I laughed at how wide his eyes got with the force I put on him.

I yanked Devon's head back.

He laughed and spit. "Fuck a Black. And tell ya mama I'll see her soon."

It was then that I picked up the hunter's knife. My choice was clear, and I vocalized that, as I ran a blade across his neck. I enjoyed the blood that spilled out in a ruby rush. In my mind, I went over everything that had happened. Every bit of emotion I had about it all simmered just under the surface. It was then that I knew that it wasn't over. I grabbed my Glock and squeezed the trigger to rain bullets into his body as I snarled, "Fuck a Royal and fuck Guerilla. Blacks will always rise."

Chapter 24

Devon Royal Jr.

I went into my father's office to find him dead the next morning. Wasn't a shocker for me as I knew what would happen. See, Mom and Pops had to die for the greater good. They'd gotten too big for their britches, as pops used to say. They were reckless and would bring down the whole Royal empire. Pops was starting to think with his heart and not his head. Same with Mom.

Most people needed a reason to betray a person they loved. Not me. I was born vindictive. I wanted what I wanted and didn't give a shit who I had to step on to get there. I was the best and worst kind of person to be around as you had only one time to do something that I felt was an affront to me and all bets were off. Pops made that mistake. He promised me the whole Royal enterprise when I turned twenty-one but, like always, he reneged on me. I was tired of waiting. I'd worked hard, done everything he'd asked of me; and then he went back on his word.

As luck would have it, I happened to come to his office one day sooner than expected. I lucked out and found out some shit I shouldn't have. There began my plot to dismantle his whole empire. I had to do it in a way that it didn't fall back on me or my little sister. Shit, poor London. She probably didn't know what had hit her. But Saint was my ace in the hole when it came to London. He would protect her. I had no doubt about that. Saint would protect her and because Saint would protect her then so would Sin. I swore God was on my side when my sister actually fell for Saint. Shit couldn't have worked out any better than it did.

So like the grief-stricken son I was supposed to be, once my mom had been found by my sister, I rushed out to find my father only to learn that Saint and Sin had left their marks. I'd dismantled all security cameras before. I had to, just in case those niggas were too angry to think rationally to do so. I had to make sure my ass was covered at all times. I always did. Just like I had some of my illegals attack Leon and leave him behind a building. Sin had cut my cousin up bad, damn near killed him. So we had to make it look good so nobody would question Leon's injuries. Trying to save London damn near got him killed. I wasn't expecting her to be at that urgent care center, but I was glad she wasn't hurt. Mudbuster was able to tackle her before she could do anything foolish.

After finding my father, I placed a distressed 911 call. "Oh, Jesus," I yelled into the phone. "Send help, please!"

The police were already on high alert so they got there in no time. I held my father's dead body until the paramedics had to damn near pry me away. I couldn't front like seeing my mother and father killed as they were didn't move me. I was sad to see them go out that way, but they had done some very evil and coldhearted shit in their time as Guerilla. However, to preserve their image, I made sure no trace of them being Guerilla could be found. The only persons who knew were Saint and his twin and if either of them exposed my parents to the public or authorities, I'd wreak havoc on their lives in ways that couldn't be imagined.

I had no fear of Blanket, whoever he was, coming back at me. I knew someone in the Black family was Blanket, just didn't really know who. Yeah, I'd led the police to Luther and Uncle Red, but I couldn't really say for sure it was both of them or one who was Blanket. Either way, shit worked out well for me in the end.

Don't get me wrong, I felt some kind of remorse. I shed a few tears, a few very real tears; and then I thought about the empire I'd just inherited and that made me shed a different kind of tear.

Chapter 25

London

The sun hid behind the trees. Wind whipped around the crowd that had gathered, forcing people to hold on to hats and programs they'd brought from the church to the burial. The ground was still wet from the rains the night before. A week after my mama and daddy had been murdered, we were laying them to rest.

My whole body shook as they lowered both of my parents into the ground. DJ had spared no expense for their homegoing. I couldn't even bring myself to talk about preparing for their funerals. My mind wouldn't let me come to grips with the fact that they had been murdered. Law enforcement agencies were stumped. They didn't know who had ordered their deaths, Guerilla or Blanket. And the fact that Saint's uncles had been exposed as Blanket floored me. All the while we were thinking it was one man and it was two. They were right in the community the whole time.

I didn't know how I was supposed to survive without my parents. Even with all the money and assets that had been left to me, I felt lost. I found myself wishing all the fights and arguments we'd had could be washed away. If I had known they were going to leave me so soon, I wouldn't have been so rebellious. But it was only when the man started tossing dirt on their caskets that I started to lose my grip with reality. DJ caught me as my legs gave out from under me. I'd spent my mother's last moments with her. Most of her words had confused me, but I cherished them and kept them close to me. As she gave up her ghosts, she also gave up her demons.

DJ was great in being strong enough for the both of us. Brash had been a damn good friend along with Marsha and Brandy, but Laylah refused to show up. That could have had something do with Brash being pregnant and engaged to DJ and the fact that DJ had temporary custody of Chance, Laylah's son. Instead of letting the baby go to the state, DJ stepped in and was granted guardianship until Laylah could get herself together. However, Laylah was livid. She believed DJ was somehow at fault for her losing Chance. I didn't see how. DJ was nowhere around when she allowed Chance to burn his hands on the hot stove.

Aunts, uncles, family members I hadn't seen in years, friends, foes, associates and the like showed up. But it was the one person I didn't see that hurt the most. I knew Saint had no love for my family, but I had expected a phone call or something. Even my calls to him went unanswered. Part of me wanted to say fuck him, but the part of me that had fallen for him needed to know his reason for abandoning me at a time like this.

Four weeks after the funeral, after all the interviews, well wishes, and after everyone had left my parents' mansion, I dressed in jeans and a T-shirt with some kicks and I made my way to Goodman. I was used to Goodman being alive and jumping, but it was eerily quiet. There were a few stragglers and some kids out playing, but other than that, nobody was around. I found that odd. I pulled up to the shop to find Sin sitting out front, drinking a beer. Something had changed with him.

Whereas before he would smile and say something slick when he saw me coming, now he looked at me with distrust in his eyes, disdain even. Not to mention the bruises, cuts, and scrapes on his face told me he had been in a fight. Maybe he was still pissed off about it, I thought.

"You need something?" he asked me, which threw me off.

Did he forget I wasn't the enemy? His eyes were just as red as mine. I was anxious. I wanted, no, needed to see Saint. I wondered how Maya was doing as well.

"Yeah, um, Saint here?" I asked, almost timidly so.

Sin didn't answer. He grunted and then got up to go into the shop. I slid my hands in my back pockets as I looked around. I felt awkward and out of place again. I hadn't felt that way in a long time. When Saint came to the door, the look of his face startled me. He looked as if he had been in a fight, one worse than Sin's.

"What's up?" he asked me from the door as if he didn't want to be near me.

I was already emotional so to have Saint act as if I'd done something to him threatened to bring me to tears. "What's up with you?" I asked. "Where have you been?"

He shrugged. "Around. You need something?" he asked, sounding like Sin.

Before I could answer, Dee Dee walked out the door to Saint's upstairs apartment and asked Sin if he still wanted her to cook for him. But it was when one of the chicks I remembered from the party walked up to Saint and wrapped her arms around his waist that my brows furrowed and I tilted my head.

Water blurred my vision. I closed my eyes and then opened them slowly. I was hoping shit was a dream, but when I opened my eyes she was still standing there half dressed. I nodded as if someone was speaking to me in my mind. As if they were telling me to take my anger about everything that had happened and show my entire natural black ass.

I looked around, from left to right then back at Saint and the girl again. Just as I made up my mind to slap a nigga and a broad, the last person I expected called my name.

"London," she said again.

I turned to find Maya Black walking up the walkway to the shop. She walked with a limp and a cane was in her right hand. I was used to able-bodied, fear-instilling Maya. The woman she was now was a bit different. I couldn't place why that was other than the cane and the limp.

"Yeah," I answered.

"How are you?" she asked. "Are you well?"

I was skeptical. I didn't know why that woman was being nice to me, but if she was coming at me with bullshit then, cane or not, today I was prepared to put somebody, anybody, on their ass. I was just that angry.

"I'm okay. Why?" I asked defensively.

"Come inside and talk to me," she answered.

My instincts kicked into overdrive. "No, I'm okay. I'm going to leave. Came to see Saint, but I see him and I'm good on it now."

I turned to head back to my car. My pride, ego, womanhood, and everything else that made me human dragged behind me on the ground. *Fuck life at this point. Fuck life and the hand it dealt me.*

"No, no. London, come inside and talk to me. That wasn't a question," Maya said behind me.

There she was. The old Maya I'd known. The boss bitch. The woman who demanded submission.

I whipped around on her. "I'm fine, woman! Damn. Let me leave! I don't need to talk and I don't want to talk. I'm fucking fine!"

She studied me for a moment. "You don't look fine," she then said.

"Well, I am."

"Yeah? Then why are you crying?"

I blinked rapidly and for the first time I realized the tears running down my face. I was breathing erratically and, in fact, felt like dying. Maya walked up on me and I backed away. I didn't trust that woman and I didn't know why she was being so nice to me when she hadn't been since the day I'd met her. It was odd to me.

It was when she said, "You've lost everything. I know what that feels like," that I finally took a good look at her.

I remembered my mom's words that she had loved the woman and it made me wonder just how deep their love and friendship went. My shoulders shook as I tried to keep my head up. I was well aware that Saint, Sin, Dee Dee, and her friend were still watching my mental breakdown. I tried very hard not to break down, tried even harder to keep my dignity intact and not cry about Saint being hugged up with some chickenheaded ho. But the weight of that on top of being without my parents caved in on me. I took a deep breath as if I had just come up from deep waters and the damn broke fully. The walls came crashing down.

When Maya wrapped her arms around me, I gave up holding it all in. I gave up trying to keep it all together.

"I'm sorry," Maya whispered.

I didn't know what she was apologizing for exactly, but I took it. I took it for what it was. We stood that way for at least five minutes with me crying and Maya holding me. In that moment, I didn't care who was watching or why. I didn't care about Saint being with another chick. I didn't care about anything, only the fact that my mother and father were gone and even though I still had DJ, somehow, I felt alone.

"You and Saint need to talk," she said once she pulled back. I opened my mouth to object. "Shh," she told me. "He's been going through a lot. We just got custody of my brother-in-law's, his uncle's, son. The mother has run off to God knows where. You need to talk to Saint. Don't worry about nothing and anyone else. You remember sitting in front of my home for a whole week and a day because you needed to see Saint?"

I nodded although I didn't want to. "Yeah."

"I don't know any other person who would have done that besides me or his brother. What you see is just something to do. I know my son," was all Maya said before walking toward the shop.

I saw that Saint and Sin had disappeared inside, but Dee Dee and her friend were still watching. Maya was right. I did need to talk to Saint. If not for anything other than letting him know how I felt. So I picked up my pride, ego, and womanhood, put them back on the shelf and walked forward.

Maya was speaking to Sin when I walked in. I headed past them up to Saint's door. Just as I reached it, he opened the door. We stared one another down for the longest.

"You couldn't call me, Santana?" I asked first.

"No," he answered almost too quick for my liking.

"Really? What did I do to you?" I asked.

"Some shit you don't understand, London."

"Then explain it to me."

He sighed.

"Explain it to me," I demanded again.

I could hear the baby crying and female voices in his place. It annoyed me. "Will you get them the fuck up out of here so we can talk?" I asked him.

He didn't have to answer. Maya Black was coming up the stairs. I moved out of her way so she could have more room. When she asked Saint's company to leave, they did so without thought or question. She also took the baby with her. That left me and Saint alone.

"Come in," he said after we stared at one another for a while. I did. The place was clean, but clearly a baby had moved in.

"I admire y'all taking in your uncle's son," I said.

"Yeah. Really had no choice. Me and Sin make it work," he answered. His eyes showed his heart was heavy. He looked as if he had the weight of the world on his shoulders. "I need to show you some shit. Tell you some shit, London. And this is going to change the dynamics between us like a motherfucker, but you need to know."

I didn't know what he was talking about. I was assuming he was about to break it off with me and, while it would hurt, I'd move on with time. I rationalized that I hadn't really known him or been with him that long anyway.

"Okay, you fucked that chick or Dee Dee or both?" I asked. "You want to be with somebody else?"

He frowned. "You're worried about where my dick has been and this is deeper than that."

I wanted so badly to yell yes, where his dick had been mattered to me because I felt as if it was my dick. But I caught a glimpse of something else in his eyes that unnerved me. He walked over to his closet and came back out with a huge box. He opened the box like he was angry that he had to reveal whatever there was in there to me.

He started dropping envelopes and files, then he placed an electronic tablet on the table.

"This shit you need to know, the shit I have to tell you is nothing to fuck around with, a'ight?" he said.

I didn't say anything as I had started to look through the pictures. I saw pictures of Mama and Daddy talking to men who looked foreign. Saw pictures of them handling drugs. There were video recordings of them admitting to being behind the menace that was Guerilla. My heart fell out of my chest and landed on the floor. *No, no, no*. This couldn't be right. It just couldn't be. "No way is this right," I said to him.

"You see it, London. It's right in your face," he said.

"This . . . this is madness. You're lying. Who did this? Who gave you this?" I asked, face masked in confusion and anger. "Is this why they were murdered?"

"There's more," Saint said. "Your father killed mine and my grandfather. Tamika, your mom, helped him cover it up. Everything to prove what I'm saying is true is there. It's all there."

I wanted to run away. I wanted to hide. I wanted to yell, scream, cuss, and fuss. How could this be? "Why? Why are you doing this to me, Santana? Why?" I cried. "This . . . it can't be."

"It is, London. It's true."

"Then, Blanket did this to them? Your uncles killed my parents?" I asked, forgetting all the evil my parents had done just that quickly. I was ready to fight.

"Blanket didn't kill them," Saint said defensively. "I did."

My whole world shook violently, tilted, crashed, and then exploded. "Wh . . . what?" I screamed.

"I killed them, London."

Before I could stop myself, a monstrous scream, something akin to a battle cry, erupted from my lips as I jumped from his sofa across the room to him. I didn't know if I had caught him off guard or what, but I was fighting Saint with aggression I didn't know I possessed. He'd killed my parents? Him? The man I'd fallen in love with? How could he? Most of my hits he blocked, but the kicks, slaps, and punches I did land, I knew he felt them.

I screamed like a wild banshee as I attacked him, kicked like a madwoman. I had an insatiable thirst for bloodlust and it was his blood I was after.

Saint fought with me, pushed and shoved me. He mushed my face to back me up off of him but I was relentless. I didn't even realize Sin had come in. He pulled me off of his brother who looked like he was seconds way from hurting me physically. Maya was yelling for both of us to chill, but I was too far gone.

"You son of a bitch," I yelled. "You did this to me! Why, Saint? Why would you do this?"

"I just showed you why," he yelled. "Your father killed mine. He killed my grandfather! And your mom almost killed mine. All the evil shit your mother and father put out into the world, I brought back to them. And you want to fight me?"

I wrestled to get away from Sin. If I could have gotten to Saint, I would have killed him.

"You're mad," Saint said, eyes just as red as the hair on his head. "Good, motherfucker, be mad because I am too. We are too. All this stupid shit because a nigga's ego and pride couldn't handle reality. At least you got your parents for nineteen fucking years. My father was taken away when I was eight."

"Santana, that is enough," Maya said. "Enough, both of you."

Santana and I were adversaries. We'd gone from lovers to friends to mortal enemies in a matter of minutes.

"I hate you," I told him while Sin struggled to hold me still. "I fucking hate you!"

I'd never wanted to physically harm someone the way I wanted to do to Saint in that moment. Was that why Maya was so nice to me, because she knew what her son had done? Was that why she could so easily put shit behind her now, because she had gotten her revenge?

And they knew I couldn't tell a soul. I couldn't tell anyone who murdered my parents. No way could I without them revealing that my parents, both of them, were behind Guerilla. I couldn't and I wouldn't tarnish their image. I'd been delivered a soul-crushing blow.

I needed to get out of there and quickly. I felt as if I was suffocating. Both Saint and I stared at one another with righteous indignation. Daddy had been right about the Blacks all along. I hated Saint. I hated him so much.

"Good, because every time I look at you and realize Royal bloods runs through your veins, I start to hate you a little more too," he replied.

Epilogue

Saint

I guess love isn't strong enough to withstand the street. In the endgame of the battle between the Royals and Blacks, everyone ended up losing out on more than they ever could imagine. I know I did. After everything, my goduncle Luther ended up taking the bullet for my mom, a nigga I always thought had no involvement in the world of Blanket. Like all the other lies I grew up on, I learned that wasn't factual. Luther was the third hand to Blanket. Nigga was my mother's bodyguard and low-key lover to my mom.

Against her wishes, that nigga allowed the evidence to be twisted to make him look like the bad guy. He never once admitted to being Blanket, but he for damn sure didn't fight when the law made him out to be the mastermind of an empire. As for my Uncle Red, he too played his part in the fallback plan. Because some witnesses pointed him out as being one of the main bosses who worked for Blanket, he was brought up on charges as well. Never a snitch, he held it down and allowed them to book him on whatever trumped-up charges.

Death wasn't on the records for either because the courts couldn't prove any murders on Blanket's hands, so while the courts do what they do, my uncle and goduncle Luther now sat behind bars with no parole, waiting to go to prison. As for the real deal queen pin, Blanket, she sat in her home, forced to deal with her own demons and pain. My mom almost died from that bullet, but instead she fought it and came out with partial paralysis in her leg, where she now walked with a cane.

The era of Blanket and Guerilla was over with one swift move, a move that my brother and I were going over in our heads every day. We lost a hell of a lot and in the end we didn't save not one motherfucker, except Goodman. The streets were quiet. No drugs, no bullets, no nothing. Everyone in the community seemed to shun the once mighty Blacks after my uncles came out as the men behind the mask. The Royal empire seemed to only get stronger and my community was embracing the surviving children, especially Devon Royal Jr. Since the months after his parents' murder by my hands, nigga seemed to take the loss and make it work as a profit for him. Property in Goodman was still being sold and taken from my people, and new businesses owned by the Royals were popping up. Occasionally a few community people would come and ask my mother for help but, in the end, we said fuck 'em. There's no helping ungrateful motherfuckers.

Me and my crew still linked up and did whatever, but basically since the end of everything, the majority of Blanket's units had now disappeared. I guess in the end Devon Sr. won that battle with his death. Even me and London, he won that.

Running a hand down my face, I watched my neighborhood then looked down at my cell, stopping on a picture of me with London. We were hugged up in her apartment, lying on her bed. I was shirtless as she laid her head on my chest. Both of us were grinning like we'd won some shit nobody else knew about. I wanted to text her and see where her head was at, but I knew I couldn't. London was a good girl. She was the type of female who somehow found a way under all my hardness. It was fucked up how I did her, but it had to be that way. After learning everything, and after sitting with my mother as she explained her part in taking up the mantel of Blanket, I was just motherfucking done.

Fuck a Royal, right?

Too many of them took from me and, at the end of it, I allowed myself to be manipulated by them too.

Nah, London wasn't like them, but who's to say she won't flip a switch and become her mother and father? A nigga like me couldn't muster enough caring for her in my heart to try to make it through with her, even though that heart of mine whispered secret feelings for her. I killed her people, so why would she even want to fuck with me anymore? The day I told her the truth, I pretty much saw that in her eyes and, as much as that shit still hurts, I hate to say it but ain't no ghetto romance for our asses.

I allowed the tip of my tongue to run over my lips to moisten them. It was at that same time that the slam of a door echoed around me, taking me out of my thoughts.

London and I were now at odds. I heard she was moving on and killing it in school. Me, I finished my management courses with my degree. Black Towing and Rentals was on the bust right now but, as always, I had a plan to bring it back to life.

"You sure you're going to do this?" was asked by my side.

I mindfully smoothed a hand down the front of my vest then gave a slight nod. I then glanced to the right of me and checked out my twin, which was our usual practice in making sure we had our shit together. Sin was dressed in similar clothes as me: a vest with a dress shirt, slacks, dress shoes with rubber bottoms just in case something popped off, and a nine hidden against his spine.

"If that nigga thinks he can rise off of our ill deeds, then he's not as bright as he thinks he is," I said with a blank expression.

"Agreed." Sin cracked his fingers then chuckled. "Told you that you should have killed him."

"Yeah, you did. And you should have got on that twin link and handled business, right?" I said in retort.

My brother laughed hard with a shake of his head. "Naw, see. We were still dealing with the shakes, see."

As we laughed again, we heard the sound of elevator doors chime as the view of Roanoke appeared before us. Soft music played and I heard Pac rapping about him not being a killer, but revenge being the next best thing to getting pussy. A slick smile spread across my face as we stepped out into the panoramic condo suite that once belonged to our employer and mother, Blanket.

The sound of our shoes on mahogany inlaid wood blended with the music and we walked up to greet the family who had to go underground when our war popped off. Silky, Choppa, Sassy, and Hotep all circled us. As they parted, Laylah walked up to us with fire in her eyes. See, in every battle the old must fall in order for the youth to take over. That nigga DJ started something that he didn't think my brother and I would catch on to. He probably thought my love for London would keep me blind and loyal to just her. He would have been partially right about that, but he was damn wrong in thinking he knew how I rolled.

It was my time to make my choices and, in the end, after long hours talking with my mother, I realized that the world I once belonged in was now over. It was time to carve my way and make my own way. In this, I missed London, but there was no way she'd ever join me in what I had planned. The chips fell and our love lost out to the streets. I guessed that meant that I'd just have to watch her from afar.

When I held my hand out, I felt my brother lay a tablet on my palm as I stepped forward. Like I said, I had lost a lot, but with every bridge burned, another rises. London would forever be protected by me and this was the first step in that plan. The Royals gained everything on the back of Goodman and us Blacks. My family and I had time to think about just how smoothly that family was able to gain in the end and now it was time to flip the playing field.

"In the later months as we rebuild, London will thank me and hate me even more in the end. I don't give a fuck. Devon Royal Jr. started this, and it's my mission to continue to pay that shit forward. If my family has to fall, so does his," I explained.

Sin, already doing his thing as my right, walked past me and gave his orders. "Pull up the connects in 'Nam, Dubai, and here. Then hit up whoever we can, so we can leak this video, fam."

Turning my attention on a waiting Laylah, I gave her a curious smile. "Tell me everything you know about Devon, mama, and welcome to our kingdom."

I slid my hand against her back and Laylah walked with me as she thanked me for listening to her, and for helping her work to get her son back as a new member of my team. I wasn't Superman, wasn't a hero in any way. But, gaining an enemy's weakness was also something I could get down with. Besides, Laylah was essentially more Goodman than Royal and I had no qualms with that at all. So when she came my way asking for my help, I figured that she'd be my way in protecting London. I guess I loved that girl, huh?

While casually moving round the room, I nodded at my mother who sat in a huge chair near a marble fireplace holding her nephew, my baby cousin Jamal. I had plans on trying to get my uncles off in any way, even if we made Blanket be someone else. As for now, they were our connects in prison, which were now extending. That move currently made it where I could take on a new hidden identity to shape Goodman how I wanted, while taking out the last of my revenge on Devon Royal Jr. for his games. A nigga didn't do well with threats and that fact about him deeply amused me. See, I too came from royalty, and it was now time for the Blacks to rise.

I ain't a killa, but don't push me; and I sure as hell am not a Saint. But I know one thing now.

Motherfucker, I'm a king.